# REQUIEM FOR
# GERALDINE GERBIL

A POLICE DETECTIVE WHODUNIT

ISBN: 978-1-954481-11-4

Bair Ink Books
Fredericksburg, VA, USA

Cover by All Kinds of Covers

# REQUIEM FOR

# GERALDINE GERBIL

A POLICE DETECTIVE STORY

with Detectives Metzinger and Givens

BY

## J. STEWART WILLIS

Bair Ink Books

BEAUTIFUL BOOKS

FREDERICKSBURG, VA 2021

# DEDICATION

TO CHARLIE AND WINSTON,
MY GREYHOUNDS,
AND ALL THE WONDERFUL PETS
WHO HAVE
POPULATED MY LIFE

# CHAPTER ONE

KA-THUNK!

The sound repeated over and over again... not loud... you needed to be close to the house to hear it.

It was a typical October day, overcast and gray. A light wind blew steadily, creating a draft that whipped out the open front door at 410 Crest Street in Jefferson Park, Alexandria, Virginia. It was as if a window had been left open somewhere inside. The breeze provoked the wooden front door to swing closed, but each time it was stopped. Each time it banged against the head of a body lying over the threshold, then recoiled to swing wide open again.

The screened door, with its dark wire mesh, stood open more than a foot, closed just enough to hide the inside of the house and make it difficult to see the swinging door. Still, if someone paid close attention, they could notice the variations of light and shadow as the wooden door swung back and forth.

Across the street, just before seven-thirty that morning, a garage door went up and Donald Braswell backed his Toyota out, down the driveway, and into the street. As he straightened the wheels to drive to work, he glanced at the Winslow's house. Sure enough, the front door was open and the wooden door swung in the breeze; just as his wife had said.

As usual, Harriet had been up early keeping watch over the neighborhood out the kitchen window. An active participant in the Neighborhood Watch Program, she took the responsibility seriously. At breakfast, she had told Donald about an old man with a white beard pushing his cart down the street checking the curbside trash that stood in front of each house and about the strange appearance of the neighbor's door. Donald had largely ignored her since it was typical of Harriet to make such reports, both morning and night, as he ate his meals.

Now that he was driving past the Winslow's house, he understood what she'd been talking about. He glanced at the dashboard clock and thought, *I ought to stop and let them know their door is open and their heat is pouring out into the world. He glanced at the clock again and sighed. I really don't have time. I'm pushing it as it is. The Winslows are bound to notice the cold air coming into the house.*

The front stoop of the Winslow's house had two steps down to a sidewalk which turned immediately across the front of the house and led to the driveway. Shrubbery grew on the street side of the sidewalk, and, in fairness to the neighbors who drove past that morning, the shrubbery screened the lower half of the front door. Someone driving by would have had to look vigilantly to notice the body lying there holding the door open.

According to the later police report, only the Braswells and two other people had noticed something wrong before the body was found at the Winslow house that frosty morning.

***

The Devlin boys had noticed the door on their way to the school bus stop at seven-ten. Charlie saw it first.

"Look at that! It's in the forties out here and those people left their door open! They're gonna throw a fit when they get their electric bill."

Billy had looked where his brother was pointing.

"Idiots. Seems like they'd notice the cold."

"Should we go tell them?"

"Nah. They'll just tell us to bug off and mind our own business."

And with that, they had gone on to the bus stop laughing at the foolish Winslows.

***

Beth Holden had noted something wrong when she pushed her baby stroller past the Braswell's house a little after nine o'clock that morning.

She'd looked across the street, past the garbage truck emptying the plastic trash cans into its innards and thought, *Gosh, what an awful noise. Hope it doesn't upset Anthony.* Then she'd looked down at her child, who didn't seem bothered at all. He watched the truck as if it were just another toy.

Looking back up, her eyes had caught sight of the swinging front door. *Goodness,* she'd thought, *it looks like the Winslow's front door is open. I'd better phone them when I get home.*

After Beth got home, she'd taken off Anthony's hat and coat and settled him in his playpen. She had phoned the Winslows, but there was no answer. *I could walk back down and knock on their door, but I'd have to dress Anthony up again. I'll be darned if I want to do that. I'll try calling again in half-an-hour,* she thought.

Half an hour later she had forgotten.

***

At ten-twenty a US Postal Service truck pulled up to the curb in front of the Winslow's house to deliver mail. Some houses had mailboxes on posts by the curb, some had boxes attached to the house next to the front door and some, like the Winslows, had mail slots in the door. The latter two required the postal carrier, Bennie Hastings, to walk up to the front door in all kinds of weather. (Obviously, he preferred the posted boxes next to the curb.) As usual, he gathered the mail, hopped out of the truck, and hurried to the front door. When Bennie reached for the screened door handle he noticed it was not pulled completely closed. He started to pull it open and froze when he saw a foot jammed between the screened door and the door frame. Then, he saw the body connected to the leg.

Flustered, he let go of the doorknob and jumped back. The screened door slammed against the body's leg. Bennie looked at the mail in his hand and back at the door. After a moment's hesitation, he stepped forward and shoved the mail through the opening in the screened door.

Then, he pirouetted and ran back toward his truck, fumbling in his jacket for his cell phone.

Safe in his truck, he sighed twice and dialed 9-1-1, thinking, *Oh, God, this is going to make me late for my deliveries.*

# CHAPTER TWO

DETECTIVE DRURY METZINGER finished in the bathroom, dressed in his suit and headed downstairs where his children had just finished breakfast and were heading to school. His wife, Sarah, was cleaning the dishes off the table.

"I'll have your eggs ready in a minute."

"No hurry." he said, pouring himself a cup of coffee. "You sleep okay last night?"

Sarah sighed.

"No. Bet Sterling came over and had a cup of coffee yesterday afternoon."

"Oh, Lord. She upset you again?"

"She always does. Almost wish she wouldn't come over."

"Me too. Did she give you the same spiel about Dave being a Navy pilot and landing on little boats in the middle of the ocean at a million-miles-an-hour?"

"Yes, and how she made him quit. Couldn't stand the worry... suffered severe depression. She always asks how I can stand being a cop's wife."

"Yeah, and now the poor bastard teaches delinquents in high school. I bet he went from the life he wanted to feeling like he barely gets by."

Sarah was silent for a moment.

"It worries me, Drury. I never want you to be unhappy, but it's never been easy. Bet always reminds me."

Drury walked over to her and took her hand in his.

"I'm not just a cop, sweetheart. I'm a detective. Cops get shot at. I stand behind them when they go in."

"Yeah, you were behind them two years ago on that drug raid. When the bad guys have automatic weapons, it doesn't matter where you are. Thank goodness your vest saved you."

"That was a ricochet."

"You imply that makes a difference. I know better. Get hit by a ricochet and you're just as dead as a straight-on shot."

"Doesn't hit you as hard. Loses some of its energy."

Sarah pulled her hand from his and hit him.

"Not funny, Drury. Simple fact is you were hit. It wasn't the first time you were shot at either. You know I worry."

"I know, darling, but it's my life. It's what I do. I know we've survived some rough times to get where I am, but we've got twenty-four years in, six to go. Then I can guard warehouses or something."

"God, you think that makes me feel better? You'll still be carrying a gun. There's got to be something else."

"Don't know what it would be. Security's my life."

"Be a security boss, then."

"That's an idea. Like for a corporation or something."

"Will you look into it?"

"Sure, babe."

Sarah turned back to the stove.

"Six more years."

# CHAPTER THREE

DETECTIVE LESLIE GIVENS' eyes popped open, then closed as she rubbed her face into her pillow, hoping to rub the pain away. She'd been out with Sharyn and Chantel the previous night, dancing at Chick's. Danced with that stupid Travis Lee and Kenya what's-his-face and drank too much. She knew better than to go out on a work night. Mama had warned her... said it was no good for her job... that she needed to be more strait-laced... keep respectable, but Sharyn said the job was making Leslie dull, said she needed to be something extra. So, against her better judgment, Leslie had gone out and enjoyed it.

At the bar, Sharyn and Chantel were amped and ready. Leslie had held back until Kenya came over and asked why she was just standing there looking crazy hot and pulled her to the floor.

"Damn bitch, you're looking fucking awesome tonight!"

Leslie wasn't sure if he was talking about her looks or her moral character. She'd taken it for the former and they'd danced most of the night, except for when Travis cut in asking, "Why you wanna dance with that shady bastard?"

"'Cause he's a solid dancer," she'd told him.

"He'll try to take you home..."

"No problem. I'll bail before then," she'd assured him.

And she had.

Getting out of bed, Leslie grabbed her robe from the chair and shuffled to the bathroom. Sitting on the toilet, she pushed her palms against her forehead and rubbed her hands over her short, kinky hair, trying to make her head feel right. At the sink, she started brushing her teeth. With the brush in her mouth, she studied her reflection in the mirror and decided she'd survived well enough, despite the way she felt. She ran a hairbrush over her hair contemplating the style.

*My hair's been straightened and dreaded... I've tried the works. It's all more trouble than it's worth, makes me look better, but it's all such a pain,* she thought, pulling out the electric razor with plastic shaving attachment and running it over her head.

That's better.

Back in her bedroom, she put on her suit. A little formal for the neighborhood; drew attention. She was a detective in the Alexandria Virginia Police Department living in a more guarded part of town. Leaving the house, she always moved to her Toyota quickly to avoid hassle.

But first, she needed breakfast; mostly coffee. Her mother had already gone to work. (The morning shift at Lavonia's Diner.) She'd worked there ever since Papa died. Leslie had hardly known him, but Mama said he was a good man and Leslie decided it was best to think of him that way.

Fortunately for Leslie, a pot of coffee was waiting and cereal was on the table with breakfast buns. She appreciated her mother leaving it for her but was glad she didn't have to get the once-over before work, especially on a morning-after like today.

She sat at the table drinking her coffee, eating her cereal and getting ready for the day. Getting her mind set. She talked differently at work, more like her partner Drury. Leslie wondered how her boss, Lt. Ramirez, talked at home with his buddies. *Spanglish?* Surely not the way he talked at work. *Maybe everyone has their own way of talking at home,* she pondered. *We all adapt.* She relented. They all had to communicate at work and she guessed Drury was the common denominator. He'd been there longer than most of them.

This morning, work would be bureaucracy. No active cases on the agenda. Final paperwork from the dumpster baby murders. *Maybe I can run errands, maybe just get coffee. Let Drury do the writing.*

Detective Givens finished her breakfast, checked that she had her badge and weapon, and bolted out the door. Thankfully, Old Man Davis wasn't out on his stoop across the street this early. She was clear of harassment.

# CHAPTER FOUR

Lieutenant Ramirez came out of his office a little after eleven o'clock. "Metzinger, Givens, grab your coats. We've got a dead one."

He handed Metzinger a note.

"Woman shot in the front hallway of this house. The job's yours."

Givens breathed a sigh of relief. Metzinger had put her to work writing reports. She'd managed to get coffee, but that was all. Metzinger always said it was part of her training, good for the soul, all that crap. She hated paperwork so much she was almost relieved someone had been killed. Not really, but it was better than paperwork. Her soul could wait.

\*\*\*

Metzinger wheeled right out onto Duke Street and took a quick left on Quaker Lane. Givens gaped at the large houses.

"Christ, how can people afford these things?"

"No kidding. Nice area. Guess it was once on the outskirts of town. Fairly old now. Area we're going to is not as rich, but it's nice. Old, too. Probably goes back a hundred years. Houses are above my pay grade."

Givens looked at him.

"Goodness, Drury, you've been grumpy all morning."

Metzinger groused, "No worse than you. I had my wife nagging me this morning. What's your excuse?"

"Night out."

"Night out?" Metzinger barbed.

"Gin and tonics."

"Gin and tonics on Monday night? How many?"

"Didn't count."

"That means more than three. That all you did?"

"Drank G and T's and danced."

"Danced, huh? Might have helped your muscles but did nothing for your eyes."

"At least I have an excuse. All you did was get fussed at."

"Yeah, you're not married. You don't know what a guilt-trip feels like."

"And you don't know my Mama! I know what it feels like."

*** 

They turned right on Braddock Road, left on Cameron Mills, and right onto Woodland Terrace, admiring the Jefferson Park area houses. A couple of blocks down they stopped at Crest Street and looked left. Sure enough, halfway along the short street, there were multiple police vehicles, including the vans from the morgue and forensics. The two detectives parked their unmarked police car behind the first vehicle on the right, away from the gawkers on the sidewalk. They didn't want to be caught in a crossfire of questions about the police presence at 410 Crest Street.

Metzinger slouched down in the car.

"Damn circus."

He turned to Givens.

"You ever get used to these things?"

"Hell, Drury, I only have six years in. You've how many?"

"Twenty-four. It doesn't help. You ready?"

They got out of their car, locked it, crossed the street and tiptoed along the curb keeping parked vehicles between them and the crowd of gawkers. As they walked up the driveway, past the forensics van, they were greeted by several uniforms standing on the sidewalk and in front of the garage door. They flashed their badges and asked one of the uniforms what was happening.

"Techs are in there doing their thing."

Metzinger noted that tape was stretched across the front stoop at the top of the steps.

"Where's the body?"

"Right inside the door. Her foot blocks the screened door. I didn't even have to go in. Didn't want to mar the crime scene and didn't have to."

"You were sure she was dead?"

"Oh, yeah. Rigor had set in."

"Okay, Givens," Metzinger pointed at her. "And I will have a look when the techs come out. Have you talked to anyone?"

"Just the postman who found her. He's still parked down by the curb in his toy truck. Really twitching to go. Says he's got a ton of mail to deliver."

Metzinger looked at the truck.

"Leslie, I want to talk to that man while we're waiting but first, call Lt. Ramirez and tell him we need help canvasing the neighborhood."

Down the driveway the postman was sitting in the driver's seat of his truck with his eyes closed, leaning back, listening to his cell phone through earbuds. Evidently, the surrounding excitement had gotten old.

Givens tapped on the truck's side door window but got no response. The man was clearly enjoying whatever he was listening to. She knocked again. The man jumped, pulled out his ear buds, and slid the door open.

"Sorry, just listening to a book, the new Baldacci one. Who are you?"

Metzinger and Givens showed their badges.

Metzinger took the lead.

"Drury Metzinger and Leslie Givens. We're the detectives assigned to this case. And you are?"

The postman twisted in his seat to better face the detectives.

"Bennie Hastings. I'm the postal carrier for this route."

"You found the body?"

Hastings nodded nervously. "Is she dead?"

"You didn't check?"

"Hell, no. She looked dead. Blood on her clothing. I wasn't about to get involved. I've got a route to run and there's no way I was going to mess up the scene. I've seen too much television. I called 9-1-1. How long do I have to stay here?"

"Mr. Hastings, I understand you have a route to run and very much appreciate your waiting here until we could speak with you."

Metzinger pulled out a field notebook to take notes.

"Let me start by getting your address, home and cell phone numbers, and your email."

Hastings gave the detectives the information.

Givens asked if he knew the woman's name, then corrected herself because she didn't know with certainty if the dead woman lived there.

"Do you know the property owner's name or who lives here?"

"Uh, no."

"You deliver mail. Whose name is on the mail?"

"I just go by address. This is 410 on Crest Street."

"Can't you just look at today's mail?"

"I delivered it. Stuck it through the opening in the door."

"Dumped it on the body?"

"No, -uh, on the floor. At least I hope it's on the floor," he said, looking in panic from one detective to the other. "Hey, I was upset. Didn't know what to do. Did I screw up?"

Metzinger sighed.

"Probably not. At least we know what happened. Other than the screened door being cracked and the main door open, did you see any-thing out of the ordinary? Anything odd on the porch, or anywhere else around the house?"

Hastings shook his head.

"No, but I wasn't really looking."

Metzinger noticed the techs coming out of the house.

He reached into the truck and shook Hastings' hand.

"Mr. Hastings, we appreciate your being responsible and reporting what you found."

The postal carrier didn't hesitate. He put the truck in gear and drove off.

Detective Metzinger turned to Givens.

"Ready? This is the fun part."

"Not to me."

# CHAPTER FIVE

WALKING UP THE driveway, Metzinger and Givens met Jimmy Prothro, a tech with whom they had worked many times. He was well away from the house, lighting a cigarette.

"Have to get rid of the smell. Only reason I smoke."

"Sure, Jimmy," Metzinger said. "I see Manny by the door. He the one running this?"

Prothro looked toward the door of the house.

"Yeah, got assigned to Migliano." He glanced down at the detectives' feet. "You need protective boots and gloves?"

"Yeah, you got some on the truck? Save us walking back to the car?"

Prothro grinned, "No problem. Truck's stocked for a disaster."

Prothro climbed into the back of the van and returned with the goods, handing them to the detectives.

He looked at Givens assessing her size, "Might be big," he apologized.

Givens took them with a nod.

"Better than walking back to our ride. Thanks."

The detectives turned and walked to the stoop where Metzinger offered his hand in greeting.

"Hey, Manny, we've got to stop meeting like this."

Migliano wouldn't shake the hand, holding up his own hand to show it was gloved.

"Old joke, Drury," he waved at Givens. "You two ready for the reveal?"

Metzinger nodded as the detectives slipped on the disposable plastic boots and gloves. They started to follow Migliano through the screened door but came to an immediate halt.

Migliano swung the screened door open wide to show the body. The victim's foot that had been wedged in the screened door flopped. Metzinger thought, *rigor mortis is letting up. Killing must have happened last night, or late yesterday afternoon.*

He studied the mail. Magazines and a letter were on the floor, two letters lying on the woman's hip.

"I think we can get rid of the mail. Save it with the evidence. The postman dumped it on her this morning."

Metzinger picked up one of the letters.

"'Oliver Winslow', is that who owns the house?"

Migliano shook his head.

"Don't know. I leave that to you guys."

Metzinger picked up the magazines, Bookmarks and Publisher's Weekly. Both addressed to Daphne O'Hanlon. He looked at Magliano again, and then at the body.

"Think that's her?"

Again, Migliano shook his head. "Your job."

Metzinger smiled at Givens.

"He's giving us all the work."

Turning back to Magliano he asked, "So, what have you learned?"

"Victim's a middle-aged woman. Well dressed. Might even say expensively dressed. She's wearing four rings, two bracelets, a gold necklace chain with some kind of medallion. Looks like the perpetrator had no interest in them or in things in the house. As I said, I haven't really cased the place, but the hallway's unruffled. A bullet was fired at close range. Through the screen door, up at an angle. Went in just below her breasts and didn't come out. Like it was shot from the hip, or by a short person. Don't believe she died instantly, probably immobilized. Lot of blood. The red Persian rug soaked up a lot of it, so you don't see as much as there is. I'd say she bled out. Don't know how long it took, but she didn't move around much. Blood's not smeared around."

"Close range, huh? Residue on the clothes?" Metzinger inquired.

Migliano nodded, "Mostly on the screen."

"Any sign of muffling... pillow feathers... plastic from a bottle... any odd materials?"

"Nope. Clean through the screen."

"Must have been loud then."

"I'd guess."

Givens asked, "Was the light on in the hallway? What about the two outside lights adjacent to the door?"

Magliano looked up at the hanging light in the entrance hallway.

"Haven't touched them. They're out now so they must have been out when we arrived. Lights are on in the kitchen and living room. Funny they're not on here."

Givens offered, "Was it still daylight when she was shot? I would still think the hallway light should be on."

Metzinger asked, "Did the killer turn out the lights? Might explain why the screened door was open. Any prints on the light switches?"

"We got a million prints, but nothing usable on the light switches, the screened door, or the main wooden door. What's there are all smudged."

"Killer may have wiped everything down."

Migliano nodded, "Could be... a quick swipe, or they used gloves. It's possible the killer never touched anything. Maybe the victim opened the screened door without turning on the lights. Who knows but let me show you something."

Stepping out on the stoop, Migliano pointed at the doorbell.

"Camera bell. The killer covered it with a Band-Aid. No prints on it either. That's why I say gloves. Hard to handle a Band-Aid without leaving prints. We'll check and see if the camera caught anything."

Metzinger looked down at the body.

"Head's pretty banged up."

Migliano nodded.

"Yeah, the wooden door kept hitting it. There was a draft through here, swinging it back and forth. I had to wedge the door open."

Metzinger held up his hand.

"Can't feel one now."

Migliano put his hand up.

"Yeah, seems to have stopped."

Metzinger stood back on the front edge of the stoop and considered the scene while Migliano kept hold of the screened door.

"Manny, what about a casing?"

"One for the one shot. Found it next to the stoop. 32 caliber... old... maybe seventy or eighty years. Seems like something out of the attic."

Givens came and stood beside her partner.

"What do you think?"

Metzinger drew his jaw back, mulling it over.

"I think the dead woman recognized her killer. I think she answered the door. She probably started to step out on the stoop and was shot almost immediately."

Metzinger turned, acting out his imagination.

"She fell back, leaving her foot partly outside jamming the screened door. Then, the perpetrator flicked off the lights, maybe wiped down things he or she had touched... or they wore gloves, as Manny suggested. The killer left the body to be found much later."

Givens said, "How'd the killer know no one was in the house?"

"Good question," Metzinger replied. "It's hard to imagine that someone in the house wouldn't hear all this noise."

He looked at Migliano.

"Anyone else in the house?"

"No. Uniforms got here first, but they didn't go in. I shouted when I got here and got no answer. Been here half-an-hour with no sign of anyone. I don't make a lot of noise, but it's hard to imagine anyone's here. I didn't go beyond the hallway though. Figured we'd need a search warrant to go further."

Metzinger turned to Givens.

"Do we know who else lives here?"

He looked back at Migliano.

"Is the woman married?"

Migliano looked annoyed.

"Drury, you know I don't know any more than you do. Your job! I've got to get the body off to the medical examiner and then try to identify a bunch of partial fingerprints, process the crime scene, take photos, and all that crap."

Metzinger nodded.

"Hopefully you'll find the perpetrator's prints, it seems like he or she has been here before."

Givens cocked her head.

"So, we have to identify the victim, find out who owns the house, who Daphne O'Hanlon is... any chance this is her? And who's Oliver Winslow... husband... homeowner?"

Metzinger turned back to Migliano.

"Check for powder around the wound. See how close the gun was."

"Already done. It was close... foot or two."

Prothro stuck his head under the crime scene tape and looked at Metzinger.

"You've got two uniforms here to help you."

"Great, we'll put them to work screening the neighborhood."

Metzinger looked pleased.

"All right Leslie, you and I will take the next-door neighbors and the house across the street. Hopefully, someone knows who lives here and will save us some time."

# CHAPTER SIX

J UST AS METZINGER stepped off the stoop to give the uniforms directions, he, Migliano, and Givens all turned their heads to what sounded
like a toilet flushing.

Givens shouted, "Hello. Is somebody there?"

A voice shouted back, "Hello? Who's that? Mom? Who's there?"

The voice was definitely inside the house.

Metzinger stepped into the hallway past the body. As he did, a teenage
girl in pajamas and robe emerged from the back of the hall. Her mouth
gaped when she saw Metzinger.

"Who are you?!"

She saw the body and her hand shot up to cover her mouth. "What's
happened? What's going on?"

Metzinger took her arm, leading her away from the body into the kitch-
en. He pulled out a chair from a kitchen table while holding up his police
badge.

"Have a seat. I'm with the police."

The girl sat down and looked up at him.

"What's happened to my mother?"

Metzinger hesitated and turned to Givens, who had followed him into
the kitchen, and then back to the girl. She looked about eighteen... a little
older than his own daughter.

"I'm Detective Metzinger and this is Detective Givens. We're here in
response to a 9-1-1 call."

Looking worried and uncertain, the girl managed, "But... my mother?"

"I'm sorry. The woman in the hallway is dead."

The girl's eyes darted around the kitchen as if desperately searching for something.

"She wasn't that old. What happened?"

Metzinger looked at Givens in desperation.

Givens asked, "Do you recognize the woman?"

"Of course. She's my mother. Did she have a heart attack?"

Metzinger sat at the table.

"I'm sorry. She was shot."

"Shot? When? How?"

"We're trying to find out."

The girl picked up a paper napkin and began twisting it nervously between her fingers.

"This isn't real, is it? We had dinner together last night..."

Metzinger tried to console her.

"I'm sorry. I know it's a hard time. Detective Givens will stay with you for a minute. I need to go out and talk to the other police officers to get our investigation moving, but I'll be back."

The girl vacantly nodded.

Metzinger turned to Givens.

"I'll put the uniforms to work and be right back."

He left Givens sitting at the table.

"May I ask your name?"

The girl looked up.

"Josceline Winslow. They call me Joss. No one wants to be called Josceline."

"I don't know. It sounds like a pretty name to me."

"Yeah, but no one wants a pretty name. You want a name that's easy to say. Two syllables at the most. No one has time for a longer name."

"Yeah, I guess. Elizabeths and Rosalees don't exist much anymore."

Joss looked at Givens in horror.

"Rosalee? No one should do that to a child."

Givens replied, "Got to admit, I don't know any Rosalees."

She changed pace.

"How about your mother's name? Can you tell me that?"

"Daphne. Daffy O'Hanlon."

"Daffy?"

"Yeah, Daffy. She writes children's books. That's the name she uses on the books. I always tell her it makes her sound like a duck, that it's stupid, but she ignores-- ignored me. She said readers wouldn't recognize her by any other name."

Givens considered that.

"That's interesting. She do well with the books?"

The girl studied her fingernails.

"Yeah. Real well."

Givens hesitated; she was always reluctant to ask about fathers in case there wasn't one.

"And what's your father's name?"

"Oliver Winslow."

Again, Givens hesitated.

"And where might we find him?"

"He's on a trip. Works for the Department of Agriculture. He's out doing something about meat packing. Mexican meat packaged in the U.S.... Makes all the small cattle farmers mad. They try to stir him up."

"Sounds like that might keep him busy."

"Yeah, he gets all kinds of pressure. Just floats with it."

"Do you know his cell phone number?"

Joss got up and moved toward a pad of paper by the telephone.

"Yeah, I'll write it down for you and my sister's too."

"Your sister's?"

"Yeah, Winifred, there's a name! She goes by Freddie Winslow."

"Okay, and where might she be?"

"Probably with her boyfriend, Sage Berenson."

"Sage? At least that's one syllable."

"Yeah, never thought about that. Simple, and that tells you a lot about Sage."

Just then, Metzinger returned. Givens let him sit down and read her notes back to him. When she finished, he turned to the girl.

"May I call you Joss?"

The girl nodded.

"Joss, we appreciate the information you've given us. We know this is hard on you and we're sorry to have to question you so much. I need to ask how old you are."

"Fifteen."

Metzinger caught Givens's eye, finding it hard to believe this girl was so young. She looked at least eighteen.

"Well, that means that legally you're a juvenile. We're required to have your father, or his representative, present before we can talk to you about all of this. We'll need to talk to you again after he comes home. May I ask how old your sister is?"

"She's eighteen."

"Okay, you can't stay here tonight. Right now the house is a crime scene. We can't let anyone be here until we've obtained a search warrant and gone over the place. Can you stay with your sister?"

Joss looked at Metzinger in distress.

"Stay at Sage's? You've got to be kidding."

Metzinger grabbed for straws.

"I take it Sage is not someone you admire. Where else can you stay?"

"I'll go to Ginger's."

"Okay. Who's Ginger?"

"My father's sister-in-law."

Metzinger felt like he was pulling teeth.

"And do you know her phone number and address?"

"'Course."

Joss took the paper with the other phone numbers back from Givens, added the information, and passed it to Metzinger.

"She lives a few blocks from here, down in Beverley Hills."

Metzinger nodded and then sat for a minute trying to decide what else to ask. Joss sat still, looking nervous. Finally, Metzinger startled everyone by standing up.

"Okay, I'll phone Ginger Winslow."

He looked at Joss.

"Am I correct, that her last name is Winslow?"

Joss nodded.

"Okay, I'll phone your Aunt and see if I can arrange for you to stay with her. While I'm doing that, please go upstairs and get ready. Detective Givens will go with you."

Joss's head came up. She looked from Metzinger to Givens and back to Metzinger.

"What, am I some kind of criminal? I can't go by myself?"

Metzinger shook his head.

"Just don't want any questions later."

He pulled out his cell phone and concentrated on dialing as Givens got up from her seat and led Joss toward the stairs.

# CHAPTER SEVEN

JOSS AND THE detectives left through the back door and Joss locked up behind them. The girl's aunt, Ginger Winslow, arrived a moment later. Metzinger explained what he knew about the murder so far, which was not much, and instructed her to keep Joss safe and available for questioning. He and Givens gave the woman their cards and told her to call if she had any concerns.

Once Joss and Ginger departed, Givens turned to Metzinger.

"Was that the right thing to do? The girl didn't cry or anything. Just looked somber. What if she's the killer?"

Metzinger sighed.

"Hell, I hope not. I'd like to assume the poor girl is innocent, but maybe I'm naïve, or in denial because I have a teenage daughter. If I'm wrong, it's on me. My bad... really my bad."

Givens looked off in the distance.

"Well, she's young and hopefully innocent." Then she quipped, "Your call senior detective. Let's check the yard."

They walked carefully around the house, paying special attention to the shrubbery and how it obscured the view. The killer had to leave the front stoop some way. Crossing behind the bushes seemed likely, but there were no broken limbs, snagged clothing, or any other clues.

"Hell," Givens expostulated, "looks like he left clean as a whistle. Probably just walked down the sidewalk."

The detectives proceeded around the house, covering the back yard in detail, but found nothing.

Metzinger shook his head and sighed.

"Let's get back to the car and make notes before I forget everything. Then I'll phone the husband and the other daughter."

As they sat in their car, the forensics truck and the morgue wagon switched places in the driveway. Givens commented, "The vic will be gone soon. When you call the next of kin, you'll have to tell them they have a death in the family, their house is a crime scene, and eventually, they'll have to clean up. Sounds like a triple whammy."

"There's nothing easy about it. Nobody has to clean up in the movies."

"Emily Blunt and Amy Adams did."

"An anomaly. Tried to make it funny, but there's nothing funny about cleaning up a crime scene."

Metzinger took out his notebook and began jotting things down to transfer to the murder book back in the office.

He glanced at Givens.

"You need to write too. I need all the help I can get."

Givens jerked alert to the situation and diligently pulled out her notebook.

"Yeah, I know. Just thinking it's not a neighborhood where you would expect this, but, then again, I guess you never know."

They both wrote in silence.

Finally, Metzinger snapped his notebook closed and stuffed it back in this pocket.

"You need more time?" he asked.

Givens sighed.

"Another few seconds."

When she finished, she said, "Okay, what's next?"

"I'll phone the husband and daughter. I've put it off as long as I can."

"Privilege of seniority," Givens pointed out.

Metzinger nodded as he took out his phone and unfolded Joss's note.

"Your time will come. While I'm doing this, how about stepping out of the car and giving Lt. Ramirez an update from your cell?"

After updating Lt. Ramirez, and waiting for Metzinger to be off the phone, Givens climbed back into the car.

"Tough?" she asked.

"No, not really. The husband was just silent for a while and then said he'd be home tomorrow, that he'd phone me after he landed. I asked him to give me a heads-up as to when that would be, after he's bought his airline tickets. The sister, Freddie, answered the call in a surly mood. When I told her that her mother was dead, she said 'Shit, what happened?' Like Joss, there wasn't much, if any, emotion. Told her not to come to the house because it's a crime scene. Told her to be available tomorrow. That we will need to talk to her. Again, she said, 'Shit', but agreed to be available."

"Sounds like a charming family. Also, sounds like a full day tomorrow. Interviews with the victim's daughter, and with her father, after he comes home, and a search of the house. What's next?"

"Canvas our part of the neighborhood. Let's start with the house to the left of the crime scene."

Metzinger pulled his notebook back out and wrote 408 Crest Street, along with the date and time.

# CHAPTER EIGHT

UNLIKE ITS NEIGHBOR, 408 Crest Street had a sidewalk straight from the street to the front door with only one step up to a flagstone stoop... a single-story frame bungalow, which was a rarity on a street of two-story houses (mostly brick houses, or brick on the lower half and frame on the top).

Givens rang the doorbell and almost immediately the door was opened by an elderly man.

The man had white hair that hung loosely in all directions around his head; combed barely leaving a vague part in the middle of his head. A small, gray-haired woman stood behind him, hands clasped in front of her, looking like terrible news was coming.

The man spoke uncertainly, "Yes, may I help you?"

The detectives showed their badges

"Yes, I'm Detective Metzinger and this is Detective Givens. We're sorry to bother you, but we need to ask some questions."

"We saw the commotion next door but were afraid to interfere. What's happened?"

Metzinger replied, "I'm sorry to say, we found a woman's body lying in the doorway of the neighboring house. Can you tell us who lives there?"

"Yes, of course. The man's name is Oliver Winslow. His wife doesn't use the same name. Her name is Daphne O'Hanlon."

"Thank you. That agrees with the information we have. Can you tell us anything about them?"

"A little. They're probably both in their early fifties. She writes children's books about a gerbil. He works for the government, one of the departments, I think."

The woman behind him nodded and added, "Yes, the Department of Agriculture. He seems to travel a lot, comes home late."

The man agreed.

"His job must be demanding. As Emma says, he comes home late. But on the weekends he really parties. His back-yard barbecues keep us awake... at least they used to. Didn't do much of that this last summer, although one of their daughters had parties, mostly when the adults were away. Never were quite as loud as the parents' parties."

"Can you tell us what your neighbors look like? Physical descriptions."

"Adults or daughters?"

"All of them."

"Well, he's medium height, not very fit. Hair is brown, beginning to gray. Has a mustache. Wears suits to work, athletic clothes on the weekend, although I never see him exercise. The woman, Daphne, dresses up every day like she's going to meet someone and wants to look nice. I shouldn't say it, but she's a bit plump. I think her hair is dyed. Auburn."

The woman nodded.

"Definitely dyed. Nothing wrong with that, but yes, dyed."

Metzinger and Givens looked at each other with slight nods.

The man picked up on it.

"She's the one who's dead?"

Metzinger answered, abashed.

"Might be. What about the daughters?"

The man chuckled before describing the daughters.

"Sandy blonde... always looks angry... we don't see much of her."

The woman chimed in, "Wears her clothes tight enough they should split. Only started that in the last year or so, like she's rebelling. Runs around with what I would call a young gangster."

"That the older daughter, or the younger one?"

"Uh, the older one."

"How about the second daughter, the younger one?"

"Only see her now and then. Doesn't wear as much makeup as her sister but seems to dress for an older crowd. We still see her walking to catch the school bus."

Again, the woman chimed in to contribute, "Prettier than the older one, but both are attractive."

Metzinger nodded.

"Well, thank you. You've been very helpful. We didn't get your names."

The man stuck out his hand.

"Charlie and Emma Sutton. We've lived here seventeen years. Seen all kinds of people next door. You say the woman's dead? If I may ask, how'd she die?"

Metzinger hesitated and then answered.

"She was shot."

Mr. Sutton gulped.

"Here, in this neighborhood?"

"I'm afraid so. Probably last night. Did you see or hear anything unusual? Like a shot being fired?"

The man shook his head.

"No, not a thing."

Mrs. Sutton moved forward from behind her husband's shoulder.

"I did."

Her husband looked at her as if she'd suddenly appeared from nowhere.

"I heard a shot. Right after NCIS Los Angeles began. Didn't know what it was, but now I think it was a shot, not part of the program."

Givens jumped in.

"A little after nine?"

The woman nodded.

"About ten after."

"Thank you, Mrs. Sutton. That's valuable information."

"And I saw a car parked across the street."

"Oh?"

"But it was a little earlier, maybe half-an-hour. I didn't see it leave, but it was gone when I went to bed, near ten o'clock."

"Also, valuable information, Mrs. Sutton. What did the car look like?"

"Um, dark, boxy. It was hard to see. The streetlight's too far away."

"Was it black?"

"I don't think so, but I don't know what color it was... just dark."

"Did you see who was driving? Did they get out of the car?"

"No, never saw anyone. I wasn't watching the whole time."

Mr. Sutton continued watching his wife in amazement.

Apparently finished, Mrs. Sutton stepped back to her previous subordinate position, looking smug and pleased with herself.

Mr. Sutton turned back to the detectives.

"You think the dead woman is Daphne?"

"Don't know yet."

"If she is, a lot of kids are going to be sad. No more gerbil stories."

Mrs. Sutton spoke again.

"Geraldine."

The man nodded, "Right, The Adventures of Geraldine Gerbil."

# CHAPTER NINE

AFTER LEARNING THAT Daphne O'Hanlon wrote children's books featuring a gerbil named Geraldine who lived in Billy Dilly's back yard shed and had great adventures in the neighborhood, Metzinger and Givens thanked the Suttons and walked back down the entrance sidewalk eyeing the few remaining gawkers across the street.

Metzinger spoke, almost thinking out loud.

"Do you think we can make it to the house across the street?"

"We just need to walk fast, eyes straight ahead," Givens replied. *Avoiding hassle is my second job.*

"Let's go for it."

They walked on the victim's side of the street until they were directly opposite their target house, 409 Crest Street, and then cut across the street with purpose. The gawkers separated to let them through, one of them asking, "Someone get murdered?"

Metzinger ignored the question.

As they walked up the sidewalk to a bright shamrock-green front door, he spoke to Givens without turning his head.

"Kind of bright for a conservative brick house."

"Yeah, looks like they want to make a statement."

The detectives noticed a head move away from the front window and the door opened before they could knock.

"I knew something was wrong," said a woman with graying hair, bangs cut straight across her forehead, the rest of her hair blunt cut around her head.

"I told Donald to check that house when he left for work this morning, but he just drove off. The door wasn't closed. Something had to be wrong. Who's dead?"

Givens recoiled from the outburst while holding out her badge.

"Dead, ma'am?"

"Yeah, the morgue truck just left. Or do you call it a hearse or an ambulance when it's carrying somebody in a bag?"

Givens glanced back across the street and noticed the mortuary wagon was gone.

"I call it a wagon, ma'am. Who's Donald?"

"My husband, Donald Braswell."

"And you're Mrs. Braswell, ma'am?"

"Of course."

"And may I ask your first name?"

"Harriet. Harriet Braswell."

Givens pulled out her interview notebook and with deliberation wrote the name down next to the address.

"And Donald is your husband?"

"Of course. I already said that. Who else do you think lives here?"

Metzinger interceded.

"She's just making sure to get everything right. Do you mind if we ask you some questions?"

"Sure, but that's all I know. Saw the screened door ajar this morning. Then, later, police arrived and there was all kinds of commotion. You really know how to create turmoil."

"Just have to cover all bases, ma'am."

"So, again, who's dead?"

Metzinger hesitated.

"We believe it's Daphne O'Hanlon."

"Believe? What do you mean, believe? A few minutes ago, you put one of the daughters in a car. Are you telling me she didn't identify her own mother?"

"Yes, she did. I'm just reluctant to discuss the victim until we know more."

"Reluctant? If the woman is dead, she's dead."

Metzinger was becoming exasperated.

"Right, Mrs. Braswell. The woman is deceased. May I ask when you noted something was wrong across the street?"

"When I got up this morning. I told you that I told Donald the door was ajar."

"Right. I didn't know what time that was."

"Six-thirty. Soon as I got up. My husband left at seven-thirty. Didn't check the door like I told him to."

"Right. Did you notice anything before that? Hear a shot or anything?"

"Shot? She was shot?"

"Yes. Did you hear anything?"

"No, nothing."

"Mr. and Mrs. Sutton thought they heard a shot a little after nine last night."

"Charlie Sutton did? He's deaf as a doornail. I didn't hear anything. If she was shot, they must have used one of those silencer things."

"How about a car? Did you see a car parked on the street between eight-thirty and nine-thirty?"

"Last night?"

"Yes."

"No, that's when Donald and I watch television. I check now and then, but no, I didn't notice a car. You sure it was there?"

"I only know what Mrs. Sutton told us."

"Can't imagine missing it. She sure?"

"Says she is."

"Strange I'd miss it."

Metzinger nodded and made a note.

"Anything else you can think of, Mrs. Braswell?"

"Well, doesn't it sound to you like those other two murders, the ones last month? Don't they think it's a derelict street person who did those? There was a guy early this morning, white beard, pushing a shopping cart, checking the trash. It could be the same derelict. You need to check up on him!"

Requiem for Geraldine Gerbil                    41

"Yes, ma'am. You say he was here this morning?"

"Yes. Around six-thirty."

Metzinger made a note. Mrs. Braswell was shaking her head.

"Something else, ma'am?"

"Yes. I'm amazed I didn't hear anything. You sure she wasn't shot some-where else?"

"Doesn't appear so."

"Really strange."

Metzinger pulled his card from his pocket and handed it to Mrs. Braswell.

"Please ask your husband if he heard or saw anything. Give me a call if he did."

"Sure, but he didn't hear anything. I'd know."

"Thank you, Mrs. Braswell, but would you ask him just the same?"

# CHAPTER TEN

METZINGER AND GIVENS scurried down the Braswell's front walk past two remaining gawkers who were talking to each other. One turned to the detectives and grinned.

"Did Harriett know the scoop? She usually does."

Givens just shook her head as the detectives hurried across the street to the neighbors' on the right side of the Winslow/O'Hanlon house. Her knock was answered by a woman wearing a blue iridescent sports bra and pink yoga pants. Blonde, early thirties. Givens noted the woman's figure was toned. She looked like she worked at it.

"Hi. Welcome. You detectives?"

The detectives showed their badges and said in unison, "Yes, may we talk to you?"

"Yeah, come on in. After all the flurry next door, I've been expecting you. Come on into the living room and have a seat."

The room was all beige with few accessories. Metzinger and Givens were relieved not to have to stand in the doorway this time. Metzinger took a club chair and Givens sat on the sofa where the woman joined her.

"I'm Jeannie... Jeannie Sorley. You caught me in the middle of my workout. What happened over there?" She stuck her thumb toward her neighbor's house.

Metzinger studied Mrs.... was she *Mrs.* Sorley?

"I'm sorry, but we are investigating a murder."

Jeannie Sorley looked alarmed.

"Is Ollie all right?"

"Ollie?"

"Oliver Winslow, my neighbor."

"Yes. I talked to him by phone. He's on a trip."

"Oh, yeah. He went to Omaha."

"That's right."

"So, who's been killed?"

"Daphne O'Hanlon."

Jeannie's hand covered her mouth in surprise.

"That's terrible!"

"Yes, it is."

Jeannie looked around.

"I'm being a lousy host. Would you like something to drink? A beer, soda, or water? Oh, of course, not a beer. You're on duty."

Givens said, "A glass of water would be very nice."

"Yes, it would." Metzinger agreed.

Jeannie rose from the sofa and headed for the kitchen with Metzinger's eyes following her.

Givens watched him watching and shook her head.

Metzinger saw he'd been caught.

"What?"

"Nothing." Givens said with an expression that said keep it professional.

Jeannie returned with two glasses of water for the detectives. She then sat and picked up her own half empty martini from the coffee table and took a sip.

Givens had noted it earlier and wondered, *how does she exercise while holding a martini?*

"We wondered, Mrs. Sorley, have you observed anything unusual happening next door, last evening or during the night?" She hadn't corrected the Mrs. earlier, so Givens assumed it was correct.

"No. I haven't, but Bill and I were dining out with friends."

"Bill is your husband?"

"Oh, right. I haven't mentioned him before."

"And what time did you get home?"

"Uh, I guess around nine-thirty, more or less."

"After you got home, did you hear anything that sounded like a shot?"

"She was shot?"

"Yes. Did you hear anything?"

"No... no, I didn't. Didn't the girls hear anything?"

Metzinger didn't feel any need to discuss what Joss had said.

"No, they didn't. When you came home did you see a car parked across the street from the Suttons?"

"The Suttons?"

"Your neighbors the other side of the Winslows."

"Oh... so that's their name. No, haven't met them."

"No you didn't see a car or no on knowing the Suttons?"

"No, about the car. We came home from that direction. I think I would have noticed. No, there was no car."

Metzinger rose, followed by Givens.

"We're still asking your other neighbors questions."

He handed Jeannie his card.

"If you think of anything, or if your husband does, please give me a call. I thank you very much for your time. We may be back."

Mrs. Sorley followed the detectives to the door.

"So, Ollie's still traveling? When's he due home? I'll want to help him with a meal."

Metzinger turned his head back to the woman.

"Tomorrow, but he won't be coming to the house. It's a crime scene."

"Oh, the poor man. He's got no home?"

"For a few days, yes."

"Poor, poor man."

# CHAPTER ELEVEN

GINGER WINSLOW'S EXPLORER pulled into her driveway on Lindsay Drive in Beverley Hills. Joss had been by the house many times but couldn't remember being in it. Her sister, Freddie, said that she had been in the house when she was a little girl and thought Joss was there when she was very small.

Joss studied her aunt while they drove in silence. Joss's mother always said Ginger Winslow was a woman of questionable reputation--not someone with whom it was appropriate to socialize. She said the woman was a dancer, performing wild gyrations in skimpy costumes to the embarrassment of the family. Joss decided Aunt Ginger didn't look weird or evil. She was wearing tan slacks, a white blouse, and a blue cardigan. Very conservative. She certainly didn't look like the floozy Joss's mother had described.

Entering Ginger's house, Joss expected something wild and contemporary. It was anything but. Everything was very traditional. A portrait photograph of a younger Ginger hung over the mantle, stylized and airbrushed; the kind of portrait Joss associated with Hollywood stars; very theatrical. Other photographs were set around on tables. Ginger's husband Edwin in a coat and tie, Ginger and Edwin at Niagara Falls, the Grand Canyon, and the Las Vegas strip... even a photograph of Joss and Freddie with their father when they were little girls.

Joss picked up the picture.

"I'm surprised you have this."

Ginger stood behind Joss.

"Why? You're our nieces, the only nieces we have, and we don't have children."

Joss turned and looked at her aunt.

"You know my mother didn't like you... dissed you all the time. It surprised me when you came to pick me up today."

"Joss, I don't dislike you. I have no reason to. Ed and I have kept track of you over the years. You're our family."

"But my mother wouldn't let us have any contact with you?"

"I know. Your mother looked down on us... on me because I danced in musicals around D.C. and had dreams of Broadway. Ed and I didn't have children because of my dreams. Foolish dreams, but I loved the dancing, even though it stayed local. Now I'm forty-two and no one wants a forty-two-year-old dancer. It's the price we paid for that love, for my ego. Like it or not, you and Freddie are our family."

"But we never see each other."

"No, but we follow your lives. You probably don't know it, but Ed and Ollie have lunch together regularly. They didn't tell Daphne. I know everything about you girls, and I worry for Freddie. It's so sad she isn't in college and I'm concerned about what she's doing with her life, messing around with that boy she lives with."

"Yeah, the dummy. Dad took her down to Mary Washington University, and the next day she got on the train and came back to Alexandria. They should never have given her a credit card."

"Your father said she wouldn't talk about it. That she just seemed angry. It wasn't the life she wanted."

"Yeah well, Dad didn't take her into the dorm. If he had, maybe he'd understand, maybe he would have done something about it, and maybe Freddie would still be there."

"Oh, is it something you know about?"

"Well, her roommate had a giant photograph of a man's thing covering a whole wall. The roommate said it reminded her not to be dominated by men. Said she would have nothing to do with them. Freddie turned and left. Stayed in a motel and came home the next day. Said she couldn't deal with it."

"And now she's living with some man and it's worrisome to your father."

"She says it's temporary... an interim thing."

"Interim between what and what?"

"I don't know. We talk some, but she thinks I'm too young for a real discussion."

"I'm sorry to hear that. Do you think I can help? Should we reach out and see if she'll come here?"

"Hey, that's kind of you, but she's being independent... and hard-headed. Right now, I don't think she'll talk to any adult."

"Won't she be upset about your mother?"

"Aunt Ginger, Freddie hated our mother... felt that Mom used her. I don't think she's shedding any tears."

Ginger focused earnestly on Joss.

"Honey, you're not shedding any tears either."

Joss looked down.

"Yeah, I wonder what the detectives thought about that."

"You didn't react to your mother's death?"

"Not even when I saw her body. I'd been around her negativism too long, all her belittling of people, of Freddie, of Dad... of me."

"Oh, sweetheart, I'm so sorry. How will your dad take it?"

"Not sure. He's stuck with her a long time."

"Yes, he has." Ginger turned toward the kitchen.

"I'm not being much of a host. What can I get for you to drink and eat? I have some cookies, soda, water... what would you like?"

Joss got up from the chair where she had been sitting.

"Let me come help. Do you have some milk?"

"Yes, I keep it for cereal. You're lucky."

Putting cookies on a plate, Ginger said, "Glasses are to the left of the sink."

Joss helped herself to a glass, took the milk from the refrigerator, and poured herself a glass full.

Returning to the living room, Ginger commented, "I guess there will be no more gerbil books?"

Joss set her glass on the coffee table.

"Freddie and my mother haven't written any in two years."

"Freddie?"

"Yeah. She was pissed--uh, sorry... angry that she wasn't being given credit... or money."

Ginger gaped.

# CHAPTER TWELVE

METZINGER AND GIVENS sat in their unmarked cruiser, with their interview notebooks and pens out.

Givens leaned back knowing that Metzinger was getting ready to go through his scribbles with a fine-tooth comb and as the junior detective she was along for the ride.

"Some bunch of neighbors, aren't they?" Givens reflected. "One little-old-lady hides behind her husband, periodically pops out with vital facts and then goes back to hiding. Another old lady acts like a Spanish inquisitor. Then, the third neighbor drinks morning martinis and shakes her booty in your face."

"She did?"

Givens glared at Metzinger with raised eyebrows.

"Really? Ya claimin' you didn't notice?"

"Only interested in relevant facts."

"And you didn't notice her relevant facts swinging in front of you?"

"All relevant facts are being duly recorded."

"Maybe in your mind."

"So, let's write 'em down."

Metzinger read back his summary:

> Deceased, Daphne O'Hanlon (DO), identified by her daughter Joss, AKA Josceline Winslow (JW), a minor who says she slept through the whole incident—to be interviewed when her father, Oliver Winslow (OW), is available. JW will stay with her aunt, Ginger Winslow (GW), 807 Lindsey Drive,

Beverley Hills, Alexandria, Virginia.

The victim's body was found lying inside the front door of her house, 410 Crest Street, Jefferson Park, Alexandria, Virginia. The body was lying on its side, tilted toward her back, with one leg partially extended over the entrance threshold, keeping the screened door open a foot or so. Main front door of the house was open, swinging, banging into the head of the deceased. The victim appeared to have been shot at close range through the screened door. Bullet entered her chest, just below her breasts. Rigor appeared to be easing, suggesting victim had been dead 10-12 hours. Based on the body's position, she answered the door. Crime scene suggests she may have opened the screened door, stepping out with one leg to let the visitor in, thus leaving her leg out. Alternatively, the leg may have fallen out when the assailant reached through the door to turn out the entrance lights. After being shot, the victim apparently fell back and sideways. Jimmy Protho was on the scene and agrees.

Initially, we believed the house to be vacant. Later, we discovered JW was in the house. We talked to JW in the kitchen limiting discussions to identification of the victim and basic family information. We then arranged a place for her to stay.

OF NOTE:

A Front hallway light was out, as were the exterior lights on the front of the house. Techs checked the light switches for fingerprints, but everything was smudged.

House doorbell camera on the front door was covered with a Band-Aid, presumably by the killer. The Band-Aid is being checked for fingerprints

   —NEED TO OBTAIN A WARRANT TO ACCESS THE RECORDINGS FROM THE CAMERA.

A While inspecting the scene with the forensics

technician, Manny Migliano, JW appeared in a bathrobe, coming from the interior back area of the house. She identified the body as her mother DO. When interviewed in the kitchen JW indicated she had just awakened in her bedroom, where she'd been since 9 P.M. the night before. According to JW, her father (OW), and sister Winifred Winslow (WW) were not in the home. OW is out of town and she declined staying with her sister who is living with her boyfriend. JW's aunt, Ginger Winslow (GW), came and picked her up.

PROCEDURAL NOTE:

Before leaving, Detective Givens escorted JW to her bedroom to dress and pack an overnight bag. JW, Det. Givens, and I left through the backdoor. JW locked the door and gave me the key. GW did not enter the house —key to be bagged and tagged.

Metzinger looked at Givens.

"What else?"

"We surveyed the yard to see if the perp left any clues. We found no threads from clothing, broken branches on bushes, etc."

"Noted."

"We also learned the victim's husband, Oliver Winslow, works for the Department of Agriculture and is on a trip to Omaha. The second daughter, Winifred Winslow, goes by 'Freddie' and lives with her boyfriend Sage Berenson."

Metzinger corrected, "We don't know she's living there, only that that's where she was when we phoned her to notify her of her mother's death. And you called the father too."

"Right, we still need to talk to both of them."

"I've got all that in my individual interview notes. Then, we sent two patrolmen off to talk to the other neighbors while we interviewed the closest ones."

Metzinger returned to focus on his notebook.

"Let's see, Officer Jess Holmes and Sgt. Sidney Simpson. We need to talk to them as soon as they get back. Hope they're not too late. My daughter's playing a volleyball game tonight. It's only a pre-season scrimmage, but I catch hell if I miss it."

"You enjoy the games?"

"Yeah, I do."

"So. Why are you griping?"

"'Cause sometimes the job screws me up."

"So, live with it."

"The job never screws you up?"

"All the time."

"So, I'm not alone. Where were we?"

"Interviewing the neighbors."

"Right."

A 408 Crest Street, The Suttons, Charlie (CS) and Emma (ES). Confirmed that DO and OW occupy the crime scene residence. ES thought she heard a gunshot approximately 9:10 P.M., which fits the condition of the body. She also said that a car was parked across the street from approximately 8:30 P.M... dark and boxy. It was gone later, but she couldn't say when it left.

A 409 Crest Street, The Braswells live across the street from the crime scene, Donald (DB) and Harriet (HB). Only HB was home when we conducted the interview. She said she saw the Winslow's door was open around 6:30 A.M. and asked her husband to check on it, but he drove past going to work. She couldn't confirm the gunshot... didn't hear it. Says a white-bearded itinerant was checking the garbage cans along the street, also around 6:30 A.M. She thinks it might be the same man from a different set of murders in a nearby area. 6:30 A.M. doesn't jibe with the condition of the body.
    —Check out the white-bearded man.

A 412 Crest Street, only Jeannie Sorley (JS) was home.
Her husband, Bill (BS), was at work. She seemed to
have intimate knowledge of the Winslows, at least of OW.
She was concerned about OW being all right... not much
about the vic. Seemed strange. She was aware OW was
traveling. Couldn't confirm the shot. Says she wasn't home...
out having dinner with her husband until 9:30 P.M. at
which time she didn't see a parked car on the street.
      —ALIBI NEEDS CHECKING.

"You didn't mention how Mrs. Sorley was dressed and that she was drinking a martini in the middle of the day."

"Again, not relevant."

"You sure acted like it was."

Metzinger studied Givens for a minute.

"Hey, I'm a man. Don't pretend not to be."

Givens nodded and looked out the car window.

"Here come our patrolmen."

Metzinger waved them over.

"Anything interesting?"

Officer Simpson took the lead, "Not really. One woman walking her baby in a stroller early this morning noticed the door open. When she got home, she tried to call the Winslows but got no answer."

"That's it?"

"That's it."

Metzinger sighed.

"Okay, guys. Thanks a lot. You can go. We'll make sure the house is secured."

# CHAPTER THIRTEEN

FREDDIE WINSLOW PACED back and forth.

"Christ, she's been killed! Who the hell would do that? They said I can't go home. Told me to just stay here. What should I do? I ought to do something, shouldn't I?"

Sage Berenson leaned back on his worn sofa, smoking a cigarette. He took a drag and stretched.

"For Christ' sake, will you settle down? You can't do anything. You didn't like her anyway. You've been bitching about her for weeks."

"'Course I have. I'm trying to get out on my own and she owes me! Won't give me a cent! Made money off me all these years and hasn't given me a penny."

"Hey, you let her get away with it."

"Yeah, what's a kid supposed to do?"

"Thought you were sixteen when the last book was published. You could have stood up for yourself."

"Well, the checks were written to her. I'd've had to get a lawyer and sue her or something."

"You can still do that."

"Yeah well, she's dead, Sage."

"I know she's dead. So, who gets the money?"

"God, my dad will. He didn't have anything to do with writing the books. Now he'll get the whole thing."

"That's why you need a lawyer."

"Yeah? And how do I pay for this lawyer?"

"Don't know, but you can't do anything tonight."

Freddie flopped down in a lounge chair.

"Shit, shit, shit. Give me a joint."

Sage got up and pulled a baggie of marijuana out of the kitchen cabinet. As he rolled it, he praised himself for doing a weed run the night before.

His self-praise elicited Freddie's curiosity.

"You were gone a long time. Didn't kill my mother, did you?"

Sage turned to her, his mouth agape.

"You're shitting me, aren't you? Stopped at Gilkerson's and had a couple of beers. Didn't kill anyone," he said, handing her the joint, and then said, "I hope this straightens your mind. You were here alone the whole time. You know I could ask you the same thing... did you kill her? God knows you have reasons."

Freddie lit the joint.

"Christ. What are we talking about? Yeah, I had reasons. You think the cops will think that!? Shit, we have to protect each other... tell them we were together, okay?"

"Yeah, Okay. How much money do you think she had?"

"Hell, I don't know. Now, I'll never get anything."

"Why don't you write more books? With her dead, you'll get the money now."

"You kidding? I was having a hard time thinking that way when I was sixteen. Not sure that last book sold at all. I didn't even try."

"Is that what your mother told you? It wasn't any good?"

Freddie laughed, "My mother didn't tell me shit."

"You think she was feeling guilty?"

"My mother feel guilty? You're kidding? The money was hers. She hugged it. No way she was sharing it."

"Your father's no better?"

"Hell, I don't know. They did everything separately. Didn't even have joint bank accounts. Dad gave me an allowance. I'll say that for him. Was going to pay part of my college expenses."

"So, maybe he'll share?"

"Maybe, but I'm not counting on it."

"Did he know the stories were yours?"

"'Course. It would have been hard to live in the same house and not know it."

"So, what are you gonna do?"

"I'm going to sit here and smoke this joint. Tomorrow's another day."

"Hell, you're making me high just sitting in the room with you. Cold outside or not, I'm opening a window."

"Quit griping and light yourself up. I don't want to smoke alone."

# CHAPTER FOURTEEN

METZINGER ARRIVED TO the high school at 7:25 P.M. Late.
He glanced at the scoreboard: Home 5, Visitors 3. Must be the second game.

Drury bought himself a hot dog at the concession stand. Mary Lou Gleason was working the stand alone. At least it wasn't his night. Parents usually volunteered together. He wondered where her husband was. *Not my problem*, he reminded his detective brain.

He scanned the grandstand, spotted his wife sitting alone, and wondered where his son, Ben, was. Then, motion at the end of the grandstand caught his eye. Fourteen-year-old Ben was sitting with a friend, laughing. They were shoving each other. Drury wondered if the kid would survive to be fifteen.

After the next serve, Drury hurried around the end of the gymnasium and made his way up the stands to sit by his wife, Sarah.

"Overtime at work?" she asked.

"You'll read about it tomorrow... Metro Section... the usual... page three or four. How's the game going?"

"We're winning. That much I understand. Laura's got some spikes in, but she's not being set up much."

"Hey, it's always sporadic. Sometimes she gets runs of set-ups. Nothing we can do."

He started unwrapping his hot dog.

"My usual diet tonight. Did you fix anything tasty?"

"Filet Mignon. The usual."

"Yeah, sure. You trying to make me feel bad?"

"Always. Want you to know you're missing the good things in life… watch the mustard… don't drip it on your suit."

Metzinger adjusted the wrapper and leaned forward.

"Way it's been for twenty-four years. Good one day and shitty the next. Victim was a children's author. Wrote about gerbils."

"Oh? Geraldine Gerbil?"

"Yeah, I think so. Should I know about her?"

"If you had read Ben and Laura more bedtime stories you might. Cute picture books."

"Well, there won't be any more--great spike, Laura!"

"You can talk and watch the game at the same time?"

"I'm ambidextrous."

"That means using two hands equally well."

"Yeah, I can do that too."

# CHAPTER FIFTEEN

G IVENS HAD TO park half a block away from her house.
    She hated that. Her suit didn't exactly fit into the neighborhood; too conspicuous for comfort. At least she wasn't wearing the uniform any more. That really had been conspicuous.

The front door was locked. She should have been prepared... should have had her keys out and ready. Instead, she'd dumped them in her purse and was fumbling to get them back out when Old Man Davis caught her.

"Lookin' mighty fine, Leslie. Pretty sharp. You goin' out again tonight? Puttin' on your party dress? Looked good last night!"

Finally, she got the door open and called over, "Don't know, Mr. Davis. Go with the flow."

She closed the door as quickly as she could. Old Man Davis commenting on her looks made her more than a little uncomfortable

She dropped her purse on the bottom stair-step and shouted, "Mama, you home?"

Her mother came to the kitchen door.

"What you shoutin' for? I'm right here. Right where I am every night. Why're you so late?"

Givens sighed.

"Workin', Mama."

"Does that mean somebody dead?"

"'Fraid so."

"Black or white?"

"White."

"At least it wasn't a poor black child walking innocent on the street. They got a black suspect?"

"Upscale neighborhood. White victim, no suspects yet. It'll be in the papers tomorrow."

"Yeah, like I read the paper. Maybe someone will leave one on a table at work. Sometimes they do. What time you get home last night?"

"Why's it matter, Mama?"

"Matters, 'cause I lay awake worried. You get killed, who's going to investigate? That old man partner of yours?"

"He's early forties, Mama. Younger than you."

"Younger than me's not saying much. Who'd you go out with?"

"What's it matter?"

"Cause some of your friends are sketchy. If something happens, don't I need to tell your partner who you were with?"

"Sharyn and Chantel."

Her mother groaned.

"Sharyn's okay but that Chantel will shade you every which way. You need to watch out for her."

"Mama don't worry. I'm wise to Chantel."

"Was Bobby Riley there?"

"No, it was a work night for Bobby."

"Work night for you too—and for me."

"Just danced. Nothing extra."

"Yeah. So, you danced with the girls?"

"No. With dudes."

"Dudes? Men off the street?"

"No Mama. Kenya Green and Travis Lee."

"Lord Leslie, Kenya Green! Talk about a thug. I've known his father, Embrey, forever. Guess he's been in prison three times. Burglary. Supportin' the habit. Probably Kenya's got it too."

"Jesus, Mama. I'm not gonna to marry him. Kenya dances super fine and Travis is safe."

"Yeah. Travis is sweet, but there's no future there. You need to work on Bobby. He's sweet on you and he's solid."

"Hey, I know but he needs to ask me out more."

"Maybe you need to start asking him."

"Okay, Mama. You caught up on my life now?"

"Hey. Don't you give me any sass. You want your supper?"

"'Course. And I know I don't say enough about your workin' all day and comin' home to cook. You know I appreciate it."

"Good. Because I put in a long day. It's a wonder I survive. Two hoodlums got in a fight today... messed up the whole diner. Good thing everything's solid. Salt and pepper, sugar shakers, ketchup bottles and napkin holders were all over the place. Called your buddies in blue, but the hoodlums were gone before anyone got there."

"We do the best we can, Mama."

"Sure, but I'm the one who has to clean up. Can't start until they get there. People'd like the cops more if they helped clean up every once in a while. Pick up a pepper shaker or two."

Givens shook her head.

"We don't clean up after the bodies either. Not part of the training. You say there's some supper?"

"You know there is."

"How 'bout we eat and then I'll clean up."

"You said that's not part of the training."

"I'll improvise."

# CHAPTER SIXTEEN

THE NEXT MORNING, when Givens arrived at work, Metzinger was ready to roll.

As soon as she walked in, he picked up his notebook and headed for the door. *Should've picked up coffee at Starbucks,* Givens lamented.

"Got the search warrant for the house," he announced. "But I want to interview the daughter first."

"Which daughter?"

"The older one, Winifred. We have to wait for their father before we can do anymore with Josceline."

"Freddie and Joss."

"Yeah, but we use the full names in our documentation."

"'Course. You got Freddie's address?"

"Boyfriend's. On Duke Street. Winifred gave me the address yesterday. Basement apartment. Entrance in back. I want to get there before they get too organized with their stories."

Metzinger drove the unmarked cruiser along Duke Street, heading downtown. They found the house easily, circled the block, and pulled into the alley behind the houses, parking near the apartment entrance. Numbers at the back of the building confirmed they were at the address Metzinger had scribbled in his notebook.

There were wooden steps up to the first floor of the house and concrete steps going down to the basement apartment between cinder block walls. Metzinger noticed a drain at the bottom of the steps and wondered where it drained to. He surveyed his surroundings. It seemed everything visible was above the drain. He shook his head. *Not my problem.*

At the bottom of the concrete steps he stood on the drain and knocked on the door. There was scuffling inside the apartment and a woman's voice asked, "Who is it?"

"Police," Metzinger and Givens said in unison.

"Just a minute," the woman's voice replied. After more scuffling, the door opened a crack. A young woman peered through the narrow opening.

"Are you the police who called yesterday?"

Metzinger and Givens held up their badges.

"Yes. May we come in?"

The door opened with slow deliberation and the woman stepped back to let them in.

Metzinger glanced around.

"You by yourself?"

Givens spotted an open door, and what looked like stairs on the opposite side of the room. Without hesitating, she bolted across the room and up the stairs where she'd heard a door close above her. She found a door at the top of the stairs, flung it open, and charged out onto Duke Street. Cars were whizzing by, the morning commute headed to U.S. 1. She checked in both directions and saw a man to her right heading for the corner at a dead run. She gave chase with the cars on Duke Street honking and the drivers shouting and gesticulating obscenities out their car windows. Turning the corner, she caught sight of the man cutting into the same alley she and Metzinger had driven into moments before.

Down the alley, he headed toward parked cars with Givens running after him. When she got to the cars, he was just standing haplessly looking from side to side, apparently befuddled. Givens grabbed the man by the back of his coat, pulling him to his knees, grabbed an arm, and cuffed it.

"Give me the other hand!" she demanded.

"Shit. What does your black ass think you're doing? Who the hell are you? I'm going to sue your ass!"

Givens grabbed the other arm and finished snapping the cuffs as she swung him around. She shoved her badge under his nose.

"Since we're asking questions, who are you and why did you run?"

"What business is it of yours?"

"Don't know that it is. All I know is that we said 'police' and you ran. Interesting development. Now, let's walk back to your apartment."

"What apartment is that?"

"The one you ran from."

"You didn't see me in no apartment."

"True enough... just saw you running after we heard a bunch of noise. You deny being there? If something's wrong in the apartment, you going to dump it all on the girl you left there? Let's go see if she knows you."

"Nothing's wrong in the apartment and I bet you ain't got no search warrant."

"Nope. We don't need one to have a nice conversation. And now I've got probable cause. What were you looking for out here? Forgot where you parked your car?"

"Nothing illegal about running. Didn't know you were after me."

Givens nudged him down the steps to the basement apartment and followed him in. Metzinger was sitting on the only chair. Winifred Winslow was sitting cross-legged on a futon. The only other furniture was an ancient sofa in a gaudy orange fabric. It had bedding piled up on one end, and the legs were missing. Givens took the cuffs off the man and pushed him down onto the sofa. She sat on the sofa's arm and caught her breath.

Metzinger grinned at Givens.

"You look a little peaked. How far did you have to chase him? You think he's guilty of something?"

Givens gasped.

"Has to be. Why else would he run down Duke Street at rush hour with people honking and yelling? He turned down the alley. After all that he just stopped at the parking lot looking perplexed. I shouldn't have bothered running so hard. He was just standing there looking confused."

"Well, you needed your exercise."

Givens gave Metzinger an evil look.

"Is this the boyfriend Berenson? He wouldn't tell me."

"Yes. Miss Winslow says he's named Sage Berenson."

Sage looked daggers at Freddie.

"What the fuck?"

Freddie hunched her shoulders, her arms down and palms out toward Sage, trying to look innocent.

"They came to talk to us about my mother's murder."

Givens nodded.

"Yeah, simple as that. No big deal. As you said, we don't even have a search warrant."

Metzinger leaned back, examined his hands, and then looked over at Sage.

"That's right. And, for the time being, we'll consider the bong sitting on the kitchen counter a work of art placed there by your interior designer; part of the décor." He paused for effect and then repeated himself, "For the time being."

Freddie looked at Sage nervously.

"Okay, Sage. Leave dead dogs lie," Givens suggested.

Sage's brow wrinkled.

"Dead dogs?"

Metzinger chuckled and intervened.

"May we get back to what we came for? Just like to ask a few questions."

Sage sulked.

"We need a lawyer?"

Givens eyed him in disgust.

"I don't know. You guilty of something besides talking about my 'black ass'?"

Sage frowned.

"Didn't mean nothing by it. You were hassling me, and it hurt. Just words."

Givens shook her head. *Yeah, just words says the dumb-ass white boy.*

"So, do you need a lawyer, Mr. Berenson?"

Sage hesitated, and Freddie spoke up.

"No, no lawyer. We didn't do anything that needs a lawyer."

Metzinger continued looking at Sage.

"Miss Winslow, Sage needs to answer. He brought it up."

Sage continued to sulk, twisting his mouth, looking down at his hands.

"Nah."

"So, no lawyer?"

"Yeah, no lawyer."

Metzinger opened his notebook. He looked at Freddie.

"Miss Winslow, where were you last night?"

"Here. I was here all night."

Metzinger turned to Sage.

"And you? Where were you, Mr. Berenson?"

Sage puffed out his cheeks in annoyance.

"Here, with her."

Freddie seemed to hesitate and finally looked at Sage and spoke.

"No, you were out... shopping... just for a few minutes."

Sage rolled his eyes at Freddie and scoffed.

"Yeah, ten or fifteen minutes. Not long."

Givens face tightened.

"Shopping, huh? What did you go shopping for that only took ten or fifteen minutes?"

"Personal items."

"Personal?"

Sage turned and glared at Givens.

"Yeah. Personal."

Metzinger made a note.

"What time was this and how do you know it was no more than fifteen minutes?"

Sage looked at Freddie before he spoke as if seeking confirmation.

"Around eight o'clock. It seemed like it was about that long. I didn't time myself. Does anybody?"

Freddie nodded.

"Yeah, that seems right. It wasn't long. He didn't have to go far."

Metzinger kept looking at Sage.

"Did you see anybody who can confirm any of that?"

Sage looked down nervously.

"No. Nobody can confirm it. Just Freddie."

Metzinger nodded and wrote more in his notebook.

"So, Miss Winslow, how did you get along with your mother?"

The change in questioning caught Freddie by surprise, Sage seemed suddenly more alert.

"Uh, all right, I guess. We didn't always agree on things."

"Teenage things?" Givens interjected.

"Yeah, maybe."

"Maybe?" questioned Metzinger.

"Well, money stuff. I wanted to be independent. Thought my parents should help more."

"Thought your parents should help you be more independent?" Metzinger asked. "That why you moved in here with Sage? Sounds like you're defying your parents but still want them to take care of you."

Sage interjected, "Hey. What do you know? It's none of your business."

Now Freddie was seething.

"Yeah. It really is none of your business! I was going to college, but it fell through. I'm coasting for a year trying to figure things out."

"But not living with your parents?"

"No."

"How come?"

Freddie looked at Sage.

"Wanted to live with him."

"Sage is special?"

Freddie looked off into the distance.

"Yeah. Gives me a place to crash, a little freedom, no hassle."

"You felt hassled at home?"

"Yeah. After the college thing and the money situation. Yeah, there was a lot of crap at home."

"Enough crap that you'd do something about it?"

Freddie leveled her eyes at Metzinger.

"I was here last night, detective."

Metzinger met her glare.

"Yeah, well, somebody wasn't happy with your mother."

"She wasn't a person to be happy with."

"Oh, no. Why's that?"

"A bossy narcissist."

"That's what you think about her?"

"Yeah."

"Who else might think that?"

"Lots of people."

"Who?"

"You'll have to ask other people. I'm not accusing anyone."

Metzinger nodded.

"That's fine, we'll do that." He closed his notebook.

"We've just started looking into this case. You can expect us back to ask more questions."

Freddie glared and replied coldly, "We're not going anywhere."

***

When the detectives settled back in their car, Metzinger reopened his notebook for the routine review.

"Well, Miss Freddie wasn't happy with her parents, mostly playing the victim. Don't know if she was unhappy enough to be involved in a murder. She has an alibi, but it depends on the word of a boyfriend of questionable standing."

Givens mused, "Sounds like we have a lot to learn about Daphne O'Hanlon, the creator of cute children's books. Cute might not reflect her personal character."

"Yeah, and why, in particular, her daughter doesn't seem to like her. What's the deal with the money? Freddie's a grown girl wanting independence. Seems spoiled."

Givens looked askance at Metzinger.

"God, Drury. Not sure I'd want to be your daughter. The girl's only eighteen. If college fell through, we need to learn why. Yeah, she probably needs to grow up, but still, she's eighteen."

Metzinger groused.

"My daughter's only sixteen, but she's more mature than Miss Freddie."

"Yeah? You think she's ready to go out on her own?"

"Doesn't need to until after college."

"Exactly."

"Exactly, nothing. No way she'd be sleeping with a loser like Sage."

"We don't know that Freddie is sleeping with him."

"What do you mean 'we don't know'."

"There was bedding on the sofa."

"You think Sage is going to live with her and leave her alone?"

"Maybe having her nearby and the marijuana is enough."

"With a good-looking girl like Freddie?"

"Maybe Sage is a wimp."

"God help us."

# CHAPTER SEVENTEEN

SAGE AND FREDDIE didn't get up when the detectives left. Sage rubbed his wrists where he'd been handcuffed.

"Fucking pigs. Damned woman brutalized me."

Freddie chuckled.

"I wouldn't go around telling people a woman brutalized you."

Sage got up and locked the door.

"So, I should just take it?"

"You just did."

"Yeah, and I get shit from you too. Why'd you tell them I went out? I thought we were going to back each other up."

"Thought someone might have seen you and it would come back to bite us. The cops think it was only fifteen minutes. You couldn't have done anything in fifteen minutes."

"And what's with this telling them your mother was a narcissist, or whatever?"

"Well, she was."

"When are you going to ask about the money from your books?"

"I guess I'll talk to Dad after he gets home and things settle down. Don't want to go running to him about money in the middle of all of this. Bad timing. Meant to ask the cops when I could go back to the house."

"Go back to the house? What do you want to do... clean up?"

"Clean up? Hell no. Dad can take care of that. His house, his problem."

"So, who do you think did it?"

"No idea. You were the one gone an hour-and-a-half. Like I asked before... did you do it?"

"No! And, as I asked before, what were you going during that hour-and-a-half? At least you could smell the beer on me. How do I know where you were?"

"Yeah well, I forgot to sniff you. You know I was here. Don't even have a car."

"I know, babe. We need to keep covering for each other. Good thing you didn't ask me to kill her. I probably would have. I'd do most anything for you. Thank goodness someone else helped us out."

"Shit, Sage, you're talking like I wanted her dead!"

"Because you did."

"Thinking isn't doing."

"So, you lucked out. Admit it."

"A dead mother doesn't get me the money. I expect that Dad gets it all."

"At least you can hit him up easier than you could your mother."

"You think?"

# CHAPTER EIGHTEEN

METZINGER AND GIVENS pulled into the Winslow house driveway. As they walked along the front sidewalk, Givens whispered, "Should I wave to nosy Mrs. Braswell?"

"Don't think so. She's liable to report us to the neighborhood watch as not treating this murder with the gravity it deserves."

"Keeping it professional?"

"You got it."

"Takes a lot of fun out of life."

Metzinger didn't disagree.

Using the key Joss gave them after she'd locked the back door the day before, he unlocked the front door.

"Now we know the back-door key works on the front too. Watch your step. Persian rug's probably still sticky as hell with blood."

After donning protective gloves and boot covers, the detectives awkwardly tiptoed around the rug.

Givens commented, "Should have come in the back door. Could have fallen in the middle of all that."

"And ruined the crime scene."

"Yeah, and you would have put it in your report."

"It would be my duty."

Givens looked down at the rug and cocked her head.

"Should we center the rug?"

"Why? Isn't it where it belongs?"

"I don't think so. It's slid toward the door. Ought to be centered in the hallway."

"Moving it really would be disturbing the crime scene."

"Just seems messy."

"It is messy."

Givens turned back to Metzinger.

"Okay, so where do we start? We've already looked at the entrance hall all we can."

Metzinger considered the situation.

"I'll check the kitchen, especially around the telephone. See if I can find anything relevant. You check the living and dining rooms."

"On it."

Metzinger searched all the kitchen drawers and carefully flipped through a notepad by the telephone. He jotted down the names and phone numbers he found there. Masterson was already working on getting the phone records, but this might be quicker.

Givens shouted from the living room.

"How you coming in there? Haven't found anything here, but there's a den down the hallway. Join me when you finish in the kitchen."

Metzinger decided he'd finished and followed Givens's voice. He found her standing in the downstairs hallway, her hand on the doorknob to the den, holding it open.

A single desk stood in the middle of the floor suggesting the room was a business office. A computer sat on a side table against a wall to the right. Both the desk and the side table had office chairs. A small Persian rug covered the floor in front of the desk. A bachelor's diploma from American University and two Department of Agriculture commendation certificates hung on the wall. There was a window behind the desk, and a closet of office supplies to the left. Three pictures rested on the desk; two of the daughters and one, about fifteen years old, that seemed to be young Daphne O'Hanlon holding a small girl. Winifred? Josceline? There were no recent pictures of Daphne O'Hanlon anywhere in the room. The only other things on the desk were a telephone and an ink blotter pad.

Metzinger checked the drawers and found the usual things: check-books; bank receipts; bills; paper clips, etcetera. The checks were all for Oliver Winslow... nothing joint with the victim. There was a date book: doctor's appointments; PTA meetings; golf matches on weekends; luncheons with someone named EW. All personal. Nothing related to work other than the commendations on the wall.

Metzinger commented, "Looks like a man-cave, but not a very interesting one. No personality."

Givens quipped, "Yeah. Where's the sixty-five-inch TV? Thought all men had one of those."

Metzinger shook his head.

"Mine's forty-two-inches."

Givens snickered.

"Really. I thought you were more man than that."

"Yeah, well, I bought my house twenty years ago. There's no room for sixty-five inches."

"You still live in the same house? Never moved up?"

"I had two kids instead. Pay only goes so far."

Givens shook her head.

"Doesn't give me much to look forward to."

"Yeah. You need to plan. Marry a rich man."

"Sounds sexist to me. Think I'll run the police force instead."

"Sounds like a plan. Let's head upstairs."

There were four rooms on the second floor. One was locked. Metzinger scowled and suggested they check the other rooms first. Maybe come back to investigate that one later.

"Maybe?" Givens asked.

"Yeah, maybe." Metzinger repeated.

The master bedroom was large with a bathroom and spacious closet. The furnishings were feminine and pastel. There was one chest of drawers, low, with a large mirror hung over it. Givens checked the drawers.

"All women's stuff..."

Next, she checked the in-suite bathroom's medicine cabinet. "Same in here. Seems like this is the victim's room."

Down the hall they found two bedrooms. One had a single bed and a chest of drawers, but little else. Checking the drawers, they decided it was Oliver Winslow's bedroom.

"Separate bedroom," observed Metzinger.

"They didn't sleep together," Givens concluded.

"Not what we put in the report," Metzinger declared. "Not sleeping together is speculation, 'separate bedrooms' is observation. Gotta be careful with facts not in evidence."

In the other bedroom there were two single beds and two small chests jammed against the wall on either side of the door.

Givens sighed. "With four bedrooms, looks like the girls still had to sleep together."

Metzinger walked over to one of the beds, nudged some blankets and then looked at the other bed.

"What's this all about? Blankets piled high on one bed and the other one's stripped?"

"Yeah, I noticed that when Joss was dressing. Must have had the window open and gotten cold. An open window would explain the draft in the downstairs hallway."

"You think Joss slept like that every night? Must have been in the forties the night of the murder."

Givens frowned.

The bathroom at the end of the hall had double vanity sinks and two medicine cabinets built into the wall at either end. The medicine cabinets contained typical women's items, while the two drawers were filled with men's items.

"Two girls shared a bathroom with their dad?" Givens shuddered. *So much for affluent privilege.*

"Poor bastard wasn't even allowed to use the master bath," observed Metzinger. He turned back and walked down the hallway.

"Let's see if we can do something with the lock."

Metzinger slipped a thin strip of metal past the doorstop and into the crack between the frame and the door, then pulled it up until the door unlocked.

Holding the door open, he beckoned Givens into the previously locked room.

"After you."

A table hosting a large all-in-one computer with keyboard and a mouse was against the left wall. Boxes of children's books were stacked against the other wall with more in an open closet. Metzinger approached the computer and ran his finger over the keyboard.

"Dusty. Hasn't been used in a while. Nothing's even plugged in."

Givens opened a file cabinet at the end of the computer table. The top drawer held checkbooks and files of what appeared to be contracts. As suspected, it looked like Daphne O'Hanlon had her own bank accounts. Among the files there was one marked "Essex Publishing", another marked "Agent, Brigit Sanders", and another marked "Illustrator, Allison Jablonski". Givens commented, "Looks like more people to interview. I'll write down these addresses and phone numbers."

She opened the next drawer.

"Looks like files for each book, Geraldine Gerbil in the Back Yard, Geraldine Gerbil at Camp, Geraldine Gerbil at the Beach."

She pulled out a file.

"Looks like an original draft with stick figures and then more professional drawings of the same things. All these files are dated by year. The stick figures get better as time goes by, even start to look like animals instead of sticks."

"You think Daphne slowly learned how to draw?"

"I don't know, but they get better. Still kind of childish, but better."

Metzinger took a last look around.

"Okay, let's take a storybook, this address book I found in the desk drawer, and have forensics process the computer."

"You think the computer has something or are you just doing what they do on CSI?"

"Don't give me a hard time, Leslie. We always take the computer. Got to keep the computer guy busy."

"Actually, we need the husband's computer too. We still need the door-bell cam footage and who knows which computer that's on... or has access to the cloud."

"Good point."

Metzinger pulled out his notebook to record his notes.

"Interesting that we haven't found any weapons."

Givens looked benevolently at Metzinger.

"Not everyone has guns."

"I know. Just seems like this is a sizable house with lots of antiques, even some silver. Lots of people have guns these days—for protection."

"Do you?"

"Nah, I have my service weapon."

"Yeah. You put it in a drawer when you get home?"

"No. I usually leave it in my locker at work. If I take it home, I put it in a safe. I've done it ever since I had kids."

"So, how does your wife get to it?"

"She doesn't. Scared to death of the things."

# CHAPTER NINETEEN

IT WAS AFTER lunch by the time Metzinger and Givens returned to the office; if a ten-desk bay can be called an office. Arley Masterson was waiting for them.

"Gather round, master Metzinger and sidekick Givens. Your dog robber has a report to make."

Masterson's partner, Gertrude Sorenson (a six-foot-two woman who they called Big Gert when she wasn't around), was grinning.

"Good thing you gave him something to do. No dope addicts shot each other yet today. Arley'd be pacing if you guys weren't around to keep him busy."

Arley nodded.

"No cases on our desk, addicts and domestics are taking a break today."

He flipped his hand at Metzinger and Givens.

"You two catch all the interesting cases anyway."

Metzinger sighed.

"Dead people are dead people."

Arley nodded in agreement.

"That neighborhood you're working in is better than where Gert and I usually crawl around. I bet the neighbors are even willing to talk... not afraid of retribution, not knowing what the word 'snitch' means. Most of the degenerates we interview don't even know what 'retribution' means. They're just afraid of the other bad guys."

Givens shook her head in understanding while Metzinger consoled, "Arley, you have my deepest sympathy. Hope our leg work brings some sunshine into your life."

Arley gave a sardonic smile and picked a notebook up off his desk.

"You make my day, Drury. Now, let's go over the headlines. Got you your search warrant for Sage Berenson's pad."

Metzinger nodded.

"In case I need it."

Arley frowned and glared.

"Don't tell me you're just wasting my time."

"I'll never tell."

"Better that way. Number two... Oliver Winslow called."

Arley looked across the bay at Officer Joey Constantine and pointed, "Joey took the call."

Constantine waved back.

"Just passing through."

"Where to Joey?" Metzinger asked.

"Stakeout."

"Sounds like fun."

Arley resumed, "Anyway, Winslow said he was in Chicago at O'Hare on his way back. Said he gets into Dulles at 3:30 P.M. and will let us know after he's checked into a hotel and settled in. Said he'd rather meet you at his brother's. Does that make sense? He said that there you can talk to him and his daughter together."

Givens groaned, and Metzinger frowned.

"Yeah, it makes sense and ruins the evening."

"Hey, service to the people."

"Yeah, Arley, you and Gert think about us when eating that steak and drinking your wine tonight."

Arley grinned.

"Hey, how do you know what I do in the evening? Been spying on me?"

"I Just assume nothing but the best for you guys."

"Good, it's what we deserve. Item three... there were a million finger-prints in the hallway, but nothing usable. The prints on the light switch in the hallway, the door, and the screened door handle are all just smudges. And nothing on the Band-Aid either."

"No surprise. The killer probably wore gloves. Damn useless. Lights or no lights, nobody saw anything."

"You still haven't explained why you sent the Band-Aid for prints."

"Killer stuck it over the doorbell camera."

"Okay, clever. Next item... One round in the vic, cut through the aorta, lodged in the backbone. Small caliber. Casing was found in the bushes. Old... maybe seventy-five years old."

"Yeah, we knew that. Sounds like it was a quick death. Screwed up the heart. Casing sounds like it's been sitting in an attic somewhere. Not bought off the street."

Arley nodded and looked back at his notes.

"Next item."

"Four or five?"

"Stopped counting. Vic had a low-level blood alcohol, consistent with a glass of wine."

Arley paused before finishing his report.

"Finally, a lady named Denise Devlin called—lives down the street from the victim—says her sons saw the Winslow's door open on the way to the school bus. Thought the people were just being stupid and didn't do anything. Got her address and phone number if you're interested."

Metzinger shook his head.

"I'll make a note, but we already know the door was open. Doesn't seem to add anything."

Arlie snapped his notebook closed.

"That's it, other than Lt. Ramirez getting pressure to close this thing out. The woman was enough of a celebrity to get covered in the papers and get blurbs on the evening news."

"Yeah. You don't get that with the addicts unless a civilian gets caught in the crossfire."

"So, now let Gert tell you about her morning."

"You busy too, Gert?"

"Oh yeah. Patrol picked up your white-bearded trash diver. Brought him in. Arley and I questioned him. Offered him a lawyer. Said he was his own lawyer. Turns out he lives in the woods, in a little commune. Has a wife and everything. They beg on the road divides. All scheduled out. He was off schedule yesterday morning and decided to sift through the trash. Says the rich neighborhoods throw out gold. Rifles them regularly. Said he was home the night of the murder. I chauffeured him home to the commune to check his alibi. Confirmed he was home."

"Thanks Sherlock. Nothing's too good for the innocent." Metzinger nodded. He hadn't expected the trash diver to be their guy.

"Well Givens, we'll have to let Mrs. Braswell know."

Givens sighed.

"Yeah, WE will have to do that."

Arley continued on as the emcee.

"Gert, you got more?"

Gert stood up to her full height and glared down at her partner.

"What the shit, Arley? Half those notes you just read are mine. You got any more?"

Arley tried to look humbled.

"Okay, Drury. What else have you got for us?"

"I'd appreciate your making a couple of appointments for me for tomorrow." He opened his notebook and scribbled it down on a sheet of paper.

"These two women. Got the names from inside Daphne O'Hanlon's file cabinet along with their phone numbers." He held up the books he'd confiscated from the crime scene.

"Allison Jablonski is the gerbil illustrator. Says so on the book. Brigit Sanders is the agent our vic thanks in the back of the book."

Masterson studied the paper.

"Looks like this Sanders lives in DC. You really want to go there?"

"Not really. Hoping you'll set up a telephone interview, so we don't have to cross into the District."

Arley was thumbing through the Geraldine Gerbil book.

"How about the publisher, Essex Publishing, in New York?"

Metzinger grinned and turned to Givens.

"Sounds like fun, Leslie. You want to go?"

Givens gave a rueful smile.

"Yeah, I can see Lt. Ramirez approving that."

"Might be important. Might solve the case."

"In your dreams."

# CHAPTER TWENTY

GIVENS CALLED HER mother with a heads up she would be late getting home. Her mother responded, in no uncertain terms, that supper was already being prepared. Leslie needed to give warning earlier. Everything would be cold and ruined when she got home. She should learn to be considerate.

"Mama, it's the job. I have to be flexible."

"Not my job. I've got a schedule. Work till three, come home and make meals. Weren't for you, I could come home and just gel. You need to 'preciate me."

"Mama, I do appreciate you. Always do. I'll hurry the best I can."

"Yeah, I know what that means. I'll leave the food on the kitchen table under plastic wrap. You can heat it in the microwave if you want."

"Okay, Ma—"

Givens stared at the phone and shook her head. Her mother had hung up. She looked at Metzinger.

"Your turn."

Metzinger nodded and returned the sigh. He pulled out his smart-phone and asked it to phone Sarah.

Sarah answered.

"Damn, Drury, don't tell me you're working late. We have a teacher's meeting tonight. Supposed to be there at seven."

"You make it sound like 'Damn Drury' is my name."

"Does it fit?"

"Yeah, I'm afraid so. I need to do interviews. Not something I can put off. If I finish in time, I'll try to join you. Which school?"

"Laura's."

"Damn, high school's a bunch of teachers."

"Yes, that means I'll be there a while so try to come. Good for them to think we're both interested."

"Do my best. Love you."

"Yeah, love you too, I guess."

***

Metzinger and Givens parked on the street in front of Oliver Winslow's brother's house a little after 5:00 P.M.

As they approached the front door, Metzinger spoke to Givens out of the side of his mouth.

"You knock, lady like. I don't want this to sound like a police raid."

"You're telling me that even door knocks are sexist?"

"Shit, Leslie, don't give me a hard time. I was born twenty years too early for 'me too'. Just do the best I can. I'm fine with equal rights. We've wasted brains for too long. Just knock on the damned door."

"Okay. I'll work on tolerance even if it doesn't keep the faith."

Givens knocked and it sounded like a police raid.

"Jesus Christ!" said Metzinger. "It's like I'm talkin' in the wind!"

Givens grinned.

"Not sure the word's 'talking'."

Ginger Winslow opened the door.

"Hi, detectives. Ollie's in the living room. Joss is upstairs. I'll call her."

Metzinger quickly intervened.

"No, leave the girl alone. We'll talk to Mr. Winslow first and return to you later."

"Okay, but I don't know what happened."

"Just gathering background."

"Okay."

Ginger led them into the living room where Oliver Winslow was standing, waiting.

"Hi. I'm Ollie."

He extended his hand and shook those of the detectives, who gave their names, as they shook.

"Leslie Givens."

"Drury Metzinger. We're sorry for your loss and hate to put you through this, but it's necessary."

"No problem. I understand. Please have a seat."

Before he sat, Metzinger turned to Ginger.

"May we talk to you later?"

Ginger understood.

"I'll be in the kitchen when you need me. May I get you drinks, water, or soda? I think that's all I have that's not alcoholic."

Metzinger shook his head and looked at Givens.

"Thank you, no."

Oliver pointed to the glass of water on the coffee table, then at Ginger and shook his head. He turned back to the detectives, who were opening notebooks.

"How can I help?"

Metzinger pulled a pen from his shirt pocket.

"You're the husband of the deceased, Daphne O'Hanlon?"

"Yes."

"How long were you married?"

"Twenty years this past June."

Givens interjected.

"I'm always curious about a woman who doesn't take her husband's name. Do you mind explaining that? It's usually professional, but sometimes it's retaining personal identity."

"No, I don't mind. It was some of both. Actually, she took my name when we married and changed it back to her maiden name when she published her first book. She wanted her own identity. She didn't want to be a housewife who wrote books on the side."

"When you attended book fairs and the like, how were you introduced?"

"I didn't go to books fairs, award dinners, interviews, or anything involving her business."

"Why not?"

"I wasn't invited. She said it was her thing."

Metzinger inquired, "It's personal, but I need to ask. Were the two of you independent? I noticed, inspecting your house, that you two had separate bank accounts."

"Yeah, and separate dens, phone lines, internet connections, whatever. She went her own way after the second book."

"Still, you stayed together."

"We have two children."

"Yes, we've met them, Winifred, age eighteen, and Josceline, fifteen."

Givens observed, "These questions would upset a lot of people, Mr. Winslow, but they don't seem to bother you. You seem to accept them as facts of life."

Oliver looked at Givens, a sad sheen in his eyes.

"As you say, detective, they're facts of life. I stopped loving my wife twelve or thirteen years ago. I travel a lot. If you dig into my life, you'll find I often have affairs on my trips. I'd just as soon that the girls, Ginger, and Ed don't know."

"Ed?"

"My brother, Edwin Winslow. Ginger's husband."

Metzinger made a note.

"It sounds like you not only did not love your wife, but that you actually disliked her."

"I detested her. We were two separate people. I paid the mortgage, the utilities, bought the kids' clothes, food, the essentials of life. She paid for her phone, internet, clothes, and travel. I suspect she has a good bank balance."

"With her death, who gets her money?"

"No idea. Don't even know if she had a will."

"If she doesn't, wouldn't you get the money in probate?"

"I guess. I stuck with her, at least with the family. It would seem reasonable."

"Did she have any life insurance?"

"Again, I have no idea. I have my own life insurance, but the girls are the beneficiaries."

Givens interjected, "I have to ask, Mr. Winslow, did you dislike your wife enough to kill her?"

"That's an interesting question. Haven't really thought on it much. I've just gone my own way. Anyway, I was in Omaha."

"Yes, and we'll verify that."

"I can provide the hotel receipt."

"We'd appreciate that. However, being away doesn't always keep a man from killing his wife."

"I understand that. I watch television, although I generally avoid the true crime programs. I don't know anything about the world where you can hire people to do in wives."

"If you did, I wouldn't expect you to admit it."

Oliver looked at Givens coldly.

"That's not funny, detective. I didn't kill Daphne."

Metzinger rejoined the conversation.

"Do you have any idea who might have?"

"Her publisher, her agent, anyone involved in the books."

"Did she argue with all these people?"

"Loudly."

"What about?"

"She wasn't delivering the books she's contracted for and she'd been paid an advance."

"Why didn't she?"

"Because Freddie wouldn't help her."

"Oh? What did Freddie need to do?"

"Write the books."

"Write the books?"

"Yeah. Freddie wrote all the books... did rough illustrations."

"Freddie wrote all the books?"

"Yeah, since she was five- or six-years-old."

"Did she get any credit, any acknowledgment for it?"

"No. Daphne did most of the work... got the books formally illustrated, got the agent and the publisher, did the publicity, took the credit."

"Freddie was happy about this?"

"She was a kid. She didn't know any better. She was just happy to see Geraldine Gerbil in real books. Didn't get unhappy until much later. She did a lousy job on the last book, at least Daphne said she did. They really fought over it. Freddie wanted credit... and money. As she put it, 'it was only fair'. Daphne said that she did the work... the books wouldn't be published, wouldn't be successful without all the work she put in."

"And what did you think?"

"They both were correct. Freddie should have been recognized."

"So, did you do anything about it?"

"What, and wreck a good thing? A little scandal would have screwed up the whole business. If the publisher found out who knows what would have happened."

"So, you did nothing?"

"Tried to get Freddie away from Daphne, off to college. Daphne fought it all the way. One day she was going to help pay the tuition and the next day she wouldn't. She'd say Freddie should stay home and write Geraldine books. Kept Freddie uncertain and confused. Finally, she said she wouldn't help pay for college and Freddie ran away from it all. Ran away from college and from home. Moved in with a loser. Throwing away her life. Daphne screams at her, calls her worthless and begs her to come back, all at the same time."

"Screamed at her," Givens corrected.

Oliver nodded, humbled.

"Yeah, past tense. Won't scream anymore. Maybe Freddie will come home."

"You and Freddie get along?"

"Yeah. I wanted her to go to college but couldn't pay for it all, so maybe she's a little frosted, but I think we're all right."

"What's your other daughter, Josceline, think of this?"

"Joss? Hell, Joss is in her own world. Seems to ignore it all. Does great in school but seems above it all. Doesn't socialize there. Thinks all the kids are juvenile."

"Sounds like both you and your daughter, Freddie, didn't have any reason to like your wife. Maybe disliked her enough that we should keep you on the list of possible killers." He gestured toward Givens. "I certainly think Detective Givens thinks so."

"Do what you like, detectives. As I've said, I was in Omaha, a long way from here."

"And you're not going anywhere?"

"Oklahoma City in a couple of weeks. To my home tomorrow if you let me."

"We'll let you know when it's clear. You haven't asked about the body... when it will be released and so forth. You'll want to arrange a funeral."

"Oh, yeah. I do have to think about that. If I cremate her, will that look like I'm hiding something?"

Metzinger looked at Oliver Winslow with a bit of disdain.

"Are you really asking me that? She was shot. The cause of death seems clear. We'll let you know when the autopsy is complete."

"You're doing an autopsy?"

"Do it with murders. Don't know what might be hidden."

"Yeah, maybe a couple of martinis. Don't be surprised. You want to talk to Joss? I understand I have to be around."

Metzinger sighed and nodded.

"Sounds like you're getting a little miffed. Yeah, I need you to be around."

Oliver Winslow called up the stairs to Joss. As she came down, Ginger came out of the kitchen.

"That was a long discussion. Are you sure you don't want something to drink?"

Both detectives nodded and Givens said, "Yes, water if you don't mind."

Ginger nodded and returned to the kitchen.

Joss entered the living room.

"I thought you'd never call me."

Givens took out some wipes.

"Do you mind if I wipe your hands?"

"What? What for?"

"Gun residue. It's a little late, but as a juvenile we couldn't do it yester-day. If your dad says it's all right, we'll do it now."

Oliver looked at his daughter.

"Joss?"

"It's all right, Dad. I didn't shoot her."

She looked at Metzinger.

"You want my fingerprints, too?"

"Yours, and your dad's."

"Okay." She turned to her father.

"Okay with you, Dad?"

"Sure. My prints are all over the house. It's my house."

"Mine, too."

Metzinger shook his head.

"It's routine. We know your prints are all over the place. If we find the gun, though, fingerprints may mean something."

Joss chuckled.

"I thought the bad guys wiped their weapons clean."

"Usually."

Givens pulled out a fingerprint kit.

"Who's first?"

Joss smiled and held out her hands.

"Wipe and fingerprint to your heart's content."

When Givens had finished both father and daughter, they all sat down. Meanwhile, Ginger had brought in glasses of water. She turned to Joss.

"Would you like a glass too, sweetheart?"

"No. Thank you, Aunt Ginger."

Metzinger took a long draft of water.

"So, Josceline, you were in the house Monday night?"

"Yeah, you know I was. And please call me Joss. Josceline was my mother's idea."

"You didn't like your mother?"

"I could take her or leave her. She wasn't around much, and even when she was, she was up in her office."

"She called it her office?"

"Dad had a den. She had an office. She said she worked there. Professional work requires an office."

"Okay, I'll get back to her profession in a minute. Tell us where you were Monday night."

"I was out with friends most of the afternoon just goofing around. Went to McDonald's for dinner. My friends dropped me off at home around eight o'clock."

"Who did you go to McDonald's with and how were you dropped off?"

"With Janet and Twiggy. Err, Janet Thorsson, with two 's's, and Twiggy, uh, Theresa Thigpen. Twiggy had the car. She dropped me off."

"You know their phone numbers?"

Joss pulled out her cell phone and walked over to Metzinger so he could copy the numbers.

Metzinger thanked her and she returned to her seat.

"So, you returned home at approximately eight o'clock. Did you see your mother?"

"Yeah, she was in the kitchen, on the phone, with a drink in front of her."

"A martini," Oliver interjected.

"One of those clear drinks with olives in a cocktail glass."

"As I said, a martini." Oliver reiterated.

Metzinger stared at him.

"Is that important?"

"Only that I told you so," Oliver said with satisfaction. "Might have made her slow jumping out of the way of the bullet."

Givens shook her head.

"At close range I don't think it would have made much difference."

Metzinger turned back to Joss.

"When you found your mother in the kitchen, what did you talk about?"

"We didn't. She was on the phone. I waved hello, and she waved back. I went to the refrigerator, took out some cold pizza and sat down to eat while she talked. That's what I call having dinner with my mother. After that I went upstairs, closed the bedroom door, turned on my music. With Mom downstairs, Dad wherever, and my sister living with a lowlife, I do what I want. No one pays much attention to me."

"Did your mother not coming up seem strange?"

"No, she goes to bed late and doesn't go into her office much lately. Plus, like I said, I'm irrelevant."

"Did you leave your room at all?"

"Not until you saw me yesterday morning. I worked on homework 'till midnight. I mean I went to the bathroom, but that's all."

"When was that?"

"Well, I used the bathroom when I got home and again when I went to bed, so around midnight."

"So, you were in your room all evening from eight 'till midnight."

"Yeah, and in my bed from then till late morning. When I got up, I spent about ten minutes in the bathroom, and then came downstairs where I found you... I heard voices, but thought it was Mom talking to someone, or the television... you were a real surprise."

"That was Tuesday morning that you heard voices, not Monday night?"

"Right, it turned out I heard you all."

Metzinger looked at Givens.

"Anything else?"

Givens leaned toward Joss.

"You called your sister's boyfriend a lowlife. Why did you say that?"

"Because he is. Twenty-one-years-old. Only works enough to buy food and marijuana and whatever else he takes. And I guess he pays the rent. Works at Seven-Eleven."

"Doesn't sound very appealing. Why's your sister living with him?"

"Because he has an apartment, and he's not a serious commitment. She doesn't want to live at home. Dad's mad at her about college and—"

"No, I'm not mad," Oliver interrupted. "Disappointed, yes. But Freddie has a home. She knows it but doesn't want to fight with her mother."

Givens used the moment.

"Right. Fighting with her mother. Your dad brought that up earlier. He said your sister wrote the children's books, the gerbil things, and your mother took credit for them."

Joss looked at her father as if he'd betrayed the whole family.

"Yeah, Freddie did, in a way. She told the stories, made them up as she went along and then made little pictures to go with them. Mom wrote them down, did all the publishing work, took the credit. When Freddie got older, she resented it. Thought she should get some credit and be paid some money. Really wanted the money once she came back from her day at college and was suddenly on her own."

"Your mother wouldn't give her any?"

"Oh, no. Mom said she did the work and the money was hers. She accused Freddie of not playing her role anymore, of killing the Geraldine Gerbil books through indifference. She said Freddie screwed it up by not putting her heart into the last book. Freddie said that should have taught Mom something about who was important when it came to producing the books and that she wasn't doing any more work until she was acknowledged. Mom said Freddie hadn't done anything for two years and it left Mom hanging, not fulfilling her contract. She said that, as a result, she owed the publisher a lot of money and Freddie nothing."

"Real acrimony between them?"

"You might say that."

"Was your sister mad enough to kill your mother?"

"How the hell would I know? You don't kill someone just because you're mad."

"On the contrary, people do it all the time."

"Yeah, well, Freddie and I don't see eye to eye sometimes, but I'm not going to kill her, and I don't see her doing that either."

"What don't you see eye to eye on?"

"Hey, we're sisters. We argue about all kinds of things, music, boyfriends, you know. I told her she was a fool when she came back from college, that she was making a big deal over nothing. A cock on the wall. Big deal. Tear it down. It was just an excuse anyway. She wasn't ready for college. And living with Sage. I've given her hell about that."

Givens gawked.

"A what on the wall?"

Joss looked around awkwardly.

"A big picture of a man's thing that Freddie's new roommate had put up. The girl hated men. Freddie claimed she couldn't live with it and came home, but I don't think it was that simple. I think it had to do with not writing the books."

Metzinger glanced at Oliver Winslow, who remained silent. Then he turned back to Joss.

"You're a pretty girl, Joss. Do you have boyfriends?"

Oliver gave Joss a look.

Joss looked at her father, "What?" she snarled and then answered Metzinger's question.

"Sure, I have boyfriends."

"Do you bring them home?"

"No."

"Why?"

"Atmosphere's not right."

"Because of your mother?"

"The whole shooting-match. My mother, my sister, and Dad's not happy. A Gothic world."

Givens looked at Metzinger, hunched her shoulders, and said, "I guess that's it."

Oliver exclaimed, "Hey, Joss makes it sound like we live on one of Dante's tiers. It's not that bad. I lived with Daphne for twenty years. I'm not a masochist, or whatever. The books were fun and my job's good. I've got beautiful daughters. I don't agree with the Gothic comment."

Joss replied uncertainly.

"I didn't mean to hurt you, Dad, but life hasn't been great the last year or so. Just the way it is."

Oliver sighed deeply.

"Then I'm sorry."

Metzinger redirected the conversation.

"Thank you for your help. We'd like to talk to Mrs. Winslow alone. Joss, do you mind going back upstairs? Mr. Winslow, is there somewhere you can go?"

Joss got up and headed for the stairs.

Oliver Winslow rose at the same time.

"I'll go back to my hotel."

"Oh, where's that?"

"Hyatt in Crystal City."

Metzinger and Givens both wrote it down.

Givens volunteered to get Mrs. Winslow.

When the two women returned from the kitchen, Ginger asked, "Where is everyone?"

Metzinger responded, "Joss is upstairs. Mr. Winslow's gone back to his hotel."

"Oh, goodness. Oliver was here so briefly. I didn't really get a chance to talk to him. He could have stayed here. I would have loved to have talked to him. I expect he's really torn up."

Metzinger hesitated and decided not to discuss Oliver Winslow's disposition.

"I guess he decided to stay at a hotel while he was on the plane coming back from Omaha since his house is a crime scene."

"Omaha? Who goes to Omaha?"

Givens offered, "Department of Agriculture people, Air Force people. There's a base there."

"Oh, yeah."

Ginger sat.

"What can I do for you?"

Metzinger met Ginger's eyes.

"We'd like to ask you a few questions, if we may."

"Of course, but I don't know anything. I haven't had anything to do with Oliver's family for years."

"How many years, Mrs. Winslow?"

"For goodness' sake, do we have to be so formal? I'm Ginger."

"It's a kind of formal situation."

"Let's see, Freddie's eighteen. Must have been ten or twelve years ago. Daphne started publishing those books... became busy and self-important... stopped socializing with us... developed new friends. Ed had to sneak lunches with Oliver. That's how we kept up with Oliver's family."

"So, there was no contact with Daphne or the daughters?"

"No... just occasional lunches with Oliver. It hurt Ed. Hurt his feelings. He loves his brother. I was never fond of Daphne... cold fish. She looked down on my dancing. Made comments to people."

"Did that offend you?"

"Of course. My profession's as good as anybody's. Not like I was dancing naked. Just showed off my legs... good as anybody's. Daphne saw me dance in a short white dress doing the shimmy one time and thought it was awful. Told Oliver it was disgusting. Ed liked it, and so did Oliver. After that Daphne said terrible things about me. I was cute and she was jealous."

Givens looked at Metzinger to see if he would be drawn in to telling Ginger she was still cute.

He wasn't. He'd been baited before.

"And you resented that?"

"Of course. She was a big-assed woman looking down on me. You'd have resented it too. Mostly I was annoyed about being ostracized, put down in front of mutual friends... I didn't like the way it hurt Ed."

"Yet, despite your animosity, you were willing to take in Josceline."

"Of course! Ed and I have always followed the girls. Oliver would sneak Ed pictures. One's on the mantle right over there."

"So, you're okay with Josceline staying here?"

"Thrilled... love talking to her... like having a daughter of my own. Especially, I care for Josceline. Oliver always told Ed he worried so much about that little girl. It's good to know she's okay."

"Why'd he worry?"

"The kid was second fiddle for so long. Freddie was writing the books... the center of attention. Daphne ignored poor Joss. Said she didn't have any value. Can you imagine? I just want to hug her... give her value. She deserves it."

"Maybe something good came out of all of this."

"You think?"

"I think no one liked Daphne O'Hanlon. How about your husband?"

"Detective, she froze us all out. Ed had to sneak behind her back to see his brother."

"Then everyone in the family didn't like her. How about the rest of the world?"

"Don't know. Can't speak for the rest of Daphne's world. Wasn't part of it."

Metzinger closed his notebook.

"What do you think, Leslie? Anything else?"

"I'm sure I'll think of something." She rose as she closed her notebook.

"Thank you, Mrs. Winslow. We'll let you know when Josceline and her father can return home."

"There's no hurry. Joss is welcome here."

***

Back at their car, Metzinger said, "You drive. I've got to think."

"Okay," Givens said, taking the keys and climbing into the driver's seat.

"Think about what? No one liked O'Hanlon. Everyone's a suspect. How are you going to separate the wheat from the chaff?"

"Well, maybe Josceline is innocent. She acted kind of indifferent to the whole thing, and didn't seem emotional about it, at least not enough for murder."

"Maybe too indifferent. Didn't even seem upset when she saw the body. Do you think anyone will show up at the funeral?"

"Maybe you and I to see who else is there. As you imply, doubt we have to worry about a crowd."

"So, what's next?"

"Arley and Gert are setting up two appointments for us tomorrow and I think we need to talk to Miss Freddie again. What time is it anyway?"

Givens glanced at the dashboard.

"Going on seven-thirty."

"Oh, damn. My wife's at the school meeting with my daughter's teachers!"

# CHAPTER TWENTY-ONE

METZINGER WAS RELIEVED to see his wife's car was still there as he pulled into the high school parking lot. *Maybe she'll forgive me if I'm in time for a few meetings.*

He hurried through the front door to the check-in table.

"Drury Metzinger. Late getting out of work and trying to track down my wife, Sarah."

The secretary looked like Mr. Metzinger had stolen her break. Having just relaxed, now that all the parents were with teachers, she had to jerk herself back to reality.

"Metzinger, you say? Let's see." She scanned some papers.

"Ah, yes. Laura's parents. Should be in Mrs. Lessing's classroom, AP calculus, room 115."

She pointed down the hall, "Down this hallway, seventh door on your right."

Metzinger hurried down the hallway to room 115. The door was open, but he knocked lightly on the door frame before entering. His eyes flashed past Sarah and her serious expression to the teacher. He stuck out his hand in greeting.

"Drury Metzinger. Sorry I'm late."

The teacher rose to shake his hand.

"Dina Lessing. We're just getting started."

Metzinger had assumed the word calculus implied a much older person, probably a man. Laura's teacher was young, maybe not even thirty. He tried not to stare.

Pulling a student desk up next to Sarah, he turned to his wife.

"You look serious."

"Mrs. Lessing is the second teacher who has told me Laura seems to be slacking off. Not working to her potential."

"Oh." Metzinger was caught off guard and looked back at Ms. Lessing.

"That's troubling. When did this start happening? Have you seen any change in demeanor, any associations with new friends?"

Sarah looked at Mrs. Lessing with sad resignation.

"My husband's a police detective. He asks questions."

Mrs. Lessing smiled wryly.

"They're fine questions and yes, she's less outgoing in my class. Last week in the hallway she was with a boy, up against the wall, holding books across her chest. The boy was leaning against the wall, one arm on each side of Laura, almost pinning her in. His face was inches from hers. I told him to move on. To break it up and reminded them about personal space."

"What's this boy's name?" Metzinger interrogated.

"Don't know. He's not in any of my math classes."

"Thank you for bringing this to our attention. Sarah and I will talk to Laura and find out what's going on," Metzinger said, rising from the chair to leave. "Is there anything else?"

Mrs. Lessing stood up as Sarah rose to join her husband.

"I'm just worried about Laura. She's a bright girl. I'd hate to see her mess up her future."

The Metzingers shook the teacher's hand and exited into the hallway.

Then Drury said, sotto voce, "What the heck? What the hell's going on?"

Sarah responded with an equally quiet voice, "I don't know, but let me talk to her before you let into her."

Drury's whisper grew louder.

"Maybe I need to let into her. Back her against the wall the way this guy does," he fumed. "She shouldn't let anyone treat her that way."

"Shh," Sarah hushed, her eyes on fire.

"Let's get out of here."

***

Arriving home, Laura was waiting on the stairs, trepidation in her eyes and body language.

"How'd the meetings go?"

Metzinger walked past her without a word and joined Ben in the living room watching television.

Laura watched him go and turned back to her mother, who waved her toward the kitchen.

When they got there, Sarah pointed at the kitchen table.

"Sit down. I get first crack at you before your father blows a fuse and we're all sorry."

"What? What's so bad?"

"Two things. You're slacking off in school. You keep it up, and you're going to pay when it comes time to apply for college, which is very soon."

"Okay. I can do better."

"I know you can, but will you? It sounds like you're more interested in some boy than you are in your future, maybe not even the greatest of boys."

"You don't know him."

"No, I don't and that's part of the problem. It might be nice if I did. If we did, your father and I, instead of keeping him a secret."

"He's not a secret."

"You've never said anything about him."

"I was afraid you might give me a hard time. It's embarrassing! Parents don't need to know everything."

"Actually, we do. We give you a lot of freedom, Laura. We don't ask a lot of questions about what you do after school... don't give you a hard time about playing your music in the evening... don't monitor your cell phone calls or texts. When you say you're going to your room to do your homework each evening, we believe you. Your father always worries about hormones and I tell him he's being silly. Now, I wonder."

Laura snapped back, "This is why I didn't tell you! Am I strange for wanting a boyfriend?"

Sarah sagged and sat down.

"No, you're not strange. But you need to protect your pride, your self-respect. Think about more than the next few days. If this guy is someone you'd like to spend your life with, realize that he may well dictate what that life is. On the other hand, if this guy is just fun for the moment, fine, but you need to protect your self-respect. What you do in life matters. You matter."

***

In the living room, Drury sat on the sofa with Ben.

"What are you watching?"

"Netflix," Ben answered. "Streaming... Jessica Jones."

"You like Jessica Jones?" *Shit*, Drury thought. *Is Ben old enough to be watching Jessica Jones?*

"Yeah, she's a good-looking woman who can throw people around."

Drury looked at the screen, trying to decide if he should say something.

"Doesn't dress very fancy... torn up jeans," Ben continued, "and t-shirts. Sometimes she strips down to her underpants. Skinny, no tummy."

As if right on cue, off came Jessica Jones' pants.

"Yeah, I can see." Drury muttered with no idea what to say.

"Laura dresses like that in t-shirts lots of afternoons when she goes out."

"She does?" *Not what I wanted to hear!*

"Yeah, but Laura's not quite as skinny. Tries to be pr-, pre-, provocative. That's the word."

Drury studied his son, searching for a response. For good or for bad, his vocabulary is growing. *I guess Jessica Jones is part of the learning process, and I'm learning, too.*

"Glad to hear your vocabulary is expanding," he mustered.

# CHAPTER TWENTY-TWO

GIVENS ARRIVED AT home after eight. The streets were quiet. Most of the lights inside her house were out. She hurried through the front door, turned off the outside light, and followed the flickering TV light to find her mother in the living room.

"Hi, Mama. Everything cool?"

"Everything's all right if that's what you mean? That Chantel girl called the house a couple of times. Don't care if you call her back. Like I've said, she's shady. There are better ways to spend your time. You've got your own phone so why's she calling here?"

"Yeah, she's been texting me, but I was busy at work ignoring her. Sorry I'm late for supper."

"Put it in the microwave. Not much good that way. What were ya doin'?"

"Interviews."

"Interviewing criminals?"

"Maybe."

"You do it someplace safe?"

"Living room of a house."

"Don't sound safe to me."

"Nice house. Lots of people around. Metzinger was with me."

"Lot of good that old man would do if a killer showed up."

"Mama, I've told you. He's in his forties. Long as he doesn't have to run, he's fine."

"Bet he watches you run."

Givens shrugged it off and headed for the kitchen to nuke her food. Chicken, mac and cheese, stewed tomatoes... it would be fine reheated. Maybe two minutes in the microwave.

Waiting at the kitchen table. Leslie wondered what Chantel wanted. Maybe to go out... *too late for that.*

When the microwave beeped, she took out her food and poured herself a glass of milk, then picked up everything and went upstairs to relax. After she ate, Givens picked up her phone and considered it for a moment before dialing Chantel. Nothing better to do.

Chantel answered after two rings.

"Where you been?"

Givens shook her head. Caller ID... no way to be anonymous anymore.

"Been working. Some of us have to do that."

"Don't jerk me around. You know I work too."

"Yeah. Secretary. Nine to five."

"Admin assistant. Some of us are smart. Get paid for overtime. Where were you?"

"Interviewing bad guys."

"What kind of bad guys. Druggies, killers, what?"

"Maybe a killer. Working on finding out."

"Well, you missed a chance to go out. Kenya called. Asked me to get your ass out."

"That's the trouble. He talks about my ass."

"You want him to talk about your brain?"

"I have other assets."

"Think he's interested in some more than others. Wants to see those moves when you dance."

"I do enjoy dancing."

"Kenya's got moves too."

"Yeah he does!"

"How 'bout Friday night?"

Givens hesitated.

"No, want to keep that night open."

"Open for what? You got something better to do?"

"Might get a call."

"Call from who?"

Givens was reluctant to answer, "Maybe Bobby."

"Bobby Riley? Straight-ass Bobby Riley?"

"Yeah." Givens shuddered at the response, even though she'd known it was coming.

"Didn't you go out with him three weeks ago?"

"Yeah, about then."

"About nothing. It was three weeks ago! Burger and a movie. I remember. Don't tell me he turned you on?"

"He's a nice guy, Chantel. Graduated from James Madison. Got a good job."

"Can't dance worth shit."

"How do you know? You see him dance?"

"I've seen him move. He doesn't walk like he can dance. I can tell."

"Well, there are other things that are important."

"Yeah, a few, but I don't know about that, either. Seems awfully strait-laced. Where's he been for three weeks? Doesn't seem like you did much of a job turning him on."

"I don't need the sarcasm, Chantel. He's been out of town."

"Yeah? He call you every night while he was away?"

"Cut it, Chantel. We're not married. Just had a couple of dates."

"Okay, you keep dreaming. If he doesn't call, come back to me and I'll set up some real fun."

"Always keep you in mind, but don't hassle me if I call."

Givens hung up and stared at her phone.

*God, I love to dance. Love to go out... dress up and show my attitude. Let go of the pretenses... live my double life, be my delusional self... my sexiest self.*

She lay the phone down on her bedside table, drew her pajamas from the closet, stripped down and promised herself that if Bobby wasn't the one, then someone else would be. In the meantime, she had a career to focus on. *Do the job, girl. Just do the job.*

# CHAPTER TWENTY-THREE

"SOME BASTARD DIDN'T restart the pot!" Metzinger vented, slamming the coffee mug down on his desk.

Givens cringed.

"Having a bad day?"

"You're just lucky. I've made a new pot."

"So, what else could go wrong?"

Metzinger scowled.

"I'm not allowed to discipline my daughter and my son has learned the word promiscuous."

"Yeah, old beyond his years."

Arley shouted from his desk, "Your home out of control, Drury? Maybe I can give you some guidance on how to run your ship."

Metzinger hit his stapler without any papers in it.

"Last thing I need, Arley!"

"Hey, be sweet to me, as long as I'm doing your work. I set up an appointment for you with Wynona for 10 A.M."

"Wynona? What are you talking about? You play the Judds on your country music station this morning?"

Arley inspected his notes.

"Winifred. I meant Winifred. Surly young woman. Doesn't like her name."

"Right. Hates her name. Wants to be called Freddie."

"Uh-huh."

"Ten o'clock, huh? Thanks. Fits my schedule."

"Good thing, because I'm not redoing it," Arley said looking back down at the papers on his desk.

"And you've got an appointment to go see Allison Jablonski at two this afternoon. Talked to her husband, Doctor Ralph."

He waved a paper.

"Got the address and telephone number here. Also, I've got a number where you can call Brigit Sanders at four-thirty this afternoon. She's in New York, at Essex Publishing, excitingly awaiting your call."

Givens took the paper. She felt like Arley was looking her up and down and tried to ignore it. *Unprofessional bastard.*

Returning to her desk, she studied the paper and dropped it on Metzinger's desk. Metzinger picked it up.

"You do good work, Arley. I'll remember you on Secretary's Day."

"Yeah, I'll remind you."

Arley looked at Givens with poorly disguised lust.

"He's all yours, Leslie. You'd better check and see if the coffee's ready. You better scurry off and pour Drury a cup before someone else gets it."

Givens rose quickly and moved out of the room with a purpose.

*Scurry before someone else gets his coffee. If Arley doesn't stop watching my ass, he's gonna have to scurry to the hospital.*

As she vanished, Sgt. Charlie Eastham entered the detective bay carrying an envelope.

Arley looked at him, appalled.

"Shit, Charlie. Who's manning the front desk?"

Eastham gave Arley an Italian salute.

"Nobody's going to break through the plexiglass and end the world in the next thirty seconds."

Arley threw his hands up in submission.

"Better be important enough to risk the end of the world."

"Express mail for Detective Metzinger. Nothing more important than that."

He handed the envelope to Metzinger, who took it with uncertainty.

Eastham waited a moment before turning away. "You're welcome."

Metzinger looked at the envelope, an office mail with multiple addresses, the last of which before him was the DISTRICT MEDICAL EXAMINER OFFICE.

"Yeah thanks, Charlie."

Metzinger unwound the string, opened the envelope, and pulled out several pages of a report.

AUTOPSY REPORT: Subject O'HANLON Daphne Arlene

He flicked through it and then sat back down to read more carefully.

Suddenly, he pounded the desk with his fist and shouted "Shit!"

Givens had just come back with two mugs of coffee and stopped abruptly, afraid to approach Metzinger's desk.

"What the hell, Drury?"

Metzinger was scrabbling through his desk drawer. He pulled out the Alexandria government phone book and thumbed frantically through the pages.

"Damn, damn, damn!" He stuck his finger on a page, picked up his desk phone and started dialing.

"Yeah, this is Detective Metzinger with the Alexandria Police Department. Need to talk to Dr. Golon—yeah, I'll wait."

Cautiously, Givens set Metzinger's mug of coffee on his desk and backed away.

Metzinger, his hand over the phone, nodded a thank you.

Givens hesitated.

"Jesus Drury... you all right? You're flushed."

Metzinger waved her off.

"Hi, Dr Golon—Detective Drury Metzinger with the Alexandria Police Department, calling on the Daphne O'Hanlon autopsy. What the hell do you mean you can't tell what killed her? She had a bullet through her aorta that lodged in her spine. That'd kill anyone—Damn, doctor, do you know what that means?—Hell, I'm looking for a killer. If I find him, his damn defense attorney is going to say maybe he didn't kill O'Hanlon, maybe the wind did it—What do you mean it's not your problem? You're going to let a murderer off the hook!—Yeah well, you need to make a choice and get off the fence."

He slammed the phone down, bit his lip and sat frowning at his desk.

Arley shouted across the room, "What the fuck, Drury. You've got this whole room shook up."

Metzinger turned vacantly toward Arley and then looked at Givens.

"The M.E. says the head wound from being hit by the door may have killed her. He can't tell if the cause of death is the bullet or the head wound."

Givens gaped.

"Can we still get the shooter for attempted murder?"

Metzinger glared at her.

"Shit, it shouldn't even be a conversation! This should be first degree premeditated, not a theoretical discussion of gun versus wind!"

# CHAPTER TWENTY-FOUR

FREDDIE ARRIVED AT 10:15 A.M. and was escorted to an interview room where she was asked to have a seat. After the door was closed, she stood with her hands on the back of the chair.

Metzinger and Givens entered the room ten minutes later. Freddie was still standing. Angrily, Metzinger took one of the chairs opposite Ms. Freddie Winslow.

He said, without looking at her, "You been standing the whole time? Have a damn seat."

She scowled and pulled out her chair.

"Is waiting part of the police procedure to intimidate witnesses?"

Metzinger was still seething.

"If you're intimidated, Freddie, that's tough. Was your being late this morning meant to intimidate us?"

"Touché," Freddie said. "We're even. Do I need a lawyer?"

Metzinger studied the young woman.

"We'll see. Are you guilty of something? You got a lawyer on call?"

Freddie sighed and shook her head.

"What the fuck are you pissed about? You know I don't have a lawyer."

"No, I don't know that. Don't know much about you. I'm here to learn."

He opened his notebook and took out a pen.

"Tell you what. If Detective Givens or I read you your Miranda rights, then you might need a lawyer. We'll get you a public defender."

"If you read my rights, does that mean you can use what I say against me?"

"Yes."

"Got it. I need to be careful. What can I do for you?"

"We're here to learn, Miss Winslow. We've had interesting conversations with your father and your sister. We understand that you wrote the Geraldine Gerbil books. Is that correct?"

Freddie frowned and gave a small nod.

"Yeah, pretty much."

"What does 'pretty much' mean?"

"I made up the stories and sketched ideas for the drawings, the illustrations... my mother wrote them down and did all the work to get them published."

"So, it wasn't a one-person operation?"

"Detective, I was six years old when it all started."

"So, you needed your mother to help you get the books published?"

"I didn't need to get them published. That was my mother's idea."

"It didn't mean anything to you to have them published?"

"Well, yeah. I got a kick out of seeing them printed up... being able to hold them in my hands but publication wasn't my idea."

"So, without your mother, the Geraldine Gerbil books wouldn't have been published?"

"Yeah. That's probably right."

"We understand that the last couple of years, you've had arguments and fights with your mother about the books."

Freddie looked uncertain. She looked away from Metzinger to Givens, who nodded slightly.

"Did Joss tell you that?"

Givens nodded.

"Josceline and your father."

Freddie looked back at Metzinger.

"Yeah, well, Joss is not so pure herself. My parents and Joss have lots of fights. Usually about her college boyfriends and their college boy expectations. Joss just gives them the finger and does what she wants."

Givens joined the questioning.

"So, your sister dates college boys. Okay, and you live with Sage Berenson?"

Freddie suddenly looked angry and turned to glare at Givens.

"What do you mean, 'Live with Sage'? I live at Sage's. At, not with. My father and sister tell you about me going to Mary Washington and coming back home? I bet they did. Well, I was persona non gratis, or whatever, after that. Had to get away from my parents. Sage's was a place to crash."

"So, why Sage's?"

Freddie blew out her breath and looked down at the table.

"Look, Joss is the good-looking one with the tits. I'm just me. Sage asked me to the Junior-Senior Prom back when I was in eighth grade. It was a big deal for me, but it labeled me. Sage was an oddball, an outsider. After prom, I was kind of connected to him in everyone's minds. I didn't get many other dates. If I wanted to go to a dance I went with Sage. He's what I had."

"You know he's got a record? Shoplifting, DUI's?"

"No, I didn't know, but I'm not surprised. He likes his beer. His pad was a place to go. That's all."

"And he provides marijuana," Givens quipped.

Freddie's eyes jerked back to Metzinger.

"Do I need a lawyer now?"

Metzinger shook his head.

"We're not looking for a marijuana bust. We're trying to solve a murder."

Freddie glared at him.

"Which I had nothing to do with."

"Didn't say you did, Miss Winslow. We're in the learning process."

"Yeah, well, Sage was convenient, and he loves me, takes care of me, protects me."

"Protects you from what?"

"From whatever."

"Your mother?"

"Yeah, she wanted me to write more books."

"And you don't want to?"

"I'm not going to."

"Why's that?"

"You know why. My father and sister told you."

"Can you tell us?"

"Why?"

"To confirm what they said."

"Okay, okay. I wrote books for ten years. Never received credit... no name on the cover, no book signings. My name's not in the Library of Congress."

Metzinger waited a moment.

"And no money?"

"And no money. I'm living with Sage and have no money. It's not fair."

"You could get a job."

"Plan to."

"You could marry Sage."

Freddie looked shocked.

"That's not funny."

"Didn't mean for it to be."

"Well, there's no way... not to Sage. I'll go to college next year... get back on track."

"So, you took a year off to smoke pot?"

"Yeah. Why not? Waste a year. Some kids hike through Europe. I hike through a haze."

Givens rejoined the conversation.

"Let's get back to the disagreements with your mother. When did you decide you were being treated unfairly?

"Four years ago."

"Did you start fighting with your mother then?"

"Started making comments, but she ignored me."

"Did you do anything? Make threats or anything?"

"Not threats. Just little comments now and then, stewed on it, tried to figure out what to do."

"Did you do anything?"

"Sabotaged her."

"Sabotaged her?"

"Yeah. She signed a contract for three books when I was fifteen years old. Took a big advance... not sure how much. I wrote a book with no new ideas, a lot of repetition of old themes. It flopped. It made the publisher mad. It made my mother mad. Fueled the arguments, incited fights. She wanted me to produce like a cash cow. From then on, her nagging became constant. The publisher was after her, and she was after me. But I wanted recognition. I wanted part of the money. There was no way she was going to give up her eminence, or her money. We were deadlocked."

Metzinger nodded.

"So, who gets the money now?"

"What do you mean?"

"Your mother's dead. There must be money in the bank. Royalties for books that will be sold in the future. Geraldine Gerbil seems pretty popular. Can't more books be written now? Who gets the money from all that?"

"Don't look at me. There's no way my mother would give me anything. I assume Dad gets everything. Isn't that the way it works?"

"Not necessarily. It depends on whether there's a will. Did your mother have a will?"

Freddie looked back and forth between the two detectives.

"I've no idea! But, even if there is a will, there's no way she would have left anything to me. If you're looking for an excuse to pin her murder on me, it's not because of a will."

"No, but it might have been because you hated her."

"I didn't hate her."

"Oh?"

"No. Hate takes energy, detective. It takes determination. It takes time. She wasn't worth it. Dislike her? Yes. And she disliked me... maybe hated me. She had the energy. Me? I'm just coasting on through life."

"In a haze?"

Freddie chuckled.

"Yep, in a haze."

# CHAPTER TWENTY-FIVE

GIVENS ESCORTED FREDDIE to the building's entrance.
"Don't go anywhere."

"You told me that before."

"Well, you have motive."

"Everyone has motive."

"Including your father?"

Freddie sighed and asked, "Have you talked to Mrs. Sorley next door?"

"Briefly."

"Maybe you need to do that again. And how about the Hales behind us?"

"No. Don't think so."

"Thought detectives canvased the neighborhood?"

"We had uniformed police do that. Don't know if they did the next street over. All the reports aren't in yet."

"What? Maybe I could do better than you."

"Yeah, well, what will we learn?"

Freddie pivoted out the front door, saying, "Your job, not mine."

Givens watched her go. Sassy little bitch.

She returned to the interview room where Metzinger sat writing in his notebook.

"Freddie says we need to talk to Ginger Sorley again, and the people behind the Winslow house, named Hale."

"Oh, what about?"

"She wouldn't say."

"The plot thickens."

"Maybe. Gives us something to do tomorrow."

"No rest for the weary. Where are you going now?"

"Having lunch with Big Gert. I need to thank her for helping us out. Seems like Arley takes credit for a lot of things she does."

Metzinger didn't doubt that at all. *Do I do that to Leslie?* he wondered.

"Have a good lunch. I'm going to stay here and finish up my notes. See you at one-thirty for our next interview."

"Does that give us enough time to get there?"

"It's in Parkfairfax... Quaker Lane again, past Braddock. Should be no problem."

After Givens left, Metzinger got to thinking

*So, Joss gave her parents the finger when they challenged her on her dating practices... I wonder if Freddie's description was figurative or described an actual event. Is it going to be this way with Laura? I wonder what her reaction is going to be when I challenge her. Can't imagine a finger but, annoyance? Anger? Sulking? Maybe all-of-the-above. Are we going to go through this with Ben too?... I have to do something...*

He shook his head. Sometimes it's easier being a hard-ass cop than being a father. If someone cries at you in the interview room, you don't have to care.

# CHAPTER TWENTY-SIX

As Metzinger turned off the main road approaching Allison Jablonski's apartment he bragged, "Two minutes early... told you we had time."

Givens made a face, "We're not there yet."

"Tiny details."

They drove into a cul-de-sac, three apartment buildings on the left and three on the right, two at the end. Metzinger parked next to a white Prius.

Metzinger shared, "The Prius is Jablonski's car. I checked it out before we came. Looks like he's home."

The Jablonski apartment's entrance was at the far end of the third building on the right, down four steps to the door.

Givens inquired, "Is this a basement apartment?"

"Yeah, a few buildings have them. Depends on the slope of the land. Hoofbeats overhead day and night."

Metzinger knocked on the door.

A slightly heavy man answered the door, puffy face, not tall—maybe five-foot-eight. His rimless glasses didn't hide the bags under his eyes. His bald head was partially covered with a comb-over, not enough to do much good. He wore a sky-blue buttoned shirt with an open button-down collar and wrinkled khaki trousers.

"Are you the detectives?"

Showing their badges, Metzinger responded, "We are. Are you Ralph Jablonski?"

The man took Givens's badge in his hand and studied it.

"Dr. Jablonski, yes. Come in and please be quiet."

Metzinger took note that 'doctor' was important to the man.

The detectives squeezed by Dr. Jablonski while he held the screened door open for them.

"Why be quiet?" Givens asked.

"My wife is sleeping."

He pointed to a woman sleeping under a blanket on the sofa.

"Please come back into the dining room where we can talk."

The detectives followed the man. Metzinger whispered, "Is that Allison Jablonski?"

"Yes, my wife" the man whispered back.

"Well, she's the one we need to talk to."

"I'd prefer you didn't. She sleeps most of the time."

"Why's that?"

"Depression." He pulled out a chair at the end of the dining room table and sat as he pointed at the other chairs.

"Please have a seat. You'll have to talk to me."

Metzinger sighed and took a deep breath.

"We really need to talk to her."

Jablonski frowned.

"Let's see if I can answer your questions. Then I'll wake her if I must."

Metzinger hesitated.

"Okay, we'll give it a try."

"So, what can I help you with?"

"Doctor, are you aware that a woman named Daphne O'Hanlon was murdered? Shot at the entrance to her home?"

The man stared myopically at Metzinger.

"I am. It was in the paper, on the evening news, probably on Twitter too."

"And did you know Daphne O'Hanlon?"

"Yes."

*Gosh,* thought Metzinger. *Brief answers... I'll have to ask lots of questions.*

"In what capacity did you know her?"

"My wife worked for her."

This is going to take a while.

"What did your wife do for her?"

"Allie illustrated children's books that Mrs. O'Hanlon wrote."

"You don't call her by her first name?"

"She wasn't a friend. She was an employer."

"Your wife is a professional artist?"

"She has a degree in commercial art."

"Oh, how did she get involved with doing children's books?"

"She was looking for work and saw an advertisement in an art magazine for a book illustrator."

"So, she applied to Mrs. O'Hanlon?" A thought streaked through Metzinger's mind—*do you call a married woman who keeps her maiden name, Ms. or Mrs.?*

"No. The advertisement was from Mrs. O'Hanlon's agent, Brigit Sanders. You know her?"

"We're going to speak to her later."

"Tough lady... but we don't blame her for anything."

"Oh? Do you blame Mrs. O'Hanlon for something?"

"Yes. She quit using Allie. Fired her. Told Allie not to bug her. Said she didn't have any work for Allie to do. Would call when she needed her. Rude about it and she didn't have to be."

"Maybe there wasn't any work."

"Okay but be nice about it."

Givens joined in.

"May I ask you, out of curiosity, why your wife didn't do commercial art if that was her training?"

Dr. Jablonski hesitated.

"She did. Tried it for a few years. Her bosses asked her to do things over or changed the whole idea behind what she was doing. She was proud of her work and eventually got mad and quit. With Geraldine, she was happy. Worked here in the apartment with nobody giving her any trouble. O'Hanlon gave her rough sketches and she made them wonderful. Allie says O'Hanlon had no idea about art, even though she got better over time. Allie took the sketches, and as she put it, brought Geraldine Gerbil to life. Allie loved Geraldine."

"And then the sketches stopped coming, a couple of years ago, right?"

"Yes. They stopped coming and the only responses to Allie's phone calls were 'stop bothering me, Allie... Stop annoying me, Allie... I've got my own problems, Allie.'"

"Did Mrs. O'Hanlon give any explanations?"

"No explanation. Just annoyance."

Metzinger rejoined the conversation.

"And how has this affected your wife, Dr. Jablonski?"

Jablonski looked at Metzinger, then at Givens, and next back at Metzinger.

"What do you think?"

"You think it depressed her?"

"She was a happy woman working on Geraldine. Worked alone, but happy. Depression started a little over a year ago. I had to quit my job. I work some, now and then, at doc-in-the-boxes. When I do, I'm forced to hire people to stay with Allie. Fortunately, I have an inheritance from my parents, but it won't last forever. We're playing it by ear."

Metzinger closed his notebook.

"We're sorry to hear about your situation, but we'd really like to speak to your wife, if it's at all possible."

Jablonski sighed.

"All right, we can try. Come with me to the sofa."

Jablonski gently shook his wife's shoulder.

"Allie, sweetheart, there are some people here to see you."

"Yes... what?" Allison turned her head and saw the detectives.

"Oh, goodness, I'm not dressed. Need to comb my hair..."

Jablonski kissed his wife's forehead.

"It's all right, honey. You've got a blanket over you. They're policemen. They just want to ask you a couple of questions."

"Policemen? I didn't do anything. Just been sleeping..."

Metzinger intervened.

"No, Mrs. Jablonski, no one says you did anything. We just wanted to ask you a couple of questions about your work on Geraldine Gerbil."

"Oh yes. Geraldine... I drew her."

"I know, and you drew her very well. You did it for Daphne O'Hanlon?"

"O'Hanlon, yes. Daffy, Daffy, Daffy. A mean woman."

Metzinger pressed on, despite a glare from Givens.

"Then Mrs. O'Hanlon stopped asking you to draw Geraldine?"

"No. No more Geraldine. No more work. I love Geraldine..."

"We know you do, Mrs. Jablonski. Do you think it's because Mrs. O'Hanlon is mean?"

"Yes, mean. Daffy is mean."

"You wouldn't hurt Mrs. O'Hanlon, would you?"

Jablonski stepped in.

"That's enough, detective. More than enough. Allie never leaves this house. It's time for you to go."

Metzinger nodded and looked down. Givens gave him a tired expression, unsympathetic.

"Let's go, Drury."

"I had to ask."

"You knew the answer."

"For the record."

"Yeah, for the record."

They got back in the car.

Givens looked at Metzinger, who looked beaten.

# CHAPTER TWENTY-SEVEN

THE DETECTIVES DROVE back to their office in silence. As they approached Duke Street Metzinger asked, "What time is the phone interview with O'Hanlon's agent?"

"4:30 P.M. Her name is Brigit Sanders."

"Yeah, Sanders." Metzinger repeated.

"You all right, Drury?"

"Just thinking about the woman."

"Mrs. Jablonski?"

"Yeah, Mrs. Jablonski. Fragile woman. Gone off the deep end. Seems like it didn't take much. I'm sorry I had to pursue talking to her."

"Dotting the i's?"

Metzinger gave a sad, brief chuckle.

"Yeah, playing the cop. Crossing the t's. Getting what we need for a report. Never know until you try. You think we can cross her off the suspect list?"

"Fragile Allie?"

"Yeah. Don't see how she could have gone all the way to Jefferson Park."

"Me neither."

"How about her husband, the doctor?"

"He'd have to have left her at home."

"Yeah, but he has help... people who come when he works at doctoring."

"Yeah, but he seems too tired and beaten down to have done much," Metzinger empathized.

"Only took one shot." Givens encouraged.

"True... yeah, keep him to the list."

# CHAPTER TWENTY-EIGHT

METZINGER AND GIVENS used a conference room for the phone inter-view. They didn't want to put a phone call on speakerphone out in the common bay... too much noise and too many ears.

A woman answered... maybe the receptionist; maybe an assistant; maybe somebody important.

"Essex Publishing. May I help you?"

"Yes, this is Detective Drury Metzinger of the Alexandria Police Department."

"Oh, yes, detective. We're expecting your call. Let me connect you to Ms. Sanders."

A moment later, a woman came on the line.

"Brigit Sanders here. Is this Detective Masterson?"

Metzinger gulped and hesitated a moment.

"No, this is Detective Drury Metzinger. It's my case. Detective Masterson set up the call for me... helping me out. I'm here with my part-ner, Detective Leslie Givens. We're working it together."

"About Daphne?"

"Uh, yes. Daphne O'Hanlon. Did you hear about her?"

"Yes, Detective Masterson told me that somebody killed her. Terrible... do you know who did it?"

"Had you heard of her death before Detective Masterson told you?"

"No. I've been in New York since Tuesday morning."

"To answer your question, we do not know who did it. We're investigating and would appreciate your answering some questions. May I put you on speakerphone so that Detective Givens can hear you, too?"

"Just the two of you?"

"Yes."

"Okay."

Metzinger pushed the speakerphone button and Givens said, "Hi, I'm Detective Leslie Givens."

"Hi, Leslie."

*Wow,* Givens thought sarcastically, *Detective Masterson, Detective Metzinger, and Leslie. Thanks for supporting women's empowerment, Bridget.*

"What time did you get to New York on Tuesday?"

"What's this? Do I need an alibi?"

"Crossing people off our list."

"Well, I got here late morning, around eleven. It's such turmoil getting out of Penn Station and catching a cab... had lunch and showed up here at Essex about one-thirty. Dinner was with some folks here. Spent the night at the Grand Marquis and was back here at nine in the morning. Mostly I repeat the same thing every day. How was she killed?"

"Shot, after opening her front door. We think she recognized the killer."

Metzinger felt no need to discuss the head injury.

"That ought to narrow it down."

"Down to a lot of people... too many. Do you know anyone who might have wanted to kill her?"

"Besides me? Hey, don't take that seriously. I don't kill people."

"Were you unhappy with Mrs. O'Hanlon?"

"Besides the fact that she was a pain?"

"She was hard to work with?"

"Hard to talk to. Hard to be in the room with. When we first started working together, she was fine... even fun. But it all went to her head, the awards, the sales, the reviews, the money, which she always wanted more of. Talked down to me. I went from a friend to an employee who never got her enough money."

"We understand she got an advance for three books."

"Yeah, I got her that, but she only finished one book... a pretty poor one. Guess the other two will never be produced. I talked to Mr. McDuffy about that yesterday."

"McDuffy?"

"Yes, William McDuffy, the guy who wrote her the advance check. He wants his money back. My commission, too. Should have gotten insurance. Does GEICO do that?"

"That I don't know. Maybe he can file a claim against the estate."

"Who's the executor?"

"Don't know."

"Her lawyer?"

"Don't know that either. Not our job. We are just working to solve the murder. Anybody else you know who might have it in for Mrs. O'Hanlon?"

"Haven't been much involved in her personal life in the last seven or eight years. There's the illustrator, of course. With no books produced in the last two years, she's been hung out to dry."

"Allison Jablonski?"

"Yeah, Allie. I hired her originally. Feel sorry for her. For me, too."

"Now, the big question. Did you know that Daphne O'Hanlon didn't write the books?"

"What!? What are you talking about? She certainly took all the credit... all the Geraldine Gerbil contracts are in her name. She accepted all the awards! Are you telling me she stole them? If she didn't write the books, who the hell did and why didn't they take credit?"

"So, you weren't aware she didn't write them?"

"Hell no! She said they were hers! Never a mention of anyone else!"

"Well, they were written by her daughter, Winifred. Began when the girl was about six. And you had no idea?"

"No! No way! Why didn't the kid protest? Shit. Are you sure?"

"When she became a teenager, she did protest... says she intentionally wrote a bad book and refused to write more until she got credit and money."

"Lord, that explains the last book. This kid still around?"

"Yes, why do you ask?"

"Maybe she has more books in her."

"You're kidding? You'd want to publish more books?"

"Hell, yes. That's how I make a living. Maybe I wouldn't have to pay back the advance—"

Metzinger cut in.

"We haven't asked you the important question."

"Oh, what's that?"

"Where were you Monday night?"

"So, all the rest of this conversation was shit?"

"No, ma'am. All information we need. Please answer the question."

"I was home."

"Where's that?"

"My apartment's in D.C."

"And you can prove you were there?"

"I was with someone."

"Someone? Does someone have a name, phone number, address, etcetera?"

"No."

"No name?"

"It's private."

"Then you have no alibi."

"I'm not giving it."

Both Metzinger and Givens were getting frustrated with the phone call.

"When will you be home from New York, Mrs. Sanders?"

"It's Ms. Sanders," she corrected. "Why?"

"We're probably going to have you come in for an interview."

"To Alexandria?"

"Yes."

"Good luck."

"What do you mean?"

"I'm not coming."

"We can make you."

It sounded like Ms. Sanders drew in a deep breath before she spoke again. Her tone dropped and timbre steadied.

"I didn't kill her, detective. My private life is nobody's business."

"That's to be determined, Ms. Sanders. So, when do you get home?"

"Friday afternoon. There. You happy now?"

"Thank you. Let me see..." Metzinger paused while checking his notebook. "Yeah, I have your local address and phone number. We'll be in touch."

"You're wasting your time, detective. Mine too."

Metzinger smiled at Givens

"We do what's necessary and appreciate your cooperation. Goodbye, Ms. Sanders."

Metzinger hung up.

"Wonder what Ms. Sanders and 'someone' were doing?"

Givens smirked, "None of your business, Detective Metzinger."

"Maybe. Let's go home. Our day's over."

"In a minute. I want to check on Janet and Twiggy. See if they verify Joss's story. Hopefully, they're home from school by now."

"Good luck. If Joss's story is correct, they were still driving around at eight on Monday evening, five hours after school ended. Hope that's not routine for teenagers around here."

# CHAPTER TWENTY-NINE

METZINGER PARKED IN his driveway, turned off the ignition, and sat for a minute. He wasn't sure he was ready to face his teenage daughter... or his wife.

He entered the house and took off his coat and tie. He was rolling up his sleeves as he entered the kitchen, where he found his wife lifting a casserole out of the oven.

"Where's Laura?"

Sarah set the casserole on the stove and turned to her husband.

"She promised she'd be home by six," she said, glancing at the clock on the stove. "She has seventeen minutes."

"So, she has three hours with Doofus between school and dinner?"

"Doofus? I hope you don't call him that to Laura."

"I'll call him worse than that if he screws up her getting into college."

Sarah shook her head.

"Laura promised me she'd get her grades back up. She also promised me she'd be home for dinner every night at six. Besides, today she is working on the yearbook. She does that three times a week. All that will limit her time with Jack."

"Jack? That's his name?"

"Yes, what's wrong with that? His real name is Jacobius Fazio. I can understand not wanting to be called Jacobius."

Metzinger pursed his lips at the name.

"He'd sound tougher if he'd call himself Jake. Jacob would be all right. Why Jack?"

"I have no idea."

"No one asked you?" Drury taunted, trying to lighten the mood.

"Nope, not a soul."

"Okay, so what did you do about the weekends?"

"Homework has to be done by noon Sunday... home by six Sunday night... dinner and evening with the family or texting friends but the phone stays downstairs."

"Sounds pretty restrictive. What time does she have to be in on Saturday night?"

"Ten o'clock, unless there's something specific, like a dance or a late movie."

"She agreed to all this?"

"Yes."

"And you did it without yelling?"

"Yes."

Metzinger wrinkled his nose and sighed.

"I don't see how it can work," he turned away, shaking his head. "I'm going to change my clothes."

***

When Metzinger came back downstairs, he stuck his head into the kitchen.

"Laura home yet?"

Sarah was setting the kitchen table.

"In the basement watching TV with Ben. Dinner's in ten minutes."

"Okay, I'll go watch TV with them."

He found Laura and Ben sitting on the sofa. Thank God it's not Jessica Jones again, he thought. Laura glanced at him but quickly turned back to the television. She looked nervous.

"You going to say something to me?"

Metzinger sat in a club chair.

"Just watching television with my children waiting for dinner."

"That's all?"

"What else?"

"You're letting Mom take care of it."

"It? What do you mean?"

Ben threw up his hands in disgust.

"Good grief. Her Jack-o'-lantern romance. Light of her life. Stop beating around the bush, interrupting my TV. Go someplace else and talk."

Laura hit Ben with a pillow.

"His name's not Jack-o'-lantern and it's not a romance. That word's from the Middle Ages. We're just dating. It's what people do in high school. He's my safety."

Metzinger was startled.

"Safety? What's that mean?"

"It means you're not standing around all the time by yourself while some guy has his arm around your best friend. It means you have a date for the dance."

Ben hit her back with the pillow and interjected, "It means you don't have enough self-confidence, don't think you're attractive."

Metzinger got out of his chair and grabbed Ben by the arm.

"Don't say cruel things to your sister!"

Ben shook himself loose.

"I didn't. It's not cruel. It's a fact. Laura's pretty. She just doesn't know it."

Laura looked at her brother and gaped.

# CHAPTER THIRTY

MAMA GIVENS WAS still in the kitchen working on supper when Leslie got home on time.

"No bad guys working you late tonight?"

Givens grabbed paper napkins and utensils and started setting the table.

"No, lots of unhappy people, but we haven't figured out who's the bad guy."

"Well, stretch it out. The longer it takes the longer you keep your job... keep getting paid."

"Pfft, takes time to figure things out. Got lots of possibilities... too many. Haven't found anyone who liked the victim."

"Maybe the woman deserved it."

"Not the way it works, Mama. The law says people don't get to kill people."

"Yeah, I know, but think of all the money wasted chasing and jailing no-goods. My tax dollars. It's a shame."

Givens sighed and sat at her place.

"Anything I can help with?"

Mama scowled at her daughter.

"You sit down before you ask?"

Givens felt the guilt.

"I can get back up."

"Good, how 'bout pouring us drinks?"

Givens got back up.

"Glad to... what are you drinking."

"Same as always... glass of water."

Givens poured the water and a glass of milk for herself.

Returning to the table, she asked, "How was your day... any more fights at the diner?"

Mama brought plates to the table; pork chops, mashed potatoes, and lima beans.

"No, didn't have anyone younger than me in before eleven, and then some street workers and delivery men for lunch... all regulars... no one with a rod up their ass."

Givens got up again to get apple butter out of the refrigerator.

"Colorful way to describe them."

"Okay, young punks looking for trouble. That better?"

"Yeah, I understood what you said before. Deal with them all the time. Them and the druggies keep me employed in between bodies."

Just then, the house-phone rang. Givens rose to answer.

"Tell 'em we just sat down for supper. Tell 'em you'll call back."

"Leslie Givens," she said as she picked up the phone and answered. "Oh, hi, haven't talked in a while—you've been out of town? Your job sent you?—Birmingham? Never been there—Still hot there, huh?"

Her mother was waving at her to get off the phone. Givens kept nodding.

"Sunday night? Sure, that'd be nice—Pick me up at seven? Okay, I'll be ready—Nah, Mama won't hassle you. I'll be ready, text me and I'll come right out. See you then."

She hung up and looked at her mother who was making an annoyed face.

"Who am I not hassling?"

"Bobby Riley."

"Bobby Riley!? When've I ever hassled him?"

"Last time he was here. Pinned him down and asked him all kinds of questions about his family."

"What's wrong with that. Just want to know if he was good enough for you."

"You didn't ask him anything about himself... where he went to school... where he works... that kind of thing."

"Don't need to. Family's what's important. I can tell from there."

"Well, he felt like he was being judged."

"Well, he was. What's wrong with that? Was he ashamed of something?"

"He wasn't ashamed... just didn't like the inquisition."

"Inquisition? I didn't even ask him where he goes to church. Should have."

"Exactly. This time he's not coming in, so you won't get a chance."

Mama Givens' annoyance continued.

"Hey, you act like I'm doing something wrong. I've got to play mama and papa... take care of you... do what's right."

Givens became conciliatory.

"I know, Mama. Didn't mean to get Bobby in trouble with you. He's a good guy."

"Always thought that too. Now, I wonder."

"No need to wonder. I'll find out where he goes to church."

"And you'll tell me?"

"If it's a good answer."

"Now, who's hassling who?"

# CHAPTER THIRTY-ONE

AFTER SUPPER, GIVENS went to her crib of a room and phoned Chantel. "Well, girl, guess who called."

"Straight-ass?"

"His name is Bobby... Bobby Riley."

"Poor bitch. Why are you into this guy? He's got no swagger."

"Don't call me bitch."

"I call all my girlfriends bitch. Term of endearment. You gettin' politically correct on me?"

"I simply don't like the term."

"Well, la-de-dah. I'll work on my English accent."

"Damn, Chantel, don't be bitchy with me."

"Thought we weren't supposed to use that word." Chantel quipped.

There was a moment of silence.

"So, you're not going out with us this weekend 'cause you have a super date?"

"I'm seeing Bobby Sunday night. I've still got Friday open. You still wanna go dancing?"

"Yah bitch, I'm in! Maybe there's hope."

# CHAPTER THIRTY-TWO

M ETZINGER ARRIVED AT his desk and found a cup of coffee sitting in its center next to some phone messages and yellow post-its. He picked up the coffee and looked around. Givens grinned.

"Thought I'd get you coffee before the pot was emptied... start you off in a good mood."

"Why? You know something I don't? Is it bad?"

"No. Just adding sunshine to the morning."

Metzinger picked up the notes.

"Well, let's see if we can do something about that."

He read a post-it.

"The computer guys went over the Winslow computers. Didn't get anything off the doorbell cam. Nothing, except Monday night when Joss came home, just some kind of smudgy movement after nine o'clock and then nothing thanks to the Band-Aid. O'Hanlon's computer had a lot of emails back and forth with Essex Publishing and Brigit Sanders. Lots of anger, but no physical threats. They're sending us the relevant messages."

Metzinger picked up another post-it.

"The lieutenant says the Winslows can go back into their house. I guess we've squeezed all the evidence we can out of the place. Give Oliver Winslow a call and ask him to contact his daughters. They can all decide how friendly they are... if they're ready to face each other at home."

Givens looked at Metzinger while she dialed, "The junior detective has all the fun."

"And you're so good at it."

"Good morning, Mr. Winslow. This is Detective Givens from police head-quarters—I'm fine, thank you. And you—Just wanted to let you know you can get back into your house—No, it's not cleaned up. Afraid that's your respon-sibility—No, nothing fun about it—No, we haven't found the perpetrator yet—Still working on it—Yes, we're anxious, too. We know it's a strain on your family—Certainly, we'll phone as soon as we know anything—Will you be returning to the house today?—Yes, just want to know where to contact you—The girls, too—No, I understand. Would you let us know when you find out?—Yes, thank you. Goodbye."

"I admire the way you jump right on it," Metzinger said after she hung up. "On the phone before I finish looking at my notes."

He was flipping through his trusted notebook again.

"You have any luck with Janet and Thiggy last night?"

"Janet and Twiggy." Givens corrected.

"Thought her name was Thigpen."

"It is, but she's still called 'Twiggy.'"

"Doesn't make sense."

"Maybe she's skinny."

"That'd do it. What'd they say?"

"They both agreed with Joss's story."

"Check that off." Metzinger made a note.

Givens closed her own notebook.

"What else have you got? Shall I keep the phone in hand?"

"Might as well. We got a call last night, late, from a neighbor named Audrey Hale. Lives in the house directly behind the Winslows. Says she wants to talk to the detectives in charge. Guess that's us."

"Same Hale Freddie mentioned?"

Metzinger nodded and said, "I'll take this one," and made the call.

"Yes, good morning. This is Detective Metzinger from the Alexandria Police Department, returning your call from last night. How can I help you?—Right, I'm investigating the murder of Daphne O'Hanlon—Yes, we had two policemen make inquiries around the neighborhood—Oh, and what else have you thought of Mrs. Hale—Mmmm, out your kitchen window. Good view of the back of the Winslow house and the neighbors—Strange goings on? In what way?—I see. Mind if we come take a look, talk to you some more?—Ten o'clock?—See you then."

Metzinger hung up the phone and looked at Givens.

"She says there's been a lot of movement back and forth over the past few months between Jeannie 'Yoga Pants' Sorley and Oliver Winslow. Seeing her at 10:00 A.M. You coming?"

"Of course. You might be interviewing a woman nicknamed Yoga Pants Soreley which definitely requires my presence in case I have to report back to Sarah."

"My Sarah?"

"We women stick together."

"You do, huh? I thought partners could confide in each other. Changing the rules?"

"Just pulling your leg, Drury."

"Well, it's a sensitive leg."

# CHAPTER THIRTY-THREE

THE HALE'S HOUSE was a frame Colonial painted yellow. The detectives arrived five minutes early.

"Do you think we should wait five minutes?" Givens asked as Metzinger started to get out of the car.

Metzinger looked over his shoulder at Givens still getting out.

"She doesn't have to answer the door."

Givens hurried to catch up.

"Look at this yellow door!" Givens said. "I told you I was bringing sunshine this morning."

"Shush, she might hear."

"So what? She must like it."

Metzinger rang the doorbell and shifted his feet a couple of times waiting. A woman pulled open the storm door. Mid-forties, glasses, small features, dark hair and bangs across her forehead.

"Are you the detectives?" she asked.

"Yes, I'm Detective Metzinger, the one you spoke to on the phone, and this is Detective Givens." He swung his hand toward the storm door, noticing the summer screens already replaced by glass.

"You've put the glass in early," he commented. "Is it going to be a bad winter?"

The woman met his hand, shook it, and smiled.

"Hi, I'm Audrey. My husband, Andy, just likes to be ahead of the game. Come in and have a seat."

"Could we check out back first?"

"Of course. Come this way."

Mrs. Hale led them out onto a deck and pointed to the kitchen window.

"We don't spend a lot of time out here. Andy doesn't like the heat, but the view from the kitchen is the same."

"And what have you seen?"

"Mr. Winslow going to the Sorley house and Mrs. Sorley going to the Winslow's, but more often Mr. Winslow goes to the Sorley house."

Givens asked, "Does Mrs. Sorley usually wear yoga pants?"

Mrs. Hale answered without batting an eye, "Sometimes. Why do you ask?"

Givens answered without meeting Mrs. Hale's eyes.

"Oh, she was wearing one when we interviewed her. I thought, maybe, it was her regular outfit."

Metzinger purred.

Givens gave him a glare.

Mrs. Hale looked back and forth between the detectives.

"Oh, you've already talked to her?"

"We tried to talk to all the neighbors."

"Yes. Right. I talked to the policemen who came by but didn't think about them running back and forth. The policemen wanted to know if I'd seen or heard anything Monday night and I didn't."

Metzinger asked, "And why do you think the neighbors running back and forth is important now? Maybe they were borrowing things or making food for each other."

Mrs. Hale became defensive.

"Well, if they were doing that, they'd be carrying things and not looking furtive. When they get to the doors, they look like they're trying to get in before someone sees them. Besides, it doesn't take a half hour or more to borrow something. Additionally, they have keys to each other's houses. They don't even knock."

"Half hour or more, huh? How long have you observed these goings on?"

"At least six months. Didn't pay much attention before then."

"So, you think there's something untoward going on?"

She looked at Givens.

"Well, you've seen Mrs. Sorley... in her outfits."

She looked back at Metzinger.

"Have you seen Mr. Sorley?"

Metzinger shook his head.

"He's a mousy little guy. Can't imagine anyone being interested in him. And they don't have any children."

"And you think that means what, Mrs. Hale?"

"It's obvious, detective. Somebody's inactive or impotent."

"And you think Mrs. Sorley might be looking for help elsewhere."

"Seems obvious to me."

Givens asked, "And when do these possible liaisons take place?"

"Weekdays, when the Winslow girls are in school."

"When Mr. Sorley is at work?"

"Right."

"Why wasn't Mr. Winslow at work?"

"No idea. Vacation days?"

"And what about Mrs. Winslow, err, Daphne O'Hanlon?"

"Don't know anything about her. I never see her."

"She doesn't come out into the back yard. They have a patio there with patio furniture."

"No, the only person who uses that is one of the girls to make out."

"One of the girls makes out on the patio furniture?"

"Necks with her boyfriends."

"So, Daphne O'Hanlon doesn't use the patio."

"Detective, I never see Daphne O'Hanlon. All I see from here is the back of the house. I can't see their front door, garage, or driveway. If the woman doesn't come out back, I don't see her."

"So, you wouldn't know if Daphne O'Hanlon was home when her husband was entertaining Mrs. Sorley and vice versa?"

"Well, no."

"Well, you certainly have a good view. A four-foot high chain-link fence with a low hedge doesn't hide much. How long have you lived here, Mrs. Hale?"

"A little over two years."

"And the liaisons have only been going on for six months?"

"That's how long I've noticed them."

Metzinger joined in.

"Thank you, Mrs. Hale. We appreciate the information. Every detail helps."

"I should have offered you something to drink."

Metzinger and Givens edged toward the front door.

"No, that's fine. We appreciate the thought, but what we needed was information."

The detectives walked down the entrance walk and got back into their car. They drove and around the corner out of Mrs. Hale's sight to confer.

"Mrs. Sorley may be more involved than she implied," Metzinger observed. "Mrs. Hale apparently believes there are vacuums in the lives of Oliver Winslow and Jeannie Sorley, and that the two have found a mutual solution."

Metzinger put the car in park, "Lord knows that nature abhors a vacuum."

Givens thought about it.

"So, did Jeannie 'Yoga Pants' Sorley have an interest in filling the vacuum and replacing Mrs. Winslow, AKA Daphne O'Hanlon? Did Oliver, or was the relationship just a temporary mutual convenience?"

"Either way, the list of suspects grows longer."

"Indeed, it does. Shall we go and visit Mrs. Sorley? After all, she's the reason I'm here... to protect your virtue"

Metzinger smirked. "And I'm grateful for that. Afterwards, we can visit Mr. Winslow."

"A full sweep. Do you think they'll admit an affair?"

"I wouldn't."

# CHAPTER THIRTY-FOUR

At the Sorley's house, Givens noticed the garage door was open with no car in sight.

"Doesn't look good," she remarked.

Metzinger turned off the ignition and opened his car door. Let's at least go knock... maybe leave a note.

As they headed up the sidewalk Givens wondered aloud, "Do you think Mrs. Braswell is watching?"

"I'd be disappointed if she's not. A neighborhood watch failure. Can't believe that would happen."

Givens knocked on the Sorley's door.

Metzinger grinned.

"Nice police knock. I'm proud of you."

"You really commending me or giving me a hard time? Sometimes I can't tell."

"No," Metzinger protested, "it was admirable... really good but wasted. No one's home."

He pulled out a contact card and his pen.

"What do I tell her?"

"That we'll be back this afternoon."

"No, I've got something personal I need to do."

Givens raised an eyebrow, but her partner kept talking, "You willing to work Saturday morning?"

"I guess... if it's not too early."

"Friday night party?"

"Maybe. Saturday morning sleeping-in means a lot."

Metzinger scribbled on the card.

"Eleven o'clock then."

"If the time changes, you'll let me know, right?"

"Of course. I wouldn't make you sacrifice your slumber for no reason."

Givens looked at the Winslow house.

"Maybe we can at least kill off Oliver Winslow."

"Careful of your terminology," Metzinger cautioned.

"Uh-huh."

"I think we're going to fail there too. No car in the driveway and the crime scene tape is still in place."

"Maybe he used the back door to avoid the bloody entrance."

"That would be smart, but still, there's no car."

"Another note?"

"Remind me to requisition more cards."

# CHAPTER THIRTY-FIVE

SINCE LAURA WAS working on the yearbook, Drury Metzinger was gambling that doofus Fazio would come straight home after school. He parked across the street and one house down from Jack Fazio's home.

The Fazio's lived in a small 1930s house with a brick façade lower half; framed white upper... a single garage, one car driveway, in the Del Ray section of town. He'd learned from Ben that the kid didn't play any sports. Still, there were other ways a young man could occupy his time on a free afternoon. Metzinger felt he might be wasting his time.

So, he sat, waiting.

It was ten minutes later than he expected when a gray Taurus, 2005 or 2006, turned onto the street and parked against the curb in front of the Fazio house. Metzinger quickly exited his car and approached the young driver who got out of the Taurus hauling a backpack.

"Jack? Jack Fazio?" Metzinger shouted as he approached.

Fazio turned, inquisitive, his eyebrows raised.

"Yeah, who are you?"

"Laura's father."

The eyebrows knitted.

"Laura Metzinger's father?"

Metzinger looked Fazio up and down... dirty brown hair in a short ponytail... t-shirt with "Don't Tread on Me" and a coiled snake spread across it... worn jeans... well-worn high-top sneakers named after some basketball player.

"Yes, that's me."

"The cop? You going to hassle me?"

"No, I just want to talk."

"Oh... just a pleasant conversation in the middle of the street."

"Yes. I'm concerned about Laura."

"Concerned I'm not good enough for her?"

"Concerned that her grades are going down since she's been dating you."

"Maybe I'm more interesting than the books."

"That's what's worrying me. She's spending too much of her time on things other than her books... other than her studies... on not maintaining the grades she needs to go to college."

"Maybe she doesn't want to go to college."

"She's always planned to, at least until she started going with you."

Just then a woman came out of the house, looking thirty or so pounds overweight, sporting the beginning of a double chin, also wearing jeans and a t-shirt from Virginia Beach.

"What's going on, Jack? Who're you talking to?"

The woman descended the front walk, looking ready to take charge.

"He's giving me shit about Laura."

"Who the hell's Laura? One of your bimbos?"

Metzinger took a defensive stance, turning towards her.

"I assume you're Mrs. Fazio."

"What's it to you?"

"First, my daughter is no bimbo. I don't know other girls Jack goes with, but Laura's not in that category."

"All the girls Jack comes home with are in that category. Can't keep their hands off him."

"Since you don't know Laura, I assume she's not a girl Jack's brought home."

"Shit, you're a snippy one, aren't you? So, why're you hassling Jack?"

"I'm not hassling him. Just trying to talk with him, to ask for his help and support getting Laura back on track."

"What's he supposed to do? Study for her?"

"No, just encourage her to maintain her goals, to do what she's capable of, and not twitter away her life."

Mrs. Fazio smirked.

"So, Jack here makes your daughter twitter?"

"I'm not trying to be humorous, Mrs. Fazio. I'm just trying to keep my daughter on track."

Mrs. Fazio drew herself to full height and puffed out her chest.

"Well, Mr. Laura's father, let me tell you about life. Girls are stupid over cool boys, they act silly, and the boys spend all kinds of time trying to get into girls' pants. That's the way it is, the way it's always been. No different now than it was when you and I were teenagers. We survived, and they will too."

"You're encouraging Jack to try to get in my daughter's pants?"

"Way it is, mister. I don't encourage anything. Life's life."

"Yeah, well, this young punk," Metzinger stuck his thumb toward Jack, "had better show my daughter some respect and encourage her in life."

"Or you'll do what?"

"Lady, I'm not threatening, but I've got one daughter and I'm going to do everything I can to get her through the next few years and into college. All I'm asking is for Jack to help. Encourage her and behave himself."

Mrs. Fazio laughed.

"Again, what are you going to do?" She turned toward the house. "Come on, Jack."

Jack glanced at Drury with a smirk and followed his mother.

"Ma, that guy's a cop."

Mrs. Fazio glanced back at Metzinger and then looked at her son. Then, turning her head enough so that Metzinger could hear, she wrapped her arm around Jack's shoulders and said, "Hope he's tougher with criminals than he is at harassing you."

Then she punched his shoulder.

"This Laura girl worth fucking, Jack? Well? Is she?"

Metzinger was relieved that Jack seemed a little embarrassed.

Mrs. Fazio took her son by the shoulders.

"You embarrassed? Damn, don't you realize that bastard thinks his daughter's too good for you?"

"That's right! That's exactly right! She's way too good for you!" Metzinger shouted at the two of them.

But the shouting didn't make Metzinger feel any better. He sighed deeply as the Fazios went into their house and closed the door. He felt like a useless fool. He wished he weren't a cop. He wanted to beat the hell out of Jack Fazio and his mother, too.

# CHAPTER THIRTY-SIX

GIVENS SAT ON a barstool at Chicks, nursing a gin and tonic with Chantel and Sharyn. Chantel was in the middle, which was fine with Givens. Instead of feeling the pressure from two sides, she could just enjoy her G&T.

The women eyed the other patrons. Some were familiar, but no one was dancing. Leslie thought the DJ was good, the music tempting, but she didn't want to dance with her friends. Platonic group dancing was fine at weddings, but it wasn't what she was looking for. She was relieved when Kenya and his friend Snooky arrived. Snooky wasn't much to look at, but he was a mighty fine dancer.

Kenya surveyed the room, trying to be casual. Finally, he and Snooky made their way over to the women.

"Glad to see my ladies are here waiting for me."

Chantel sneered at him.

"So, what makes you the king of the roost?"

"I can dance. For now, that's what you need. Later, who knows? I'm here to fulfill needs."

Chantel laughed.

"You're dreaming. Nobody was waiting for you... but you can dance. You ready?"

Kenya held out his hand to Chantel, with a charming smile.

"May I have this dance, charming lady?"

As he led Chantel to the dance floor, Kenya pointed at Snooky and then turned the finger to Sharyn.

Snooky nodded and held his hand out to Sharyn, emulating Kenya, and led her out to dance as well.

Still at the bar, Givens sipped her drink.

*Guess I'm the wallflower tonight. You trying to show me something, Kenya? Trying to make me jealous? I can out dance every woman in this bar. You'll come around.*

Her thoughts were interrupted by a smooth voice.

"You look lonely, sitting here by yourself."

Givens turned to see the man speaking to her.

"No, I've friends out dancing."

"Maybe you should be dancing, too."

Givens looked the man up and down... over six feet... light skinned... hair cut very short.

He looked back at her.

"Satisfied by what you see?"

She smiled.

"Are you asking me to dance?"

"I am."

Just then the music switched to something slow, and the man pulled her close in the classic dance posture.

"You're beautiful to dance with," he complimented, and then Kenya tapped him on the shoulder to interrupt.

"Mind if I cut in?"

"He does," Leslie answered. "You had your chance."

Kenya backed off, looking hurt as the man pulled her close, closer than before.

By the end of the song Kenya was begging, and Leslie reveled in the attention. Much later she rewarded Kenya's regard with his own slow dance, and she let him pull her in tight. His hand slipped to her butt. She knew he could feel everything about her. She could certainly feel everything about him.

# CHAPTER THIRTY-SEVEN

"You're chipper this morning," Metzinger said, looking up at Givens who gifted him a cup of coffee.

"Yeah, life's good, but I wish I could get a smile out of you on a Saturday morning. Your errand go okay yesterday afternoon?"

Metzinger sipped his coffee.

"Can't say it did. In fact, it went piss poor."

"Sorry to hear that. Takes the shine off my morning."

"Sorry to rain on your parade. I made a fool of myself. Tried to reason with my daughter's boyfriend and got terrorized by his mother."

"Ran into a buzz-saw, huh?"

"An amazon with no restraint."

"Your daughter know?"

"No."

"Let's hope she doesn't find out. Maybe I should check with Mama and ask her to get the extra bedroom ready."

"You think I screwed up that bad?"

"No doubt in my mind."

"Shit."

"Probably hit the fan. So, are we going to see what active wear she is wearing today… check the spandex?"

Metzinger gave a wan smile that didn't include his eyes.

"Yeah, I called her this morning. She didn't sound glad to hear from me. Seemed a little nervous. We're due at eleven. Hopefully take the afternoon off."

"Hope so. I'd like to take a nap."

"Oh, the cheer's running out. Short-term chipper?"

"Something like that."

***

Givens was careful not to look at Metzinger after Mrs. Sorely opened the door. She thought he must be disappointed. Her wardrobe was more varied than expected. Instead of tight-fitting exercise clothes, she wore jeans and a heavy cotton blouse.

Metzinger began the conversation.

"Good morning. As I said over the phone, we're trying to understand the whole environment of what is going on and would like to speak with you further. May we come in?"

Mrs. Sorley seemed indecisive.

"Yes, yes of course. Come in and have a seat in the living room. May I get you some coffee?"

"Thanks, just the same. This is not a social call. It's an educational one."

"God, that sounds ominous."

They all sat.

Metzinger asked, "Is your husband home?"

"No, he plays golf on Saturday mornings, all year until the snow falls."

Metzinger continued.

"That may be just as well. We've learned that you make frequent visits to the Winslow's house."

"Huh? Frequent? What the hell does that mean?"

"Just what the word implies. And that Oliver Winslow often comes here."

"Who told you that?"

"It doesn't matter."

"That nosy woman behind us?"

"As I said, it doesn't matter. We also understand that you have a key to the Winslow house?"

"Uh, yes. We're neighbors. They gave me a key for emergencies."

"And that you visit when the girls and Mrs. O'Hanlon are not there?"

"What... what are you implying?"

"We're just trying to understand what's going on. Put everything in context. Trying to understand possible motives."

"What do you mean... motives?"

Givens interjected bluntly.

"If you and Oliver Winslow are having an affair, it would give you or Mr. Winslow a motive in this case."

Sorley looked horrified.

"What? You think I killed Daphne? That's ludicrous."

"We're just trying to understand motives, Mrs. Sorley."

"Understanding, nothing, you're accusing me."

"We're just trying to dot the i's and cross the t's, Mrs. Sorley. All the visiting back and forth is kind of unusual, and we know Oliver Winslow's marriage had its problems."

"Damn you. This kind of loose talk could destroy my marriage."

"That's not our purpose, Mrs. Sorley. We have to explore all possibilities."

"If you go too far with this, I'll sue you."

"That won't help your marriage, Mrs. Sorley. You need to know we're not out to publicize anything. We're just looking for facts."

"You're basing things on innuendo, on gossip from neighbors."

Metzinger came to Givens' defense.

"We haven't based anything. We're learning. To summarize, you acknowledge that you visit the Winslow house now and then and that Mr. Winslow visits your house... that you have a key to the Winslow house, 'for emergencies', and stipulate that the visits are the result of 'just being neighborly'. It that right?"

"Yes. But that doesn't mean I was having an affair. I deny that."

"We understand. We'll talk to Mr. Winslow next."

"You... you're going to talk to Oliver?"

"We'll go there next."

"Right now?"

"Yes. Anything wrong with that?"

"Uh, uh..." Sorley looked down, "... I didn't do it."

Givens came alive.

"Didn't do what?"

Jeannie Sorley gulped and looked at Givens.

"I didn't kill him."

"What are you talking about?"

"Oli... Oliver's dead. He's lying on the kitchen floor in a puddle of blood."

"You went over there and found him?"

"Ye... yes. I went over there to welcome him home, express my condolences and see if I could help."

Metzinger tried to stay calm.

"Mrs. Sorley, give me your key to the Winslow house. Detective Givens and I are going over there. You need to stay here. Don't go anywhere!"

Jeannie Sorley took the key from her pocket and handed it to Metzinger.

"I just used it this morning."

"When was that?"

"About eight o'clock."

"Three hours ago. And you didn't do anything about it?"

"He was dead. I felt his neck for a pulse. There was nothing I could do!"

Metzinger glared, "You could have called 9-1-1."

"But you didn't want to be involved, isn't that right?" Givens berated.

"I couldn't do anything."

"Right. As I said, stay here."

Givens and Metzinger raced across the back yards along the alleged cheaters' route.

They unlocked the Winslow's kitchen door with gloved hands, trying not to smudge potential prints.

Sure enough, Oliver Winslow lay on the tile floor in a puddle of blood.

"Looks dead," Givens gasped.

"Probably since last night or maybe yesterday afternoon. Call headquarters. Get the duty officer to ruin Migliano's weekend. We'll leave the body and crime scene to him. Let's go wait in the car."

"Should I go stay with Mrs. Sorley?"

"Hell, let her stew. We'll be right out front if she wants to talk to us."

Givens shook her head. *The grout's going to be stained forever.*

# CHAPTER THIRTY-EIGHT

WHEN MIGLIANO AND Prothro arrived to process the new crime scene, they parked in the Winslow driveway. Metzinger and Givens led them around to the back door. Metzinger nudged the door open. He had left it slightly ajar to minimize handling of the doorknob.

"Key's still in the door where I left it. Body's in the middle of the floor. You can't miss it. The woman next door had a key. Says she came over about eight this morning and found the body. Says she checked his neck for a pulse and didn't find one but was afraid to get involved, so she locked the door and went home. At least, that's her story. We stopped by to ask her some questions, and she confessed to finding the body. She's at her house waiting so you can get her fingerprints."

Migliano nodded and asked, "Why do you say, 'that's her story'?"

"There's a rumor that she and the new vic were having an affair. Hell, that's what we were over there to talk to her about. We've got suspects crawling out of the woodwork and she just jumped to the head of the line."

"Okay, I'll get her prints."

"At a minimum, you should find them on the doorknob. Hope I didn't screw them up. I wore gloves and turned the knob with a thumb and a finger. Givens and I probably stepped inside three or four feet with no booties on our feet."

"You didn't touch the body?"

"No need to."

"Okay, you going to be around?"

"Questioning the neighbors. Might do a McDonald's run."

"Hey, if you do, get me and Prothro burgers and fries. A couple of Cokes would be nice, too."

"Will do. Life goes on."

"For some of us."

***

While Givens ran to McDonald's, Metzinger sat on the patio behind the Winslow's house.

*Damn weekend,* he thought. *I should have stayed home. Bet Ramirez is home taking it easy. Perks of being the lieutenant. Arley and Gert are probably enjoying their weekend too.*

He flipped open his notebook, spent ten minutes writing up notes on the morning, delaying the inevitable. Then, it was time to make the hard call and notify the victim's family. He found the telephone numbers and dialed.

A voice answered, "Morning. Ginger Winslow."

"Mrs. Winslow, this is Detective Metzinger."

"Oh, hi detective. Have you found the killer?"

"No. That's not what I'm calling regarding. By any chance, is your husband there?"

"No, I'm sorry. He's run out to the hardware store. Can I help you?"

"I have some bad news."

"Oh?"

"Yes, I'm afraid Oliver Winslow's dead."

"Dead!? Oliver!? I just saw him yesterday. Looked as healthy as can be."

"It wasn't natural, Mrs. Winslow. He was murdered."

"Migod, Oliver too?"

"In the kitchen of his home."

"Someone shot him?"

"Don't know. Forensics is checking him now."

"You think the same person did it?"

"No idea yet. The investigation has just begun. I hate to ask you this, but will you break the news to Joss?"

"Oh, God... I guess I have to. Anything else I need to do?"

"Yes, give your husband a heads up that we'll probably need to have someone formally identify the body. I'd hate to put that on the girls."

"No, I agree. Thank you for calling, detective."

Metzinger ended the call, stared at the phone, sighed, and dialed again.

He wondered if Freddie would be malevolent when answering and was given a reprieve when Freddie's phone went to voice mail. It was Sage Berenson's recorded voice that came on, "Leave your wisdom, time and date for posterity, at the beep."

Metzinger winced at the message and the idea of Sage's voice on Freddie's voicemail. Maybe they were more attached than she'd said. At the beep he said, "This is Detective Metzinger. I have important information for you. Please phone me as soon as possible."

Although he had previously given his contact information to Freddie, he gave his cell number again, and ended the call.

# CHAPTER THIRTY-NINE

DETECTIVE GIVENS RETURNED from the burger run and sat with Metzinger eating lunch at the patio table. Migliano and Prothro came out to get their hamburgers and joined them. Stripping off their white plastic protective gear. Migliano observed, "PPE clothing's a damn nuisance."

"Do we know how he was killed?" Metzinger asked.

"Knife wound in the gut. My guess it was a long knife stuck in at an upward angle. Only one thrust, but it hit something important."

"Any idea how long he's been dead?"

Migliano frowned.

"Off-the-cuff, I'd say he was killed late yesterday afternoon."

"Gosh!" Givens exclaimed. "We just let him back in the house! He should have stayed in the hotel."

Metzinger mused, "I would guess he didn't have any idea he was going to be murdered if he came home."

Prothro interjected, "Poor guy. Coming home like that probably means he was innocent. A sheep walking to his slaughter."

Givens shook her head.

"Maybe he was innocent, but it doesn't really give me any better idea of what's going on with this damned case."

Migliano asked, "You think it's the same perp?"

"Don't know. Method of killing's different," Metzinger reflected.

He looked at Givens.

"If you've finished your lunch, let's start on the next street with the Hales. They have the best view of the Winslow's back door and she shows a lot of interest. Maybe they've got a clue."

***

A man answered the door. Trim build; very blonde; light sunburn... looked like he should avoid the sun.

"Yes, you the detectives?"

"Yes."

"You look like it."

"Oh, how's that?" Metzinger responded, quizzically.

"Earnest face, lopsided suit, too old to be selling religion." He stuck out his hand. "Andy Hale. Audrey wants to talk to you."

Metzinger shook the hand.

"Detective Metzinger. And this is Detective Givens. Your wife wants to talk to us?"

"Yeah, come on back to the kitchen."

Metzinger worried and couldn't help asking, "Suit's lopsided? It's tailored to not show anything."

"No. I can tell there's a gun. Maybe it's because I know you're detectives."

"Guess it's hard to be subtle."

They found Audrey Hale standing right inside the kitchen door as if she were expecting them.

"Heard Andy talking to you. There's been some comings and goings at the Winslow's."

"Oh, like what?"

"About four o'clock yesterday, a guy in a hoodie and jeans came around the house from the front and knocked on the Winslow's back door. Mr. Winslow answered. I didn't know he was home, but anyway, Mr. Winslow let the man in and closed the door. Fifteen or twenty minutes later, the hooded man came back out, carrying a folded newspaper, and cut across the neighbor's back yard."

Givens tensed up, excited for the lead but nervous about the description.

Oh Lord, please don't let this be an innocent black boy accused of murder because he was seen in a posh neighborhood wearing a hoodie. Mama will never shut up about it.

"What did he look like?" Metzinger asked.

"Never saw his face. He kept the hood up. With the coat it was hard to tell, but he seemed slender... moved like he was young. When he came back out of the house, he held his coat crunched up in front with the hand that didn't hold the paper."

"Good information, Mrs. Hale. Anything else you can tell us about him?"

"No, I think that's all. Is the man important?"

"Yes. He probably murdered Mr. Winslow."

Audrey's mouth fell open.

"Mr. Winslow, too? That's awful! And I saw the murderer?"

"We think so. What else has happened?"

"Well, this morning the woman from next door, to the left back there, was over at the Winslow's back door, unlocked it and let herself in, like she does so often. A minute later, she came back out, looking distraught, closed the door and hurried back home. Now, I know why. She must have found the man's body."

"This was about eight o'clock this morning?"

"Yes, that's right. Did she find the body?"

"She did."

"But you don't think she was the killer, do you? You think it was the man I saw?"

"The timing's right for the man."

"This is all horrible. Makes me afraid to be in the neighborhood. Who's he going to kill next?"

"One more question, Mrs. Hale. When the man arrived, was he carrying anything? Anything that might have been a weapon?"

"Do you mean something like a pistol?"

"No. Something like a long-bladed knife. Something that might be hard to hide."

"No. Gosh, the thought gives me chills. No, I didn't see anything like that."

***

After leaving the Hale's, the detectives sat in their car sorting their notes.

Metzinger had his summarizing tone.

"We have two murders. One done in the dark, tape over the doorbell camera and no one saw anything, apart from a parked vehicle. Vic #1 got a single shot; no muffling or silencing. Bang and gone. Seems premeditated. For the second killing, a man arrives in broad daylight, comes through the front yard to the back door of the same house. Vic #2 lets him in and he stays about fifteen or twenty minutes. Then, he leaves in a hurry, cutting across the neighbor's back yard. It hardly seems premeditated, like it took some time to reach fruition. The killer was circumspect only in the sense that he wore a hood."

"Yes, but maybe he was just cold. It was chilly last night."

"True, but maybe he had a car. Maybe he parked it in front of the house. Mrs. Hale said she thought he came from the front of the house. Let's check in with Mrs. Braswell next. See if neighborhood watch was watching."

# CHAPTER FORTY

Harriet Braswell greeted them with an impatient tone. "Have you found the killer yet? Was it that bum digging in the trash? It's been a week."

Metzinger was immediately defensive.

"Five days. Not a week. And it was not the man checking the trash. There are lots of suspects, but he's not one. Right now, we're interested in what you might have seen yesterday."

"Yesterday? Something happened yesterday?"

Metzinger was reluctant to talk more about Oliver Winslow's death, although eventually the murder would be in the news. Fortunately, the word wasn't out yet. There were no reporters parked on the street. As a lead-in, he stated the obvious.

"Apparently, Oliver Winslow arrived home after we released the house as a crime scene."

"Yes, that's right. Came home yesterday. Tore the crime scene tape off the front door and went in with his suitcase. Now, some guy has put the tape back up. I don't think Mr. Winslow will like that."

Metzinger and Givens were taken aback and turned to look at the Winslow house. Sure enough, Migliano or Prothro had put up more crime scene tape. Word was going to get out to the press soon. Lt. Ramirez was going to feel even more pressure.

"Yes, Mrs. Braswell, I see what you mean. Did you notice anyone else at the Winslow house yesterday?"

Harriett Braswell's eyes narrowed.

"Something's going on, detective. What is it?"

Metzinger sighed.

"Mr. Winslow was murdered in his kitchen yesterday."

"Oh dear! You want to know about the guy in the hoodie?"

"Yes, ma'am."

"Why didn't you say so? Why the pussyfooting around? If you want to know something, come out and ask it."

"Yes, ma'am. What about the 'man in the hoodie'?"

"Came down the sidewalk from the left out there by the street. Had his hands in his pockets, hunched over like he was cold. I think it was cold. Hard to tell when you don't go out. He crossed the street and walked up the Winslow's driveway but he didn't go to the front door. Went around back like he was familiar with the place. I didn't see him come back to the front again. I was watching."

Givens asked, seemingly with little hope, "Did you see his face?"

"No."

She asked, "How old would you say he was?"

"Hard to tell with him all hunched over like that. Seemed to be moving a little reluctantly, like he was a little uncertain about what he was doing."

Metzinger pursued the comment.

"Huh? He was hesitant?"

"Yes, he stood at the curb for a few seconds before crossing the road. But then he moved out like he'd made a choice."

"Where do you think he came from? Was there a car down the street?"

"I don't know about a car. I just saw him coming from the left, walking down the sidewalk."

"Where did the man go after he came out of the Winslow's house?"

Mrs. Braswell scrunched her face in thought.

"As I said before, I never saw him come back from the rear of the house."

For confirmation, Metzinger asked, "About what time was this, Mrs. Braswell?"

"Around four in the afternoon."

Metzinger nodded.

"All you've said confirms what we've been told."

"Told? Told by whom?"

"Other neighbors."

"Yeah. He seemed conspicuous. Is he the killer?"

"We think so."

"You think he was wearing the hoodie intentionally?"

"We don't know."

"Because it was cold, or he was disguised?"

"Again, we don't know."

"Guy might have lucked out because of the weather. If I had seen him, I'd be able to describe him. Could have been your key witness."

"True. I wish you had seen him. I'm sure your neighbors appreciate you watching the neighborhood. We certainly appreciate your help."

After they left the Braswell's house, Metzinger blew out a lung-full of air.

"I'd hate to have her working me over in an interrogation room."

"At least she gave us information."

"True. Confirmed the killer arrived around four and was wearing a hoodie."

"And says he was hesitant. I wonder if he was uncertain about committing murder or reluctant about something else."

"Well, Braswell didn't see the man come back out, and Hale saw him going across the Sutton's back yard."

"Okay, so let's go talk to the Suttons."

As Metzinger and Givens started to cross the street in the direction of the Suttons, the mortuary staff came around from the back of the Winslow's house carrying Oliver Winslow's body to their van. Migliano and Prothro followed. Metzinger and Givens hurried to meet them.

Metzinger asked, "What did you learn, Manny?"

"Got one set of prints off the doorknob. Smeared, probably by you, but I suspect they're still good. Only one set though. Doorknob must have been wiped recently. Two bar stools were pulled out like the vic and perp were visiting... knocked over like there was a shoving match. The victim was lying beside one of them. A butcher block knife set was on the counter, with one knife missing... a large one. Might be the murder weapon. Medical examiner will be able to tell what kind of knife made the wound.

Also, there was a coffee mug on the counter and a matching mug in the trash, wiped clean. The counter was also wiped. We don't have much in the way of prints. I'll write it all up."

Metzinger sighed.

"All these guys watch TV and wipe everything down now, but thanks for the effort. I assume you didn't find the knife. Anything on the front doorbell camera?"

"No. No knife. He might have set it on the counter for a while. Even after being wiped, the counter showed residue of a bloody pattern. It's been photographed and measured. Unfortunately, the doorbell camera and the computer were removed as evidence after the O'Hanlon murder, so we're screwed there."

Metzinger groaned.

"Did you get Mrs. Sorley's fingerprints?"

"The lady next door?"

"Yes, I expect her prints to match the ones on the doorknob."

# CHAPTER FORTY-ONE

AFTER THEY LEFT Migliano and Prothro, Metzinger and Givens headed back to the Suttons. Mr. Sutton answered the door. Mrs. Sutton stood behind him, just like before.

"Welcome back, detectives. We see there's another commotion next door. The same vans have come and gone. I'm afraid to ask what's going on."

Metzinger sighed. *No way to keep things under wraps in this neighborhood.*

"Oliver Winslow was murdered."

Emma Sutton peered around her husband.

"The husband, too!?"

Mr. Sutton looked alarmed.

"Are we in danger? Should we go to live with relatives for a while?"

Metzinger was careful.

"There's no way I can answer that with certainty, but I suspect this is all about the Winslow family, something to do with the book business."

Mr. Sutton looked back at his wife.

"What do you think, Emma?"

"I think we get the handgun out of the bedside table drawer and keep it within reach."

Givens warned, "It's better not to shoot anyone. Call 9-1-1 if you have any concerns."

Mr. Sutton nodded.

"Emma's feisty. We'll be cautious. Thank you for coming to warn us."

As Mr. Sutton started to close the door, Metzinger put up his hand to hold it open.

"Actually, we'd like to ask you some questions."

Mr. Sutton looked perplexed.

"Oh, sure. We didn't hear any shots."

"No. Mr. Winslow wasn't shot. He was stabbed. It may have been about four o'clock yesterday afternoon. The murder may have been committed by a man wearing a hoodie. He may have crossed your back yard."

Mr. Sutton looked appalled.

"Yes, he did. I was in the shed putting away my garden tools. I'd been cleaning out the garden for the winter and as I came out of the shed this guy was crossing the yard, walking fast. I shouted at him, asked what he was doing in my yard, and he started running. Went through a few other yards and cut between some houses out toward the street."

"Could you describe him?"

"No. Sorry. He had the gray hood up. Didn't even turn toward me when I shouted. He just started running."

"What time was this?"

"I don't know. Sometime between four and four-thirty."

"Okay, thank you. That fits what we know so far. The timing's right. The clothing is right, although I don't think anyone else said the hoodie was gray."

After visiting the Suttons, Metzinger and Givens canvassed the neighbors around the Winslow house, asking if they had seen the hooded man or any strange cars. Givens was thinking, so much for taking the Saturday afternoon off.

They headed back to police headquarters to drop off their unmarked car. Then, with all the day's new information, they headed to the bullpen to write up the day's notes before going home.

# CHAPTER FORTY-TWO

WHEN THEY ARRIVED at their desks, Metzinger's phone was ringing. Givens got there first and picked it up.

"Detective Givens. How may I—"

She was interrupted and listened for a moment.

"Hey, go slow—She's gone?—Since when?"

Metzinger listened, instincts aroused.

"Wait a minute." Givens put her hand over the phone and looked at Metzinger.

"It's Ginger Winslow. Joss has done a runner."

Givens returned her attention to the phone conversation, repeating things back so Metzinger would know what was going on.

"Yes. You and your husband went shopping and when you got back, she was gone?"

Metzinger picked up an extension and joined the call.

"Metzinger here on the other phone. You sure she didn't just go out for a while?"

"No, she took her suitcase and clothes. She's gone—what's that Ed? The what's gone?—My God, she's taken our gun!"

Metzinger drew in his breath.

"What kind of gun?"

A moment passed.

"He says a Glock 19. That mean anything to you?"

"Yes, Mrs. Winslow. It does. Do you have any idea where she might have gone?"

"No, I'm just getting to know her. I don't have any idea where she would go."

"Any idea why she might run?"

"No... I shouldn't have left her. I told her about her father, and we had lunch... It was several hours ago... she didn't seem too upset, just quiet... I shouldn't have left her..."

"We'll find her, but taking a weapon is worrisome. How did she know it was in your house?"

"I've no idea."

"Okay. We'll check with her sister. If there's no answer there, we'll put out a bulletin. I'll call when we know something. Meanwhile, keep someone at home in case she comes back."

As soon as they hung up. Metzinger flipped open his notebook and began dialing.

"Freddie, uh, Miss Winslow, this is Detective Metzinger. Did you get my previous call? —No, I didn't leave a message. It's bad news. You sitting down?—I'm afraid your father is dead—You still there?—No, he was murdered, stabbed in his kitchen—No, the body has been taken to the Medical Examiner's—I'll let you know what we find out—Of course. Meanwhile, I need your help with something else. Your sister has been staying with your aunt—Yeah, Ginger—She's run away—Yes, the whole thing is a mess—I know she's not your problem—Do you have any idea where she might have gone?—No idea? Okay, if you hear from her, you have my cell phone number—Yeah, it's written on the back of the card I gave you—Call me if you hear anything from her."

He turned to Givens.

"Will you put out a bulletin? I think I better get hold of Lt. Ramirez. After that we can go home. You can get a nap but stay ready in case something comes up."

"Good thing I don't have a date tonight."

# CHAPTER FORTY-THREE

M ETZINGER PULLED INTO his driveway next to his wife's car. Another Saturday missed, Drury thought, trying to turn the detective off.

At least I'm on time for dinner.

As he entered the house, he could hear the television going in the basement. He walked into the kitchen where his wife stood over the sink. He walked up behind her, put his hands on her arms and kissed her cheek.

"Hi, beautiful, how was your day?"

She turned.

"Boy, are you in trouble."

Metzinger was taken aback.

"What, what are you talking about?"

"I told you to stay out of this business with Laura and her boyfriend."

"Yeah. I let you talk to her."

"Lot of good that did when you went and grilled the boy."

"I had to do something."

"Well, he called and broke up with Laura this morning. She's crushed."

"Just as well. He's a worthless kid and his mother's even worse."

"His mother? You saw his mother!?"

"No, I was talking to him in front of his house, just having a conversation about Laura's grades and so forth, when the woman came out of the house and gave me a piece of her mind. You wouldn't believe the language she used."

"Did you deserve it?"

"No way. I was low keying the whole thing. I would hate to meet that woman in an alley."

"Well, Jack says you threatened him... played policeman."

"Oh, BS, I was just playing the concerned father. Never said anything about being a policeman. He knows I'm a cop because Laura told him."

"Well, Laura screamed about you ruining her life and stormed up to her room. She has been there ever since, seven or eight hours."

"She's not in the basement watching television?"

"No, that's Ben. He's trying to stay out of the way, clear of the fireworks. I tried to get Laura to come out of her room, but she just cried that her life was over."

"Should I go talk to her?"

"Have you got your body armor on?"

"Do you really think it's that bad?"

"Do you mean, will she throw something at you? I wouldn't be surprised. She's mad. Says you've humiliated her in front of the whole high school. Says she wants to stay home Monday. That now she can't show her face. Something about social herpes."

"Geez, all I did was talk to him. I asked for his help getting her back to normal. You can't imagine what that woman said about her son and Laura. This whole thing is better terminated."

"Yeah, well, try to convince your daughter of that."

He hung his suit coat on the back of a kitchen chair, pulled off his tie and headed for the stairs. He climbed to the second floor with trepidation and stood at Laura's bedroom door for a minute, pulling himself together before he knocked.

An angry "GO AWAY!" answered.

"I can't do that."

"You ruined my life!"

"I was concerned about your grades and about the kind of boy you were dating," Drury pleaded.

"You threatened him!"

"I did not."

"He said you did."

"No, I didn't. Just tried to talk to him, but his mother butted in."

"His mother?"

"She came out of the house and told me off. Have you met her?"

"His mother? No."

"Count your blessings. When she led Jack back to the house, she asked him if you were worth having sex with, although that's not the language she used. Looks like he's got a rough family."

"You think he's not good enough for me?"

Metzinger hesitated.

"I think there are better people out there for you."

The door opened. Laura's face was strained with anguish, and Drury's heart felt as broken as hers.

"But he's all I have. The Halloween dance is coming up. I'm going to be the dumped girl who has no date."

"And I'm sorry about that. You're a beautiful young woman, even your brother said so. There's no way you're going to be without a date for very long. Believe me, I'm a man and I know."

"Dad, you're an old man. It's not the same."

"Old, huh? Thanks a lot."

"Ben's going to tease me."

"If he teases, it's because he loves you. Siblings do that, but I don't think he's going to tease you right now."

"Do I have to go to school Monday?"

"We can talk about that, but I think you should. I think you should show them you're above the whole thing."

He started to return to the stairs and turned back to the still open door.

"Always know I love you, Laura. I may be old and stupid and an awkward father, but I do my best."

Laura nodded and wiped her cheek.

"How was your day?"

Drury smiled ruefully.

"Not very good... but life goes up and down. With my family, it's mostly good."

# CHAPTER FORTY-FOUR

Givens was home just before five that afternoon. Her mother was in the living room, sitting in a club chair, watching television. Givens settled into the other club chair.

"Whatcha watching?"

"Hallmark channel."

"All the white folks having problems and ending up happy."

"Sometimes they're black."

"Token shows."

"At least they're happy, and the black guys aren't bad."

"That's why I watch Netflix... European shows. More diversity. There's usually darker faces on the police force with sexy British accents."

"So, why would you want to watch cop shows?"

"Darned if I know."

"How come you're home early?"

"It's Saturday."

"Lot of good that did you."

"Seems like murderers work 24/7."

"You got another murder?"

"Second this week. Same family."

"If they keep killing each other, it will narrow down the suspect pool. They might solve things for you."

"I hope not. I'm getting tired of dead people."

Mama Givens studied her daughter.

"You look tired. You don't usually grouse about it."

"Not grousing. Dead people and blood get to you."

"I can understand that. You don't usually freak about it though. Maybe you should do something else... robberies, dope sellers, something else for a while."

Mama stopped talking and stared at the television. A moment later, she turned back to her daughter.

"They're kissing. The show's over. I'll go start dinner since you're early."

"There's no hurry, Mama. I'm happy to sit."

"No dates tonight? I'm not going to ask about last night. Not my business. Just hope you know what you're doing."

Givens sighed.

"Best you can hope for... best I can hope for. Went dancing. Had fun. No dates tonight."

Mama rolled her eyes.

"Out late dancing."

"Yeah, and now I'm dragging."

Givens' mother headed for the kitchen. As she went out the living room door she said, "If you ever want to talk, you know where to find me."

Givens followed her.

"I know, Mama."

She started getting out the tableware and napkins to set the table even though dinner wasn't ready.

Her mother watched.

"I haven't started dinner yet. There's no hurry."

Leslie stopped and looked at her mother.

"I love you, Mama."

"I love you, too."

Leslie smiled, contemplatively.

"I don't mean to worry you, Mama. I've just got to be me."

"I know."

"I've got a date with Bobby Riley tomorrow night. Dinner and a movie."

Her mother was taking out a pan and almost absentmindedly replied, "Good, he's a nice boy."

"I thought that would please you."

Her mother seemed to tune back in.

"Yes, it does. Like I said, he's a nice boy."

"Yes, he is," Leslie agreed, smiling softly. *But last night was a hell of a nice night.*

# CHAPTER FORTY-FIVE

Metzinger sat with his family at the dining room table. They seldom sat there, but it was Sunday and they were together, so, even though they were only eating Italian subs, they decided to eat in the dining room.

Ben was pulling the onions off his sandwich.

Sarah banged her hand against her forehead.

"Stop. Ben, I gave you Dad's sandwich."

Metzinger looked at his sub and winced. He'd already taken a bite, so he used his knife and cut off the end before exchanging subs with his son.

"I always liked the taste of fingers on my onions," he joked.

Laura snickered, and Metzinger smiled.

"Sounds like your humor's returning."

Laura lowered her gaze.

"I thought about it overnight. I might forgive you."

"I thought you forgave me last night."

"Felt sorry for you."

Sarah laughed.

Metzinger felt himself being defensive.

"I told you I'm sorry. I only did it because I love you."

"I know, but you cost me a date for Halloween. That's hard to take."

"I'm sorry, and I won't say any more about Jack other than that the guy didn't fight for you. That says something."

With reluctance, Laura said, "Yes, it does."

Ben spoke up.

"Guy's an idiot. Good riddance."

Sarah became defensive.

"Ben, that's horrible."

Laura shook her head.

"But the twerp's right. Dad told me what Jack's mother said."

Sarah looked uncertain.

"What did she say?"

Metzinger almost choked on his sandwich and looked at Sarah. He hadn't told her that part.

"Uh, later, okay."

Sarah nodded and said, "Whatever," and looked at Laura. "We missed you at church." Again, Laura looked down.

"Thought I might see someone I knew."

Metzinger suggested, "People can't know about it that fast."

Laura laughed with a taste of bitterness and held up her cell phone.

"You have no idea. I've gotten so many text messages since yesterday. Most commiserating... a few bordering on glee."

Metzinger bit his lower lip in guilt. He didn't want to tell her he was sorry again. That only went so far.

"Still, what is, is. I hope you'll go to school tomorrow."

"Yeah, I'm thinking about it."

Ben asked, "Mom, can I have another half sandwich? Dad cut off a third of mine."

Sarah was relieved by the change of subject and rose from her chair to head for the kitchen.

"Of course, you can."

Ben passed her his plate and leaned back in his chair.

"Sis, just play it cool. Act like everything is normal. If anyone says anything about it, be sanguine. Say 'thank goodness he's out of my hair.'"

"Sanguine?" Metzinger repeated.

Ben looked pleased.

"Word for today."

Just then, the phone rang.

Laura said, "I don't want to answer it."

Ben stated, "Well, it's not for me."

Reluctantly, Metzinger got up and answered the phone.

"Hello, Drury Metzinger speaking."

It was Arley.

"Hi Drury, sorry to bother you on Sunday, but I thought you'd like to know."

"What's that, Arley?"

"I got a phone call this morning, right in the middle of mass."

"Yeah? I didn't know you were Catholic."

"There's a lot about me you don't know. We were in the third row when it rang. Interrupted the whole service when I walked out the front door. Wife's giving me hell for not turning the phone off."

"Whoo... so what was the call?"

"It was from Jimboy Drummond."

"Who?"

"The witness with the white beard. The trash can diver guy Gert checked out on the commune."

"Oh, is he a new friend?"

"Seems to think so. Anyway, he said he had something to give me... said it was interesting so after I took the family home, getting shit the whole way, I drove out to Mount Vernon Avenue near Glebe Road where Jimboy was doing his begging today. Said he was scheduled, treated it like a work shift, and couldn't bring the items to me. Anyway, he had some things in a plastic bag... a dirty old plastic bag that may have screwed up the evidence inside."

"What evidence?"

"A bloody knife wrapped in a bloody newspaper. Butcher knife with an eight-inch blade... and a bloody sweatshirt."

"The shirt have a hood?"

"Indeed, it does."

"Is it gray?"

"Yep."

"Where did Jimboy say he found these things?"

"In a dumpster behind the McDonald's at the intersection."

"Hey, Arley, I appreciate the help. If you'd called me, I would have picked the things up."

"Apparently, he trusts me and Gert, but she didn't answer her phone. Anyway, I'm at the office now. I've started making out the paperwork, already bagged the evidence."

"I appreciate that. I'll be right down. We'll courier it to Manassas Lab first thing in the morning. Maybe this is the break we need!"

# CHAPTER FORTY-SIX

G IVENS WAS AFRAID to answer the phone when Metzinger called late Sunday afternoon and she could feel her date with Bobby going down the drain as soon as he said, "new evidence".

It was a relief that he was taking care of things. He'd gone to work and finished the documentation on Jimboy's find. Everything was done. He'd even been out to the McDonald's dumpster and talked to the employees. It was a bust and not worth calling it a crime scene. No one saw the stuff get dumped or Jimboy fish it out. He'd see her Monday

She finished her makeup; more reserved than for dancing. Lighter lipstick, no eyeliner, natural shadow after all, it was just a movie. She chose a conservative blouse and a knee-length skirt and wondered if a sweater would be enough.

*Nope,* she thought, *better go with a light jacket.*

She didn't often get picked up at home, more evidence that Bobby was a nice guy. Old Man Davis would definitely be sitting on the stoop across the street, ready to whistle at her tight, short dress. He would be disappointed tonight.

Downstairs, Mama seemed pleased with the outfit.

"Nice and reserved tonight! No eye-popping for Bobby?"

"Hey," Givens replied, "I can be girlie-sweet with the best of 'em. Mama."

"Well, that's okay. Husbands should be for the long term."

"Husband, huh? Conservative is what you want. Not sure about what I want."

"So, you think you can pick and choose?"

"Yes, ma'am. I do and I am."

There was a knock at the door.

Givens opened it.

"Hey Leslie. You ready?" Bobby said.

"As soon as I grab my purse."

"Okay, I'm double-parked."

"You think I'll give you a ticket?" she asked, picking up her purse.

Mama's voice called from the living room, "I guess you're leaving now?"

"Yes, mama, I'm gone. Love you."

Bobby tried to help her down the steps... give her an arm, but Givens didn't know how to handle that. She was on the sidewalk ahead of him.

As predicted, Old Man Davis shook his head and shouted, "Show was better Friday night."

Givens glared, but kept her mouth shut.

Bobby asked, "What happened Friday night?"

He tried to help her with the car door, but she was already half in.

"So," she segued, "Where we going?" pulling the car door shut.

Bobby hurried to the driver's side.

"Movies off Eisenhower... AMC. You can decide which one when we get there. There are a couple of grills across the street. We'll pick one."

***

At dinner, they mostly talked about their jobs, although she didn't say much about the current case. She did talk about murders in general, what she and her partner did, what the forensics people did, the lowlifes they often had to deal with, and so forth... trying to be more Leslie and less Givens.

Bobby talked about the design work he did, about buying what he called "off the shelf" hardware and putting it together... electronic stuff, and about he was just getting back from an installation job... a cable was pinned wrong. That meant nothing to Leslie, but she listened with feigned fascination.

At the movie theater, Bobby bought sodas and a huge box of popcorn. They sat in the fourth row from the front. (She preferred to sit further back, but she forced herself to be accommodating.) They were early for the feature and had to endure almost twenty minutes of advertising.

Afterwards, when they came out of the theater, Bobby asked how she liked the movie. She offered a polite answer but was thinking more about how much Mama would like this date. Bobby seemed like perfectly nice husband material.

Leslie remembered to let Bobby open the car door even though she didn't see much sense in it. She was perfectly capable of opening her own door. Still, it was nice when he had bought the tickets.

Bobby got in the car and started the engine, but as he put the car in gear, Givens suddenly reached over and put her hand on his arm.

He flinched and looked at her.

"What?"

"Pull out slowly and turn to the right."

"Why, what's going on?"

"That girl with the guy is Joss."

"Joss? Who's Joss?"

"A girl we're looking for."

"The police are looking for her?"

"Yeah. Drive slowly. I want to follow them."

"Jesus, what did she do?"

"Could be nothing, but she's wanted."

"Okay, I'll try. Is she dangerous?"

"I don't think so, but she might be armed."

"Yeah, well, that sounds dangerous to me."

"We'll be careful."

"Have you got a gun?" Bobby asked.

"No, I don't usually take it on dates."

"Do you sometimes?"

"In some parts of town."

"Really?"

"No," she laughed, "not really."

Joss and the unidentified man with her got into a RAV4. The car's headlights turned on and they backed out of their parking space.

Bobby had come to a full stop, wondering which way the RAV4 would turn. Fortunately, it turned in the direction he was going.

"Guess we're in luck. How close do we follow them?"

Givens replied tensely, "We just don't want to lose them."

"Okay, I'll stay close and hopefully not have to run any red lights."

The RAV4 turned right onto Eisenhower Avenue. Bobby squealed out, cutting off a car already on the avenue. The car honked. Bobby winced.

"I'd hate to be a victim of road rage."

"Don't worry. My badge is in my purse."

"Hope he asks to see it before he shoots."

Givens looked through the back window at the car that had honked.

"Looks like he's staying back there. We kind of want to avoid drawing attention to ourselves though."

They traveled a couple of miles and turned right on Van Dorn. A car behind them honked three times and turned left.

So much for being inconspicuous, Givens thought.

At Edsall Road, the RAV4 turned left, and then left again on a road they didn't know. The RAV4 turned right into an apartment parking lot. Bobby slowed.

"Keep going," Givens barked.

They passed the parking lot entrance and as soon as the lot was out of site, Givens ordered, "Stop."

She turned to Bobby.

"I'm going to get out and go back there. You can go home."

"No, I can't." Bobby protested. "I can't just leave you here... with no idea what you're doing. I don't know if it's dangerous or what. And you've got no way to get home."

Givens opened the car door to get out.

"I'll be fine. This is police work and I don't want you involved," she urged and fluttered her hand at him. "Go!"

Then the car door slammed shut and Givens was gone.

Bobby tried to follow her with his eyes, but in a blink, she was out of sight.

He pulled the car forward and parked. Quickly, he got out of the car and headed for the parking lot. *Gotta hurry or I'll lose her.*

Bobby rounded a patch of bushes that had been screening him from the parking lot and looked down a sidewalk. He saw three figures and headed toward them.

"Leslie, you okay?" he shouted.

Givens whirled around.

"Jesus, Bobby, get away."

"What's going on?"

Joss was holding the Glock in her hand.

"Who the hell are you?" she demanded.

Bobby froze.

"Leslie's friend."

"Leslie?"

"Uh, Detective Givens."

"Oh," Joss pointed with the gun, "Guess you better join us. Were you driving?"

"Yes."

"Boy, talk about being obvious."

"I'm not police," responded Bobby, wondering why he was defending himself.

"Well, this is a hell of a mess," Joss concluded.

The man with her wasn't moving. He was looking wide-eyed at Joss.

"Joss, what are we doing? Where'd you get the gun?"

"Doesn't matter, Earl. I told you I was scared when I came here to hide. We shouldn't have gone to that movie."

The man backed away.

"He said this woman is a detective, as in, police detective? Why can't she help you?"

"She just can't. She'll give my hiding place away."

Givens held her ground.

"Joss, threatening a police officer with a gun is against the law."

Joss waved the Glock.

"What I know is that I'm standing outside holding two people at gunpoint. If anyone comes along, I'm screwed. We need to get inside."

She turned to the man, whose name seemed to be Earl, and whom Givens concluded was hiding Joss.

"Earl," she said calmly, "you lead the way to your apartment. We all have to go there and talk."

Earl led them to an apartment where he unlocked the door and opened it as if letting everyday guests in.

As Givens passed by, she looked him in the eyes.

"Now you've added kidnapping to everything else."

Earl protested, "I don't have a gun."

Givens rolled her eyes.

"Accomplice."

Joss ordered everyone to have a seat. She continued to stand, holding the Glock up at an angle, as if ready for anything.

Givens sighed. So much for a nice night. I guess I'm always on the job.

"Joss," she tuned in, "have you ever handled a gun?"

"No. I'm trying to be careful. I don't want to shoot anyone."

"Okay, do you know how to put in a magazine?"

"What?"

Givens got back up and walked slowly toward Joss.

"Because the magazine is not all the way in that gun."

She reached out hoping to take the gun from Joss, but Joss pulled it away, pointed at the floor and pulled the trigger.

It fired.

Givens grabbed the gun away from the horrified girl.

"Christ, there was a round in the chamber," she said pulling out the magazine and checking the chamber. "Safe, now."

She looked at Joss.

"Now, sit down and tell us what's going on."

Shaken, Joss sat down.

"Freddie killed my father. I have to hide before she kills me, too."

"Hold on... How do you know Freddie killed your father?"

"She wants the money. She's killing us all off so she can get it."

"How do you know that?"

"She's angry! Bitter! She wrote all those books and got nothing for it... no praise... no money... my father's going to get it all. It's logical. She killed my mother, whom she hated, and then had to kill Dad to keep the money from going to him. I'm next so she doesn't have to share the money."

Givens shook her head.

"You're assuming a lot of things. Freddie had an alibi for your mother's death."

"What alibi?"

"Sage said she was with him."

"Sage!? That's some alibi. That wimp will say whatever Freddie tells him to."

Just then there was a knock at the door.

Everyone was alarmed, uncertain.

Givens turned to Earl.

"Get rid of them. Make an excuse."

Everyone was tense as Earl moved cautiously to the door and opened it.

As soon as he did, he was thrown back against the entry wall and Sage burst into the room wielding a knife.

Surprised by the number of people in the room, he headed for Joss, who was cowering by the sofa. As he passed Givens, she grabbed him, wrestling him away from Joss.

Sage tried to pull away and swung the knife, cutting Givens in her side, but she hung on to him, working to batter the knife away, only to get cut on the arm. She was weakening and Sage pulled away from her, but Bobby had already pulled down a lacrosse stick that Earl had hanging on the wall and clobbered Sage across his head. As Bobby drew back to hit again, Sage bolted for the door. In quick response Earl tripped him and Sage fell out onto the sidewalk. He scrambled back to his feet and ran.

Earl started to go after him, but Givens shouted for him to stop.

"Earl! He still has a knife! We don't need anyone else stabbed. We know who he is and will track him down... bring him in safely."

Earl closed the door and locked it.

Givens held up her hand.

"Everyone, stop. I need to call for help."

Joss sat back down.

"What'd I tell you? Freddie must have sent him. She's trying to kill me."

After calling the police department requesting help, Givens held the hand of her bleeding arm against the side wound, trying to keep pressure on it.

She looked at Joss.

"All we know right now is that Sage attacked you. We don't know anything about Freddie's involvement. We don't know that she's trying to kill you. I need to get over to Sage and Freddie's apartment and check on things."

With concern, Bobby said, "You can't go anywhere. You're bleeding."

Earl said, "Yeah, and you're getting it on the carpet."

Givens looked down at the carpet.

"Oh, I'm sorry," she said sarcastically and moved to the tiled kitchen area.

Suddenly, Joss seemed to come out of shock.

"God, Earl, the woman's been cut."

Givens pulled up her blouse, exposing the cut.

"And it ruined my blouse."

She tore paper towels off a roll, folded them and pressed them against the cut.

"Earl, or whatever your name is, do you have some four by four bandages and tape?"

Slightly embarrassed, Earl headed down the hall toward a bathroom.

"I've got Band-Aids... maybe tape."

"Good. Get me three Band-Aids for my arm and lots more if you don't have any gauze."

Earl hurried back with a box of Band-Aids and a roll of tape.

Joss took them from him, turned to Givens and said, "I'll fold up more paper towels. That will have to do until you get to a hospital."

"Thanks. I need to brief the officers when they get here and then they need to get you to police headquarters for safety. I'll meet you as soon as I get fixed up at the hospital."

Temporarily bandaged, Givens groaned and sat on a kitchen stool to call Metzinger.

Sarah answered.

"Hi, this is Leslie Givens. I need to talk to Drury—Yeah, I know it's late—Yes, you can say that I'm working—Thank you."

Metzinger came on the phone and Givens told him the long story.

"Can you get over to Sage's apartment while I go to the hospital?—Don't forget about the steps up to the front door."

# CHAPTER FORTY-SEVEN

METZINGER HUNG UP the phone. His eyes starting to adjust to the dark.

"Sorry, honey, I have to go out."

"Anything dangerous? I don't like you going out at night. These emergencies scare me."

"No, I just have to pick up a guy. I doubt if he's even there, but we can hope."

Sarah sat up.

"You're rushing. It worries me."

"Don't worry. It's not like I've never done this."

"They might shoot. Happens more and more."

"This guy uses a knife. Don't worry."

"That doesn't help."

Metzinger went into the closet, partly closed the door, and flipped on the light.

*Whoever installed that light was one of the smartest people in the world,* he thought.

He pulled clothing off the hangers, turned the light out before he left the closet and moved carefully to the bureau for underwear and socks, before he went into the bathroom to dress. As he sat on the toilet, he used his cell phone to call headquarters to request support.

The desk sergeant complained, "Your partner already has half the force with her. When will you be here?"

"Fifteen minutes. Get me what you can."

***

Metzinger had two cars of uniforms to support him. They all parked a block away from Sage's apartment. Metzinger stationed two officers at the front door, explaining that it was the alternate way out of the apartment. The other two followed him around to the alley and the back door. The walls down to the basement door put Metzinger in the line of fire as he knocked. With weapon drawn, Metzinger squeezed his back against one stair wall. He heard noise inside, a woman's voice. The door opened and Metzinger stepped in front of it, his weapon down by his side but ready to rise.

"Jesus, Christ!" exclaimed Freddie. "What the hell?"

Metzinger eyed her for weapons and looked past her.

"Where's Sage?"

Freddie backed from the door.

"For God's sake. Put down the gun."

"Where's Sage?" Metzinger repeated.

"Haven't seen him since yesterday." She turned and headed for the bathroom. "Let me get a robe."

"Wait a minute," Metzinger directed. He turned to a policewoman who was hurrying down the steps behind him.

"Go into the bathroom with her. Make sure she doesn't have a weapon in there."

"A weapon?" Freddie retorted. "Be real. I just want to cover my pajamas."

Coming out of the bathroom, Freddie squeezed past the supervising policewoman. She pulled on her robe as she pushed the covers on the sofa aside to sit.

"What the hell is this about?"

Metzinger glared at Freddie and then turned to the policeman who had just come in.

"Tell the guys at the front door they can leave," he directed. "They can go back to whatever they were doing. Then come back here. I need both of you as witnesses."

"Witnesses to what?" groused Freddie.

"Just following the rules, Miss Winslow."

"Miss Winslow, Miss Winslow, shit. I'm Freddie. Even to the cops I'm Freddie. Now, will you answer me? What's going on? I was sleeping like a lamb before you came in here, guns blazing."

"Your boyfriend tried to kill your sister, and he stabbed my partner."

"Boyfriend? What boyfriend? You talking about Sage? Hell, he's no boyfriend. You're saying the idiot tried to kill my sister? That's crazy. Why would he do that?"

"That's the question I came to ask you."

"You think I told him to do it?"

"I don't know, Miss Winslow, but before we talk more, I need to read you your Miranda rights."

Just then the policeman returned to join his partner.

Metzinger acknowledged him and his partner. "Good, you two are my witnesses." He looked at the policewoman.

"What's your name?"

"Angie Wilcox, and my partner is Jeremy Soto."

"Wilcox and Soto," Metzinger said, committing their names to memory, "Thank you. Please observe and listen."

He turned back to Freddie and read her rights while she gaped.

She was shaking her head.

"This can't be real. You're just trying to intimidate me, right?"

"Real as can be, Miss. Winslow. Someone knifed my partner. I take that very seriously."

"Look, I don't know what that idiot Sage did, but it's got nothing to do with me. I haven't seen him since lunch yesterday. His car's gone and I'm stranded. Just been sitting, watching television and twitching. He left me with hardly any food, drinks, or money. He's not answering his phone either. I'm pissed."

"Well, when we catch him, you can come tell him that in jail."

"Yeah, I'll do that."

Metzinger sat down and opened his notebook.

"Sage tried to kill your sister. He may have killed your mother and father as well. We have the knife that may have been used to kill your father... we're working on the prints. Let's start at the beginning with your mother's murder... You gave Sage an alibi, said he was only gone a few minutes. You want to confirm that? Remember, anything you say can be used against you in court. We need the truth."

Freddie hesitated.

"He was gone over an hour... maybe an hour-and-a-half. Said he stopped at a bar to drink a couple of beers."

"What bar?"

"I don't know... Darcy's Pub, or Gilkerson's... maybe both."

"So, in reality, you don't have an alibi for the time of your mother's death."

Freddie looked down.

"Yeah, I guess not."

"Well, we can check the bars around here... investigate Sage's alibi. How do we know about you?"

Freddie looked off in the distance.

"I was here the whole time."

"Anybody confirm that?"

"You know the answer to that."

"I'd like you to answer."

"Then, no."

"'No' what?

"No one can confirm I was here."

"Do you own a firearm, Miss Winslow?"

"No."

"How about Sage? Does he own a pistol?"

"Not that I'm aware of."

"Did you ever discuss your feelings about your mother with Sage?"

"All the time."

"How about your father? Did you talk to Sage about your father?"

"No. There was nothing to discuss."

Metzinger speculated, "What did you think about your father inheriting the money made from your books?"

"It worried me."

"It didn't anger you?"

"I didn't get that far. If you think I wanted my father murdered because of that, you're crazy."

"So, did you discuss it with Sage?"

"The money, well, yeah. You have to understand my mother wasn't normal. For all I know, she planned to give all the money to charity."

"That's maybe true, but I suspect you assumed your father would get the money."

"Either way, I deserve part of the damned money."

"Did you tell Sage that?"

Freddie pondered the question before conceding, "Yeah, we talked about it."

"Does Sage love you, Miss Winslow?"

Freddie sighed.

"Yeah, the dumb shit does."

"And you use him for sleeping accommodations."

"I'm not welcome at home."

"Not welcome or not comfortable?"

"Some of both."

"And Sage knew that."

"Yeah, but like I say, he loves me."

"Do you love him?"

Freddie drew a deep breath.

"I've got a life ahead of me. No way it will be with Sage."

"Does he know you don't love him and plan to leave him some day?"

"I guess he has dreams... and no, I've never told him I plan to leave him."

"Would Sage do anything for you, Miss Winslow?"

"Maybe."

Freddie looked Metzinger in the eyes.

"Maybe, detective. I don't really know."

"But you can guess?"

"But a conjecture is just that, detective. A conjecture."

Metzinger nodded.

"I understand. Now, for the record, did you ever discuss, in any manner, with Sage Berenson, the killing, death, or murder of either of your parents or of your sister, Josceline."

Freddie looked at Metzinger sternly.

"I already answered that."

"Not in those exact terms."

"Then, let me be specific. I did not."

"Okay, now the interesting question. How did Sage know where your sister was?"

"How did he know she's at my aunt's? We all know that."

"No, Sage found her at her boyfriend's apartment."

"At Earl's?"

"Yes, as I told you previously over the phone, she left your aunt's after she heard your father was killed."

"Why?"

"She thought you might kill her over the money. She figured she was next after your father."

"Boy, a trusting sister!"

"She was scared."

"Hell, we're all scared."

"So, again, how'd Sage know where Joss was?"

"I assume he guessed. Maybe checked out my aunt's and when he didn't find Joss he went to Earl's."

"So, he knew about Earl?"

"Sure, I check out all Joss's boyfriends. Worry about the idiot. I had Sage drive me by Earl's apartment."

"What 'idiot' is that?"

"My sister."

"Did Joss know about your drive-by?"

"Don't think so. I snoop privately."

"Your snooping almost did your sister in."

Freddie sighed.

Metzinger closed his notebook.

"Thank you for your time, Miss Winslow. I hope you sleep well."

"Fat chance."

# CHAPTER FORTY-EIGHT

MONDAY MORNING, METZINGER sat down at his desk, coffee cup in hand, slumping numbly in his chair. Givens was nowhere in sight.

Big Gert was across the room doing paperwork.

"Where's Arley?" he called to her.

"Said he'd be a little late. Said he had to do your work for you yesterday and has to get things done at home to make up for it."

She studied Metzinger.

"You look awful, Drury."

"Yeah. Arley picked up some evidence. Didn't ask me for help. Told me he didn't want me messing with your new friend Jimboy. I only got three hours sleep last night."

"Jimboy? What's he got to do with anything? Did he keep you awake?"

"No, Jimboy found evidence in a dumpster, a bloody knife and sweatshirt. I would have picked it up, but Arley took care of it."

Gert mused, "Well, you never know about Arley. Guess he wants to keep his low-placed friends to himself. You think it's the knife that killed your man?"

"Good chance. It's off to the lab."

"So, again, what kept you awake?"

Metzinger told her about Givens' confrontation with Sage and his interview with Freddie, trying to keep the story straight with his fuzzy mind.

Gert looked appalled.

She responded, "Yeah, I heard about Sage's attack. Have you heard from Leslie this morning? Any follow-up to her being stabbed? How's she doing?"

"Stabbed? What are you talking about?" Metzinger panicked. "She didn't say anything about being stabbed!"

Gert raised her eyebrow.

"Your partner gets stabbed and you don't know about it?"

"Shit!" Metzinger exclaimed. "She called and told me she was with Joss and that Sage came at them with a knife, but she left out the part about being stabbed!"

Metzinger immediately picked up his phone and dialed Givens' home. Mrs. Givens answered.

"What you want? My girl needs to sleep. You need to give her time off from this job. She needs to give it up anyway. Goes on a date with a nice boy like Bobby Riley and gets stabbed by one of your suspects!"

Metzinger didn't like the way Mrs. Givens said 'your'. It made him defensive.

"Mrs. Givens, I didn't know about it until just now."

"She's always finding problems."

"She's a good cop."

"Too good for her own good."

"Part of the job, ma'am."

"Yeah, and, where were you?"

"Didn't go to the movies with her, Mrs. Givens. Wasn't invited on her date."

"Not likely you would be."

"Anyway, how is she?"

"Hurting. Can hardly bend over. Doesn't want to get out of bed. I'm worried about leaving her, but I've got to get to work."

"Remind her to call me if she needs anything. She has my cell phone number."

"Okay, but don't bring trouble. She doesn't need it right now."

"I promise. No trouble."

He hung up and looked up to see Gert sitting on Givens' desk.

"So, what the hell? Is she okay?"

Metzinger settled his shoulders and sighed.

"In bed... sleeping it off. Don't really know how bad it is."

Gert listened and said, "This Sage, guy. Did you track him down? Was he there when you talked to Freddie?"

Metzinger sighed again and pounded his desk with balled-up fists.

"Obviously not. He's still on the run. He hasn't been at his apartment for two days. We've got an APB out on him."

Just then, Lt. Ramirez came out of his office and pointed at Metzinger. "Drury."

He waved for Metzinger to come to his office.

Metzinger got up.

Gert raised her eyebrows.

At the door to the office, Metzinger started talking.

"We're making progress, lieutenant. Good chance we know who killed the husband."

Lt. Ramirez held up his hand to stop Metzinger.

"I know what's going on. That's not why I called you in."

"Well, Givens will be all right. Cuts not--"

"Not what I want to talk about."

"What, then?"

"You're in shit, Drury."

"What? What are you talking about?"

"A woman filed a complaint. Says you threatened her and her son. Says you brandished a gun at them."

Metzinger gawked.

"My weapon was back here. Secured in my locker."

"So, did you threaten them?"

"No... hell no. I just talked to them."

"Talked... how strongly, how loudly?"

"Just talked... I didn't go as police. It was personal. No uniform, no fire-arm. I didn't threaten anyone."

"How do they know you're a cop?"

Metzinger hesitated.

"The kid's been dating my daughter."

"So, he knew?"

"Yeah, but I didn't say anything."

"Sometimes, that doesn't matter."

"It should."

"Well, you should know better. What were you doing there?"

"My daughter's been dating the guy. Her grades have gone down, behaviors have become questionable. I was asking for his help getting things back to normal."

"Did you think rationality would work?"

"Yeah, until his mother came out of the house... a real piece of work... loud, offensive, rude, vulgar..."

"God damn it Drury, you're a cop. You can't respond in kind."

"I didn't."

"Not what she says. Says it was the other way around. Demands an investigation."

"So, I'm guilty by default?"

Lt. Ramirez shook his head.

"That's the way it is. Until this is cleared up, you need to stay away from the Fazios."

"I'm just a father looking after his daughter."

"And you're a cop, a public servant. There are rules, fair or unfair."

"Not fair, lieutenant. You know it's not."

"Yeah, well, for now I think it's best that you stay home."

"Stay home? Lieutenant, I'm right in the middle of an investigation!"

"No one knows that better than me, detective. Leslie says she'll be back in a couple of days. Arley and Gert have been on the case's periphery. They can take over."

"When will the investigation start?"

"Don't know, but I expect it to be soon."

"This is hell, lieutenant. I really didn't do what his woman says."

"I'm sorry, Drury. Sorry for you, me, and the department. Life's a bitch."

Metzinger nodded and turned to leave.

"Truer words—"

Lt. Ramirez cut him off.

"Your piece and your badge, Drury."

Metzinger turned back, aghast.

"For real?"

"I'm afraid so."

Metzinger placed his weapon and his badge on the lieutenant's desk, looking sadly into his eyes.

"This is crap, lieutenant."

Lt. Ramirez nodded as Metzinger left the office.

He beelined straight to his desk, avoiding eye contact with his fellow detectives. While he straightened his desk, Gert came over. Metzinger moved close to her.

"You and Arley have my case. Leslie should be back in a couple of days, that's all you need to know. I'm on my way home."

"What the hell, Drury?"

"A woman filed a complaint on me. Says I threatened her and waived my gun at her."

"Did Leslie see this?"

"This was after work. I was by myself."

"Hey, you don't even take your weapon home."

"I know. Tell that to the investigation!"

# CHAPTER FOURTY-NINE

METZINGER ARRIVED HOME a little after ten in the morning and let himself in the front door.

Sarah was in the kitchen, putting away the dishes, not expecting anyone.

"Who's there?" she demanded.

He came through the door.

"Just me, honey."

"You frightened me."

He put his hands on her shoulders.

"I'm sorry."

"Why are you home?"

He kissed her forehead, sighed, and turned toward the kitchen table.

"I'm suspended."

"Suspended!? Why?"

He sat at the table and motioned for Sarah to sit. She filled two cups with coffee and brought them to the table. Then she sat.

"All right, talk to me."

"Don't worry. It's not drinking."

"Thank God."

"You know Laura's former boyfriend... and how I went to talk to him and ended up being berated by his mother."

"Yes, and I know I had a hell of a time getting Laura to school this morning."

"Yeah, I'm sorry."

"We all are. So?"

Chagrined, he continued.

"That woman filed a formal complaint. It has to be investigated. Says I threatened her, using my position as a policeman and waved my gun at her."

"That's not what you said you did."

"It isn't what I did. I didn't even have my gun with me."

"I hope you can prove that."

"How can I? It was in my locker at headquarters."

"And they suspended you?"

"The word wasn't used, but Lt. Ramirez took my gun and my badge. Told me to go home. That's what happens when you're suspended."

"What happens next?"

"He said there'll be an investigation."

"And you sit here until then?"

"Looks that way."

"This is the second time, Drury."

"I know."

"It's been fifteen years. You think they still hold it against you?"

"I'm still just a detective. Never been promoted beyond that."

"Yeah, but you like your job."

"I do, but who knows what our lives might have been."

"Our lives have been good, Drury."

"I know, but I'll always wonder."

"I don't. It's good. You know I get scared, but it's been good."

Metzinger nodded.

"I love you, Sarah."

"I know. And I love you. What do we tell the kids?"

"Just that I'm taking some time off."

***

Laura came home from school a little after three-thirty and found her father watching television. He was clicking between channels, growing frustrated at the programming available.

"What are you doing here?"

"Taking some time off. It was a long weekend."

"Yeah, I never heard you get in last night."

"Well, it was about three in the morning. How was your day?"

Laura hunched her shoulders.

"Not terrible. Most people ignored me. Dee pushed to find out what happened. Jack says he dumped me. I told people to believe whatever they want."

"I'd like to say I'm sorry, but I don't think I am. I am sorry I hurt you. I never want to do that."

"Dad, I know you were trying to do what you thought was right."

"But you don't think it was?"

"No, it wasn't smooth, Dad. I'm sorry. It just wasn't"

***

Ben came home after JV football practice. He found Laura in her room.

"What's with Dad?"

Laura looked up from her homework.

"He says he's taking time off after a rough weekend."

"You believe him?"

"Not sure."

"Him taking time off in the middle of a case? No way. Something's screwy."

"You think so?"

"I know so. I'm going to call Ms. Leslie."

"He won't like that. She won't either. Remember when we tried to send her a birthday cake? It didn't go over well."

"Well, I don't know who else to call. Something's not right."

Ben pulled out his cell phone and used the 'for emergencies only' number, and dialed Detective Givens' house

Mrs. Givens answered.

"Mrs. Givens?"

"Um-hmm."

"This is Ben Metzinger, Drury Metzinger's son. Could I speak to Detective Givens?"

"MAY I speak to her." The woman corrected.

"Yes, may I?"

"Your father know you're calling?"

"No."

"This secret?"

Ben rolled his eyes at Laura.

"Yes, ma'am. It's important. May I please speak to her?"

Mrs. Givens hesitated.

"I'll check. She's still hurting, hopefully sleeping."

"Hurting?"

"Didn't your father tell you? She got stabbed last night."

"Gosh, no, I didn't know that. He doesn't like to talk about work."

"Huh, seems like he'd tell you when his partner got stabbed. You wonder what else he doesn't tell you?"

"Yeah, sometimes. Will you check on Detective Givens, please? Ask if she'll talk to me?"

"Yeah, okay."

Ben made a face at Laura and whispered, "She was stabbed last night."

Laura whispered back, appalled, "What!?"

Ben held up his hand to tell her to be quiet.

"Hello, Leslie, it's Ben Metzinger. I hate to call... know you don't like it."

Givens replied, "It's okay, Ben, I assume it's important."

"Don't know if it is or not. I'll let you decide. First, your mom said you were stabbed! Are you all right?"

"Yeah, a little sore. Nicked my side, but I'll be all right. What's worrying you?"

"My Dad's home. Says he's taking time off, that it was a hard weekend."

"It was that, but I don't understand him taking time off."

"Aren't you in the middle of a case?"

"Yes."

"Does it make sense, him taking time off in the middle of a case?"

"No."

Ben became quiet, trying to decide what to say next. Givens was also quiet and then said, "I wasn't at work today. I'll call Gert and see what I can find out."

"Big Gert?"

"Gert, to you. I'll call you back."

Ben hung up.

"She says she'll call back. Her mother said she was stabbed, but Leslie claims it's just a nick. Stayed home from work, though, and she doesn't know anything about Dad. She's calling Big Gert."

Laura was clearly concerned.

"We don't ever know what's happening with Dad, when he's in danger and when he's not."

"Yeah, he's a policeman. Anything's possible. Sometimes I forget."

Leslie called back as promised.

"This is a little awkward to tell you. Seems your father has been suspended."

"Suspended! Why in the world?"

"Something about him talking to your sister's boyfriend and his mother?"

"Yeah. I know about that."

"Well, the woman filed a complaint. Says your father made verbal threats and threatened to shoot them."

"He said he just talked to them," Ben told her.

"That's what he said to Gert, too, but there's going to be an investigation. Your dad's been suspended until then."

"Jesus, what does that all mean? Will he be fired?"

"Hopefully, the investigation will clear him."

After he hung up, Ben told Laura everything.

"Do you think you can get Jack to clear it up?"

Laura shook her head glumly, "Not if it means challenging his mother. He's afraid of her."

Ben thought a while.

"Okay, pick me up after football practice tomorrow and we'll go talk to Jack-o'-lantern's neighbors. Maybe someone saw something."

Laura looked at her brother with uncertainty.

"Okay, what time?"

"Five-thirty. I'll skip my shower."

"Ew."

"Ew, nothing. You can live with it. Dad's more important."

# CHAPTER FIFTY

THE APB PAID off, and the case moved forward even though Metzinger and Givens were both sidelined.

A call came in late Monday night.

Virginia State Police picked suspect Sage up on I- 95 just south of Petersburg and had him locked up in a holding cell. His old green Taurus had been easy to identify. Lt. Ramirez dispatched Detectives Masterson and Sorenson to transport him back to Alexandria since it had become their case.

Early Tuesday morning they took a prisoner transport van with a screen between the back and the front seats and shackles to secure Sage. In Petersburg, Masterson filled out the paperwork in the front office while Gert collected Sage from the holding cell.

"Jesus, they sent an amazon to get me," he said looking up at her.

Gert frowned and told him to stand still while she shackled his wrists and ankles. Sage held out his hands and shook the chains.

"What is this, some kind of medieval torture device? What do you think I'm going to do?"

None too gently, Gert grasped his shoulders and turned him toward the door.

"Just limiting your options. Move. And no more amazon shit. I've heard it before and don't respond very well."

Arley caught up with his partner as she led Sage out the door and over to the van. They both had to help him into the back seat as the shackles limited his movement.

"Sit still and the shackles won't hurt as much. They're uncomfortable to fall down in. Hard to get back up. The ride's a couple of hours. We don't plan to stop."

Arley handed Gert the keys and they were soon on I-95.

Arley put on his friendly detective face and looked at Sage over his shoulder.

"Smooth ride from here. Relax and enjoy." He picked up a recorder from the console between the front seats and turned it on, making sure Sage noticed. "Just in case you've got something important to say. Let me read you your rights, just in case."

Sage kept his face blank and stared straight ahead, avoiding eye-contact.

After Arley finished reciting his rights, Sage nodded with satisfaction and said, "Okay, let's get it on record that this big lady detective roughed me up... brutalized me."

Arley and Gert ignored him.

"Well Berenson. The lady detective here is named Detective Sorenson. She's Scandinavian. You sound like you might be Scandinavian too. What are the chances you're related? Ever done one of those DNA ancestry tests? Hey, Detective Sorenson, you think you're related?"

"Hope the hell not," Gert responded.

Arley continued.

"You know my name's Masterson. Ends with a son too. Maybe I'm Scandinavian too, Swedish or something? The master's son. What do you think my ancestral father was master of?"

Sage made a face.

"Probably the outhouse."

Arley made a sour face.

"Hey... be nice. We've a couple of hours together. Actually, I think Masterson might be Irish. I think Bat Masterson on the old TV program was Irish. You know... the gunslinger?"

Finally, Sage looked at Masterson.

"What the hell are you talking about? Jabbering to yourself."

"What do you want me to talk about... your trying to kill Leslie? That kind of pissed me off. Didn't make Detective Sorenson here very happy either."

"Who's Leslie?"

"The detective you stabbed in that apartment off Duke Street."

"The black one?"

"Yeah, the black one. We work together."

"Is that who's blood I saw on the knife when I was running?"

"Yeah. What did you do with the knife, Sage?"

"Didn't mean to stab her. Guess she got herself stabbed when she tried to grab me. Don't know about the knife. Lost it somewhere when I ran."

"Okay, we'll have to look for it. You can show us where you ran."

"Don't think so. Think I've forgotten. It was kind of wild."

"Yeah, well, maybe you went back to your car. Maybe you know where it was parked."

"Vaguely. Only vaguely. Not sure I could find the place again."

"Well, sometimes memories come back. Time will tell. You're just lucky Leslie was there. Kept you from killing anyone."

"What do you mean, 'kept me from killing anyone'? I wasn't trying to kill anyone."

"Is that right? You pushed in the door and ran across the room toward Joss brandishing a knife... they said you looked intent on stabbing Joss and might have if you hadn't been tackled and hit with a lacrosse stick."

Sage tried to reach up to touch his head where there were a couple of Band-Aids but had to bend his head forward when the shackles limited his movement.

"Yeah, son-of-a-bitch hit me, bunch of times, and I didn't do anything to him."

"Are you saying that you were running toward people with an open knife, not intending to do anything?"

Sage decided he'd talked too much but couldn't quite stop.

"Hell, it wasn't even the right apartment. I was returning a knife and ended up in the wrong apartment. Wanted to tell the guy I was returning it to that the blade was dull. Had the blade out to show him. Accidentally went to the wrong apartment and got attacked."

Arley turned back to the front of the van and sighed deeply. Everyone has a story.

"You accidently went into the apartment where your girlfriend's sister happened to be and just happened to be waving a knife around? Is that your story, Sage? Are you sticking to it?"

"What do you mean, story? That's what happened. Maybe I'll sue them! Hell, he cut my head. I'm still having headaches. They tackled me and beat me with a lacrosse stick. Hope you've got that on your recording. And now I'm illegally imprisoned. I'll sue the whole bunch of you."

Arley turned off the recorder.

"You're full of shit, Sage."

"Abused, detective. That's the term. That's what I am. Abused."

***

South of Fredericksburg, Sage leaned forward.

"Detective?"

"Yes."

"I need to shit."

"It's just another hour."

"Can't last that long."

"Damn it... okay. I think there's a truck stop at the next exit. Let's pull off. It's got a restaurant. Should have a john."

Gert pulled the van up to the front door of the truck stop diner. Masterson helped Sage out of the van. Sage shuffled through the front door and across the floor while four truck drivers and a waitress stared at him. Arley was relieved that there were only a few patrons in the restaurant.

He led Sage into the men's room and to a stall. Sage held up his hands.

"How about unlocking me?"

Arley looked at the proffered hands.

"What hand do you wipe with?"

"What kind of question is that?"

"I'll unlock one hand. Which will it be?"

"Damn, man. Talk about cruel and unusual punishment."

"Which hand, Sage?"

"Left."

"Left it is."

With one hand free, Sage shuffled into a stall and latched the door.

Arley leaned against the sinks and considered the occasional unpleasant parts of his job.

Eventually, Sage opened the stall door, came out, and went to the sinks to wash his hands.

When he was done, he said, "Let's go."

Arley positioned himself between Sage and the men's room door.

"Need to reconnect the cuffs."

"Shit, man," Sage said as he held up his hands.

Gert saw Sage and Arley coming out of the diner's front door behind a couple of truck drivers and started the van. Suddenly, Sage pulled loose and began shuffling away.

Arley watched, looking tired.

"What the hell are you doing, Sage?" he called out.

"I'm leaving."

Arley shook his head.

"Running away at a tenth of a mile-per-hour? Be real."

Sage continued to shuffle away. He looked at one of the truck drivers, who seemed amused.

"Hey, man, you got a cell phone you can use to cover my jail-break? Get some pictures of police brutality when they attack me."

The truck driver took out his phone and began recording the scene while the other driver laughed.

Gert got out of the van and joined Arley in slowly walking behind Sage.

"What do you want to do?"

"Wait for him to fall down."

"If he doesn't, we can spend the rest of the day following him down US 1, maybe he'll get part way to Fredericksburg. Should I get the van to follow behind?"

"Hell, Gert, would you really have the patience for that?"

"No, but I don't want to be filmed picking the guy up."

"Me neither."

Arley looked at the truck drivers.

"Okay, you guys have pictures of us looking dumb and following this guy. Now, how about helping us out?"

The truck driver with the cell phone pocketed his camera and laughed. He hitched his shoulder toward the other driver.

"Okay, if Dave and I pick up his legs, will you get him by the shoulders?"

"A pleasure," Arley chuckled.

Arley and Gert took Sage by the shoulders while the truck drivers pulled his feet from under him.

One of the drivers asked, "What'd he do?"

Masterson raised his eyebrows in place of a shrug.

"Probably killed a guy, tried to kill a girl, and stabbed a cop."

The truck driver's eyes opened wide.

"This little shit did that?"

All the time Sage was screaming, "Let me go. I'll sue your asses."

He looked around hoping to find more witnesses, but there were none. Vehicles driving down the highway slowed to gawk, but no one stopped.

At the van, Gert used one hand to slide the side door open. Then, they unceremoniously but forcibly deposited Sage in the back seat, as he complained, "Damn, you hurt my arm. Damn, Masterson, get these guy's names so that I can sue them too."

Arley slid the door closed.

"What guys?"

"Son-of-a-bitch, Masterson, I'm filing a complaint."

"You do that."

He smiled at the truck drivers.

"Appreciate the help, guys. Hope you have a tale to tell. I do."

He turned to Gert, "Let's roll. If he wants to go to the bathroom again, he can wait."

***

As the van traveled north through Dale City, Arley's cell phone rang. He answered, "Masterson—Yeah, headed north, just past Quantico—No shit, his prints huh?—Yep, see you in half-an-hour or so."

As he ended the call, he turned toward Gert.

"Guess whose prints were on the knife that killed the Winslow guy?"

Gert glanced at Masterson.

"Those of the gentleman in the back seat?"

"You 'betcha."

Masterson turned to Sage.

"You hear that, Sage. We've got you for murder. All tied up with a ribbon."

There was silence from the back seat.

After a while, Arley said, "Lot to think about, isn't there, Sage? You know, Virginia has the death penalty."

Another moment passed.

Then Sage spoke, almost under his breath.

"I didn't mean to kill him."

Arley perked up and turned on the recorder.

"You remember, Sage, I read you your Miranda rights. Now, what did you say?"

Sage twisted his face in resignation.

"I said, I didn't mean to kill him. It was an accident."

Arley raised his eyebrows skeptically.

"The knife blade went in to the hilt. Hell of an accident."

Sage became defensive.

"I was just there to talk to him. Freddie worked so hard on those books. She deserved the money. I wanted her father to share with her."

"And he didn't want to."

"He said he knew nothing about the money, which you know is not true."

Arley considered that.

"You know, I'm not thoroughly read-in about the case, but I doubt the will has been read... if one exists. I'd guess he didn't know anything about the money."

"Shit, the guy had to know he'd get it."

"Don't know, Sage. You never know with wills. Especially when people don't seem too fond of each other."

"You're saying he wasn't going to get the money?"

"Just sayin' I don't know."

"He didn't deny he would get it."

"No? So, what happened? He told you to get lost?"

"He said I had no business messing in his family's affairs. That his wife had just died and no worthless bastard had any business hassling him. I told him I resented being called a 'worthless bastard' and that I have every right to be involved because his daughter loves me. You know what he said? He said Freddie never loved me, that I was just a dork she was using. He laughed at me! I shoved him and told him that wasn't true. She loves me. Son-of-a-bitch shoved me back."

"When he shoved you, what did you do?"

"I couldn't just stand there looking stupid. I shoved him again. Then he slapped me with the back of his hand, called me a stupid prick, and turned to walk off. Stupid prick? Hell, he was the stupid prick. I grabbed the knife out of the set on the counter and shouted at him 'don't you dare walk off'. When he turned back, I stabbed him... just once and pulled the knife out. He looked surprised, and just kind of sat down. Blood was going all over the place. I wiped off the counter and the doorknob and wrapped the knife in newspaper. I didn't know what else to do. I left, tried to walk casual, but when the guy next door said something to me, I ran."

"So, you just left Oliver Winslow to die?"

"What the hell else could I do? I couldn't just stand around and wait for the police to come."

"You could, if it was an accident, but it wasn't, was it, Sage? It was something you did in a rage."

"He provoked me!"

"Maybe he did and maybe he didn't. Doesn't justify killing."

"He called me names and said Freddie didn't love me. And he pushed me. He started it."

"Yeah, okay. So, after that, you went after Freddie's sister."

"I told you before. That was an accident, too. Wrong apartment."

Arley studied Sage dubiously.

"All because Freddie loved you."

"Yeah."

"And she told you to go talk to her father so she could get money?"

"No, she didn't know! I was trying to help her out… make her love me more."

"And now she doesn't have a mother or a father."

"I don't know shit about her mother."

# CHAPTER FIFTY-ONE

Off THE CASE, Metzinger was up early and sitting in the kitchen with morning coffee. He couldn't remember when he had last made it in his own kitchen.

When the kids came down, Ben looked at his father and shook his head.

"If you're taking time off, you need to do it right and bag in."

Metzinger smiled.

"Been getting up early for over twenty years. It's automatic."

"You don't always get up early. We've known you to sleep in a little on weekends."

"Well, today's a weekday."

"How does your body know that?"

"Yeah, good question. I've no idea, but I'm awake. Want me to make you two some eggs? Save your mother the trouble?"

Laura glanced at her watch.

"Why not? I have ten minutes."

"Ten minutes? What do you usually eat?"

"Cereal. Fill the bowl, pour the milk, and eat. I'm usually halfway through when Mom comes down."

Drury rushed around the kitchen getting eggs from the refrigerator, Pam from a cabinet, and a pan from under the stove. He sprayed the pan and began cracking eggs into it, dripping egg on the floor as he carried the shells to the trash.

"You guys get the butter from the fridge, put the bread in the toaster. Where's the spatula?"

Laura said, "In the drawer next to the stove. Use the plastic one."

Ben got the bread and watched his father panic. He looked at Laura while putting the bread in the toaster.

"Do you want jelly?"

Laura shook her head.

Sarah walked in and observed the chaos. She got a mug from the cabinet and poured herself some coffee. Then she sat at the table on the side away from the commotion.

"Looks like I'm off today," she said.

Ben advised. "You're safe if you stay on that side of the table."

Metzinger found the spatula in a drawer and scrambled the eggs. He scooped them onto plates and headed for the toaster.

"Where's the butter?"

Ben jumped up and headed for the refrigerator.

"I forgot it."

While the children ate, Drury served another plate with eggs and carried it to Sarah.

"I'll put some toast in for you. It'll just take a minute."

Sarah smiled.

"That would be wonderful. Such service. I could get used to having you around."

"I guess there are some good things about it."

The children looked up from their plates with concern but said nothing.

Sarah put her hand on top of her husband's.

After the children left, he sat with his eggs half eaten. Sarah got up and refilled their two mugs with coffee. As she set them back on the table, she leaned over and kissed Drury on the cheek.

"You're a good man, Drury Metzinger. It will be all right. Keep me company and eat your eggs."

***

After breakfast, Metzinger put on old clothes and went out to the garden shed. He scraped caked-on grass from under the lawnmower and checked its oil. He looked around for more oil to add but didn't find any, so, he decided to go buy some. He decided to get a new air filter at the same time. He checked the old filter, so he'd know what kind to buy, and returned to the house to let Sarah know he was leaving.

At Lowe's he picked up the items he needed and then wandered through the power tool section. There was nothing he needed, but he enjoyed browsing, especially the specialized tools that he couldn't believe anyone would keep as personal tools, but, he reckoned, some people have to have everything.

He strolled out into the garden area to peruse the plants but found the offerings sparse.

*I guess it is October,* he thought.

Back home, he replaced the air filter, topped up the oil and looked around for something else to do. Soon they would need to rake leaves but didn't want to do it too soon and end up doing it all over again.

He went back into the house and turned on the television. He didn't want a talk show or the talking heads on the all-day news channels. He found an old movie that he hadn't seen and settled in to watch it.

At lunchtime, Sarah brought him a sandwich.

"You okay? I'm going to the gym and then shop for groceries."

"Sure. You've got to go about your day."

He looked enigmatic.

"How long will you be gone?"

"Maybe three hours. Is that all right?"

"Oh, sure. See you later."

After Sarah had gone, Drury wandered around the house. He checked the kitchen to see if dishes needed doing, but Sarah had already loaded them into the dishwasher and the machine was running. He checked the refrigerator for a dessert, but he couldn't find anything. He took out a slice of cheese, ate it, and returned to the television.

By mid-afternoon, his fidgeting had gotten worse. He wanted to know what was going on at work, what was happening with his case, but he'd been ordered to leave it alone.

*Being relieved of the responsibility sucks,* he thought.

He wondered how Givens was doing They'd agreed to keep out of each other's private lives and he rarely phoned her at home. But, he thought, this is different. She's laid up. I should check on her. She might enjoy talking to someone.

He took his cell phone off the kitchen counter where it had been charging. As he disconnected it from the charging cable, he wondered if the guy who invented kitchen islands had any idea that he was inventing the charging center for modern communications.

In the living room, he settled in his favorite chair and dialed Givens' cell number.

She answered during the second ring.

"Hey, Leslie. It's Drury. Hope you don't mind my phoning."

"No, that's fine, Drury. What's up?"

"Just wanted to check on you and your wound."

"Oh, thank you for asking. I'm doing all right. Hobbling a little, but I'm managing. A friend asked me to go bowling next weekend, but I put him off. Think it will be two or three weeks before I can bend like that. Question is, how are you doing?"

"What do you mean?"

"Heard you were home."

"You know about it, then?"

"Yeah."

"The suspension... the whole thing?"

"Don't know what 'the whole thing' means, but the suspension, yeah."

"How'd you find out?"

"Ben called me, and I called Gert."

"Ben? My Ben?"

"Yeah, he and Laura were concerned. They can tell when something is wrong. They couldn't help worrying. Don't be mad at them."

"Jesus, I won't. Makes me sick that they worry about me."

"Part of being a cop's kid. No way they can help it. You need to talk to them."

"Yeah, okay. Then you know the boyfriend's mother filed a complaint?"

"Yes."

"Are you going to tell me you told me so?"

"No."

"Okay, thank you for that. I probably deserve it, but the woman is lying."

"Completely?"

"For the most part."

"How are you going to prove it?"

"My word against hers."

"Will they believe you?"

"Probably depends on how sweet she is when they interview her."

"Balancing your sweetness?"

"Yeah, I'm good at that. Time will tell. You hear anything from work?"

"Yeah, they've been busy. Gert just called me. The State Police picked up Sage last night on 95, south of Petersburg... saved a lot of problems by getting him before he got to North Carolina. The lieutenant sent Arley and her down to pick him up this morning. Gert said they had an interesting trip back. Sage all but confessed to killing Oliver Winslow."

"Why would he do that?"

"Lt. Ramirez called Arley on the way back and said the lab found Sage's prints on the murder knife along with Winslow's blood. Arley told Sage about it and the man started protesting. Said Winslow attacked him and he was defending himself."

"What did he have to say about stabbing you?"

"Said he was returning the knife and went in the wrong apartment. Said I got stabbed because I tackled him for no reason. Says he's going to sue me, but his claim will never stand up."

"Did he kill the O'Hanlon woman, too?"

"Emphatically denies it."

# CHAPTER FIFTY-TWO

SINCE HE WAS home Metzinger decided to be an involved parent and go watch Ben's JV football practice. He parked and walked over to a grandstand. Everyone on the field seemed too big.

Of course, he realized, it must be the varsity. Only natural that they should have the good field.

"You lost, old man."

Metzinger whirled around to see Jack Fazio sitting at the near end of the grandstand.

"No," Metzinger responded, thinking you little shit.

"You look like a whirling dervish with no place to go."

"You like being smartass'd?"

"Ah, the man speaks," Fazio sneered. "You recover from my mother yet?"

Metzinger remained silent.

"Authorities got your tongue? Told you to keep your mouth shut?"

"Your mother complained."

"Sure, she did. Doesn't take well to someone messing with her little boy."

"Yeah, little saint. You a high school junior, too?"

"Too?"

"Like Laura."

"The girl my mother describes as my sex object?"

"Yeah, your mother has a vocabulary."

"She unfair to your little angel?"

"Laura's a better person than you, sitting here watching the big guys practice. How come you're not out there?"

"With those lummoxes? I wouldn't be caught dead with them, grunting and sweating."

"Yeah, I bet you tried out, and they battered you. Hurt you, and you quit."

Metzinger noted Fazio flinch, just a little, but enough. He'd hit a sore spot. He was pleased and smirked.

"Since you're so smart, tell me where the JVs practice."

Fazio laughed.

"JVs? Those runts. You got one of those? They play by the kid's playground... where else?"

"Which direction?"

Fazio pointed.

"You'll probably stumble over it. Don't hurt yourself."

Drury turned in the direction Fazio had pointed. He was steaming. He'd said too much... but not enough. He'd tried to behave. He wished he could smack the little prick.

He finally found the playground, and a motley group of kids in handed-down football uniforms. There was no grandstand, no chairs, no nothing. He wondered why there was a playground by the high school. Guessed it was public property serving the community. Probably, the equipment was budgeted and needed a place to go... this open field was convenient.

Metzinger sat in one of the swings to watch the rest of practice. Eventually, he identified Ben. It looked like he was playing tackle.

Lord, a hundred-and-thirty-pound tackle. He'll grow, but not that much.

He guessed the more aggressive kids took the good positions... or maybe the faster kids. He wondered how fast Ben was. Hell, what do I know about my kid? I'm at work during the day.

Metzinger started to swing, but then felt embarrassed. He got up, feeling conspicuous, and looked at the football players to see if they were watching. They weren't.

He moved to a bench, seemingly placed for parents to watch their children, and sat facing the practice field.

As he watched, he noted what a ragtag group the JVs were. Some were good, but most were not. It was hard to watch Ben. It seemed like he was always smothered in the pile of players at the line.

Finally, practice broke up and the coach sent the players running laps. Metzinger remembered his younger days. He'd run a lot of laps. It's what coaches had their players do.

*Tradition,* Metzinger mused. *The way it's always been done, the way it will always be done.*

As the players ran by the playground, Ben kept his arms down, but he did flip a hand at his father.

Metzinger smiled. Recognition. Hopefully, Ben's not embarrassed.

# CHAPTER FIFTY-THREE

LAURA ARRIVED AT the front of the school only to find her father waiting by the front turnaround.

She froze.

*Do I drive away? No, he's seen me. I have to stop.*

She pulled next to her father and rolled down the passenger window.

Metzinger stood by the car window and leaned down.

"Hi, baby. What are you doing here?"

"Picking up Ben. He asked me to meet him after practice."

"Well, I'm here. Came to watch practice. Sorry you wasted your time. I can give him a ride home."

Laura panicked.

"Um, he wanted me to pick him up. Wanted to talk or something... private sounding."

"Secret, huh?"

"Don't know, but he made it sound important."

Ben came out the door and stopped, looking indecisive.

Metzinger hunched his shoulders and said, "Okay."

He waved to Ben.

"Your sister says she's got you. See you at home."

As their dad walked off toward the family car, Ben approached Laura's car feeling relief. He threw his backpack into the back seat and climbed in front. He took a deep breath, then looked at his sister.

"Hey, you're on time," he teased.

She looked at him with annoyance. "Yeah, want to see what you're up to. Then she added, "No shower, huh? You could at least have combed your hair."

"I was in a hurry. Let me borrow your hairbrush."

As Laura drove off, headed for Jack Fazio's home, Ben reached for her purse. She grabbed it and moved it past her body to the space next to the door.

"What makes you think I have one?"

"I know because you just grabbed the purse away from me. Besides, I've seen you use it in the past."

"You're all sweaty."

"Yeah, so what?"

"You'll get the brush gooky."

"It's clean gook."

"No such thing."

"And it will wash out."

"You'll wash it out?"

Ben looked at her soulfully.

"Yeah, I'll wash it out."

"Okay, but don't ever go in my purse. It's private space."

Struggling, while driving, she pulled out the brush and passed it to Ben who pretended to try seeing into the purse while she had it open.

"What secrets do you have in there?"

"Nothing."

"At home, you'd better keep your purse hidden. Sleep with it at night."

"You wouldn't."

"Just worried something might crawl out."

"Not if you wash the brush."

Ben laughed, "Cooties, cooties, cooties!" Then he sat straight.

"We're on your boyfriend's street."

"Do you mean Jack's?"

"You have any other boyfriend?"

"Now I've got no boyfriends, and you know it."

"Yeah, do you miss the All-American Boy?"

"All-American Boy?"

"Yeah, like on that radio show Grandpa listened to as a kid, Jack Armstrong, the All-American Boy."

"You're listening to Grandpa? Listening to his reminiscing?"

"Yeah, reminiscing. I'll add that to my vocabulary."

Laura parked a couple of houses away from Jack's. Ben saw her slumping down in the seat and opened his door.

"Get out. You can't hide."

At the first two houses they visited, Ben asked if the people had seen an altercation on Friday afternoon between a man (they showed a framed picture of their father that Ben had taken from the mantle at home) and Jack Fazio and his mother. The people in both houses said that they worked and weren't home, although one offered that she was not surprised Jack's mother was in an altercation.

Finally, they arrived at the house across the street from the Fazio's. A woman, wearing a dark green apron decorated with huge pink flowers, answered the door. She looked to be around fifty. Short, heavy, with graying hair and florid cheeks. Ben said his spiel.

The lady shouted, "Melvin!" A man, two-thirds the woman's size, shuffled in from the back of the house. "These kids are asking about the shouting match last Friday."

The man laughed.

"Yeah, Fazio entertainment. Watched it a few times since."

Laura was incredulous.

"You watched it since it happened?"

"Yeah, the doorbell recorded it. Records all kinds of fun things."

"But you've got the discussion recorded?"

"Not the discussion... too far away for audio. It would have been fun to hear Bea Fazio's rant, but, yeah, only the action is recorded. I preserved the clip for entertainment. You want to see it?"

The man led them into a den in the back of the house.

"I'm Joe, Joe Compton. Who are you and what's your interest in all this?"

Laura and Ben hesitated a moment but saw no way out of answering.

Laura said, "We're Laura and Ben Metzinger. The man talking to Mrs. Fazio is our father."

Ben interjected, "And Mrs. Fazio says he threatened her with a gun."

"Gun? If there had been a gun, I would have called the police. Thought about doing it anyway... to protect the guy from her."

He worked the mouse on his computer. The recording started, time stamp and all. They saw their father walk up to Jack and start talking to him, and then they saw Mrs. Fazio walk into the scene and begin waving her finger at him. Laura and Ben saw their father withdraw with diffidence. Ben felt embarrassed for him but understood why his father didn't fight back.

Mr. Compton said, "She really gave it to him."

Ben said, "May I make a copy?"

Mr. Compton looked perplexed.

"How you going to do that?"

Ben pulled a flash drive from his pocket and held it up.

Mr. Compton grinned.

"Have at it."

As Ben copied the file, Laura watched him with admiration.

"Ben, you surprise the dickens out of me sometimes."

Ben smiled as he watched the computer download.

"Expert at clandestine activities thanks to Jessica Jones."

When Ben finished, he carefully put the flash drive back in its plastic case and into his pocket.

"Pure gold."

They thanked Mr. Compton as they went out the front door. Mrs. Fazio was standing at the end of the sidewalk by the road.

"You're on your own," Mr. Compton said and closed the door.

Mrs. Fazio pointed at Ben and Laura.

"You! Come here!"

Laura bit her lip.

"Jack says you're the girlfriend."

Laura glanced around, grandstanding a little.

"Was."

"Was what?"

"Was his girlfriend."

"He's inside... pointed you out."

"Afraid to come out?"

"Afraid nothing. I told him to stay inside. What the hell are you two up to?"

"Learning the lay of the land."

"Yeah, what did you learn?"

"Well, I met you. That's certainly been part of the learning process."

"What does that mean?"

"Tell me, Mrs. Fazio, did you really ask your son if he was having sex with me in front of our father?"

Mrs. Fazio shrugged indifferently.

"I asked him if you were worth fucking."

Laura glanced at her brother, turning slightly red.

Ben shrugged his shoulders.

"Already part of my vocabulary."

Mrs. Fazio looked perplexed.

Laura smirked.

Laura and Ben joined hands and walked back to their car.

Mrs. Fazio sputtered and shouted after them, "You're rude and worthless."

Ben laughed, "Rude and worthless. Sounds to me like a new t-shirt."

Laura and Ben got in their car and drove off. Laura asked, "When did you add that to your vocabulary?"

Ben smiled insouciantly.

"When did you?"

"Touché."

Ben patted his pocket.

"Yeah, Touché."

# CHAPTER FIFTY-FOUR

BEN CALLED HOME while they drove, hoping their parents' irritation would partially dissipate. They were late after the rogue mission. It was going to be rough.

Metzinger opened the front door as soon as they pulled into the driveway.

Ben looked at Laura.

"You ready?"

Laura nodded.

"Don't stop. Go straight to the computer in the den."

There was no mistaking the trouble they were in. Both their parents were clearly agitated.

"Do you know what time it is? Your mother had dinner on the table over an hour ago. She's been worried and fretting. What do we have a family meal-schedule for?"

Immediately Metzinger realized the hypocrisy and hoped no one else noticed.

Ben and Laura kept their heads down and walked past their father. Their mother was standing in the middle of the living room.

"You worried your father to death."

Ben and Laura both mumbled something about being sorry, but they didn't stop.

Metzinger followed them down the hallway as they headed for the den. "That's all you can say? That you're sorry... no explanation... nothing?" Sarah followed, chastising them all the way down the hallway.

"Where are you going and what are you doing?"

Ben plugged the flash drive into the computer, played with the keyboard and the mouse, and swung the screen around toward their parents.

"You need to see this."

At first, Metzinger protested.

"What's all this? What are you up to?"

Then he recognized the scene on the computer screen and watched in awe.

"Where'd you get this?"

Ben grinned.

"From the doorbell across the street. Nice people. Don't think they care for the Fazios."

Sarah was unclear about what was happening.

"What's all this about?"

Elated, Drury explained, "It's a recording of my encounter with Mrs. Fazio!"

Sarah was confused.

"I don't see any gun."

Metzinger grinned.

"Exactly!"

He high fived Ben and hugged Laura.

"You guys are wonders."

Laura leaned back and nodded toward Ben. "Looks like you've got a rival in the detective field."

Ben smiled.

"Can we reheat dinner?"

Sarah gave a love-punch to his shoulder, but Ben ducked out of the way.

"Hey, I'm a child. Be gentle."

# CHAPTER FIFTY-FIVE

GIVENS TRIED TO dance into Chick's, doing a pop singer's high-stepping runway strut... trying to look bulletproof. She lasted three steps and staggered against to the bar. Sharyn ran to catch her.

What the hell am I doing here? she groaned inwardly.

"Get me to a booth!" she told her friends.

Sharyn took one arm and Chantel hurried to take the other.

"Can you walk at all?"

Givens bit her lip as she settled into the booth.

"I got here, didn't I?"

Sharyn shook her head, "Barely. Why'd you come?"

Givens glanced at Sharyn and pointed at Chantel.

"Dominatrix here wanted to hear my story."

She put her palms on the table, pushing past the pain.

"Don't expect me to slide over."

Chantel defended herself.

"I didn't know how bad you were. You didn't protest."

"No, I know. Hate to let the world dictate my life."

She caught sight of Kenya dancing across the floor. He stood over her, "Where you been, cool lady? Slide over and whisper in my ear."

Leslie glared up at him.

"If you make me slide over, I'll be screaming in your ear. Stand back. Stand way back!"

Kenya backed up and held up his hands in defense.

"You mad or something? Thought we had a good time Friday."

Chantel rose and addressed Kenya, hands on her hips, looking formidable.

"Dummy. Can't you tell when someone's in pain?"

"In pain? What's she talkin' about Leslie?"

"Stupid got stabbed." Chantel admonished.

"Stabbed? How the hell was I supposed to know that?" He looked at Givens.

"That why your holdin' your side? How you gonna to dance?"

Sharyn looked past Chantel, who was retaking her seat.

"She's not."

"Then why's she here? No other reason to be at Chick's."

"To drink and tell us what happened."

"Oh, okay, let me pull up a chair."

Givens looked up, exaggerating her pain, "Get me a drink first, G and T."

"Yeah, okay. You got money?"

*Really?* She fished a twenty out of her purse. "Get yourself one for your efforts."

As Kenya took the twenty, he feigned protest, "Ah, you don't have to do that."

As he danced toward the bar Chantel said, "There goes your twenty."

Leslie nodded.

"I needed breathing room... and a drink."

Kenya returned with two drinks and no change. He put the drinks on the table, while Givens gave him a probing look.

He turned up his hands in innocence.

"I had to leave a tip."

Chantel tried to cover her mouth as she snickered while Givens frowned into her drink and offered an obligatory thank you.

Pleased with himself, Kenya said, "Anytime, babe. Now, tell us, tell us, tell us everything."

Givens stared into the distance for a moment.

"Well, Bobby Riley took me to the movies Sunday night."

Kenya sputtered, "Bobby Riley? He can't dance worth shit. The way you move, how can you go with a body who can't dance?"

Givens exhaled, her chain of thought already broken.

Chantel slammed her hand on Kenya's arm, causing him to slosh his drink

"Jesus, Chantel." Sharyn said.

"Jesus, nothing. He's the one who interrupted."

"Sharyn, I just want to hear the story."

She turned away from Chantel.

"Go on, Leslie. We can talk about Bobby Riley later."

"Well, when we came out of the movie, I spotted this girl, young woman, that we police were looking for. Bobby and I followed her to her boyfriend's apartment where she was hiding," Givens summarized.

Chantel looked up from sipping her drink.

"Woman a murderer or something?"

"A person-of-interest."

"Doesn't that mean you're in the process of proving her guilty?"

"Uh, sometimes... not always."

"So, did you capture her?"

"No, she captured us."

"What!?" they exclaimed.

"Bobby doesn't tail people very well. She spotted us and had a gun. Surprised me from behind some bushes when I was following her and her boyfriend to his apartment."

Chantel continued as the interrogator.

"So, what did Bobby do?"

"He parked his car and came back to check on me... walked up and got captured too."

"Dumb fuck."

"No, he came out of the whole thing as my hero."

"No shit?"

"Just listen. So, we all go to the boyfriend's apartment where the woman pulls the trigger on the gun, thinking it's not loaded, and shoots a hole in the floor. Scares us all to death. While we're recovering, there's a knock at the door, and the boyfriend goes to open it. As soon as it's open, another person-of-interest bursts through, knocking the boyfriend aside, wielding a knife. He charged across the room at the woman person-of-interest."

Kenya shook his head.

"How many persons-of-interest are there?"

"Lots."

Chantel waved her hands impatiently, trying to draw the story out.

"Go on," she urged.

"Well, I grabbed the guy before he got to the woman and we kind of wrestled and I got cut."

"The bastard stabbed you?"

"Uh, not really... kind of a gut slice. Didn't go in very deep."

"So, you saved the fair damsel person-of-interest and wrestled the other person-of-interest to the floor?"

"No, not exactly. Bobby grabbed a lacrosse stick from the wall, beat the guy over the head, and chased him out the door."

Kenya groaned, "He got away!"

Leslie suddenly felt chagrined.

"Yes."

Sharyn cheered in triumph.

"Leslie saved the woman. That's what's important."

"And Bobby saved me."

Kenya shook his head.

"Oh, God. You're going to have to date him again."

"I'll teach him to dance."

"You kidding? There's not a dancing bone in his body."

# CHAPTER FIFTY-SIX

METZINGER RECEIVED A call from the Office of External Affairs and Professional Responsibility at three minutes past eight Wednesday morning. He was still sitting at the breakfast table with his family, expecting the call. A secretary said that Captain Pearson would like to interview him at eleven o'clock to discuss an ongoing investigation.

He apologized to his children.

"I'm sorry to keep you two out of school for so long. I'll call and let them know you won't be to school until after lunch."

Laura and Ben nodded. Laura said it was all right. She'd get some studying done. Ben decided to play video games.

\*\*\*

Metzinger was escorted into a small interview room and instructed to take a seat on the side where persons-of-interest and suspects usually sit. He felt uncomfortable. He was used to being on the other side of the table.

Captain Pearson came in, flipped on the recording device, to include the digital camera. A woman carrying a legal pad followed. He stated everyone's names and the date and time, then he faced Metzinger.

"Detective Metzinger, I think you know what we're here to talk about."

"I do."

"This is always uncomfortable, but necessary to maintain the confidence of the citizens of Alexandria in our conduct of police operations and our interfaces with the public. Mrs. Beatrice Fazio has filed a complaint that you threatened her and her son in the middle of the street in front of her house last Friday around four o'clock in the afternoon. She says you threatened them both verbally and with your weapon, waving the weapon and telling them that you are a policeman and will, and I quote, 'take care of them' if her son continues interacting with your daughter. This is a serious charge. It alleges misuse of your position and a threat of physical harm with your city-issued service weapon."

Dismay flashed on Metzinger's face.

Pearson continued, "I interviewed Mrs. Fazio yesterday afternoon at her home. She described the incident, and her son corroborated her statement. Her husband also confirmed her story."

Metzinger protested, "Her husband? He wasn't even there. I don't even know what he looks like."

"The husband said he watched the whole thing from the house window."

"So, he was hiding?"

"I only know what he said. Now I would like to hear your side of the story."

Metzinger nodded.

"May I have representation?"

Pearson groaned.

"Of course. You're entitled to it. How long will it take to get someone here?"

"Only a few minutes. They're waiting in the lobby."

Metzinger walked out the interview room, leaving Captain Pearson with his mouth open.

"They?" he asked the woman with the legal pad.

A few minutes later, Metzinger returned with Laura and Ben.

Captain Pearson protested.

"What is this? You asked for a lawyer."

"No. I asked for representation."

He introduced his children and then turned to Ben.

"Please set it up."

While Ben set up his laptop in the middle of the table, Metzinger inquired, "In your investigation, did you interview the Fazio's neighbors?"

Captain Pearson became flustered.

"Not yet. Were they part of the incident?"

"Not directly, but their doorbell camera was."

Ben started played the video.

Metzinger narrated.

"This is the recording from the doorbell camera across the street from the Fazio's residence. You probably recognize the house from your visit yesterday. Here you see me talking to young Jack Fazio... and now you see Mrs. Fazio coming out to join our conversation. Note that I didn't show them a badge. I'm not holding anything. I'm not animated, although Mrs. Fazio is. I didn't wave or even show a gun. I couldn't have. I keep it in my locker here at headquarters. Without audio I can't prove what she said... just know she was berating me with offensive language that I will not repeat in front of my children."

Pearson paused the recording and backed it up.

"Jesus, Metzinger, it looks like she had you cowering."

Metzinger's face colored.

"I've had better moments."

"How'd you know to get this?"

Metzinger grinned and swung his head around to the children.

"Laura and Ben did it."

Pearson reached out and shook their hands.

"You must believe in your dad."

Ben mumbled, "Don't like anybody messing with him."

Pearson laughed.

"I wish you had my back."

He turned to Metzinger.

"You're reinstated. The paperwork will be in your office by the time you get there."

"Thank you for your patience."

"My patience, heck. You're the guys who played it cool."

Metzinger looked at Ben and Laura and said, "I'm taking these guys to lunch. I'll get the paperwork when I get back."

# CHAPTER FIFTY-SEVEN

ARLEY LOOKED UP as Metzinger walked into the detective bay, trying to look casual.

"Good Lord, the outlaw is back. Are you legal, been cleared and all?"

Metzinger plopped his briefcase on his desk.

"No badge or weapon yet. Feel too light. Waiting for paperwork."

"Yeah, well, Lt. Ramirez isn't back from lunch yet. Does he know you're clear so he can return your badge?"

"I can wait."

"Well, I can't. Gert and I are tired of doing your work. Sage Berenson's ride just got back from Petersburg on a flatbed. Shame what citizens pay for. I'm going down to check it out. You might as well tag along."

They found the car being unloaded in the parking lot. It was coming off one of those flatbeds that tilt up: the kind used in lieu of a towing truck for hauling cars, carrying tractors, or whatever. Two gloved up forensics techs in white suits were ready to inspect it. Arley walked toward it, suddenly realizing he was alone. He looked back at Metzinger who was just standing there staring.

"What are you staring at?"

"It's a dark green Taurus."

"Yeah, so what?"

"There was a dark, boxy car parked on the street for a while the night Daphne O'Hanlon was shot."

Arley looked back at the car.

"Guess you could call it boxy. What does that mean?"

"It means Sage Berenson might have been there... or Freddie Winslow. Let's see if we find any blood inside the car."

***

Metzinger and Gert were in the interview room at the jail waiting for Sage to be brought it. He missed Givens, but on the upside, Gert Sorenson was more intimidating.

As Sage was brought in, he looked at Metzinger.

"Where've you been?" he said, "I'm getting to know the whole police department."

He looked at Gert as he was cuffed to the interview table and said, "Missed seeing you."

He turned back to Metzinger.

"You 'cuffing me 'cause you haven't got that black girl to run me down."

"You know why she's not here, Berenson. You cut her with a knife."

"Accidental. She tackled me... I didn't mean to do it. She kind of did it to herself."

"Yeah, if she hadn't tackled you, you would have stabbed Josceline Winslow."

"Nah, it was the wrong apartment. I was trying to return a knife."

"Care to tell us who you were returning it to?"

"Don't remember the name. I can show you."

"Well, we found the knife in the bushes just outside the apartment building's door."

"Yeah, that dude was beating me over the head with a stick. I was afraid for my life! Left out of that house to save myself. Just trying to get away. Someone tripped me as I was leaving, and I fell. Must have dropped the knife by accident."

"It only had your prints on it. No one else's."

"Of course. I cleaned it. Wouldn't want to return it dirty."

"And killing Oliver Winslow was an accident, too?"

"No. Really, it was self-defense. He was pushing me around. Had me freakin' out."

"Fifty-year-old man was a threat to a young guy like you?"

"Yeah, fifty's not that old. He was pushing pretty hard. Didn't know what he was going to do. I've got a right to defend myself! When a guy gets rough with you, you don't know what he's about to do."

"You left him to die."

"I was scared."

Metzinger sighed.

"You've been working on your story?"

"Just saying what happened."

Metzinger nodded.

"Different subject."

"Huh? I've told you all there is."

"The night Daphne O'Hanlon was shot, you said you went out and left Freddie Winslow behind for twenty minutes."

Sage gave Metzinger a suspicious look.

"I think I said ten or fifteen minutes."

Metzinger nodded, "Trouble is Freddie says it was more like an hour-and-a-half."

Sage gaped.

"Freddie caved! Hell, all I was doing was having some beers. First at Darcy's and later at Gilkerson's. Drank and talked to the people there."

Metzinger nodded in understanding.

"Nothing wrong with having some beers, other than that it doesn't match your previous story."

"Hey, I didn't kill O'Hanlon. Just trying to keep from being hassled."

"Did you drive your car?"

"You trying to get me for drunk driving?"

"No. It's a little late for that."

Metzinger hesitated, looking at Sage.

"Well, did you drive?"

"No, the bars were all within walking distance."

"Did you drive your car before or after you went drinking?"

"No, like I said, I just walked."

"When Detective Givens chased you down the next day, she says you looked like you couldn't something. Was your car not parked where you had left it?"

"Not where I remembered."

"So, it had been moved?"

Sage became cautious.

"I don't know. I may have forgotten where I parked it. I never get the same spot twice."

Gert stood up.

"Terrible when the memory goes. What are you... twenty... twenty-one years old? Sad as hell."

Metzinger rose as well.

"Think that says it all."

He walked to the door and knocked, signaling the prisoner escort to enter.

While the escort unlocked Sage's cuffs from the table, Metzinger inquired, "Is the rent on your apartment paid up or do you want us to tell Freddie it's time to leave? I'm going to talk to her as soon as we can get her into headquarters."

Sage protested.

"Why? She didn't do anything."

"So, she can stay in the apartment?"

"Good to the end of the month."

"Bet she'll be relieved."

"Can't she go to her house?"

"It's kind of bloody."

# CHAPTER FIFTY-EIGHT

FREDDIE WAS ANNOYED to be back in the interview room with detective Metzinger. This time Gert was with him.

"You came to see me the other night. Now you've hauled me back here. You're treating me like a damn criminal," she complained.

"Maybe you are."

"What? Be real. I haven't done anything."

She looked up at Gert.

"Who the hell is she? Where's your partner? I'm starting to miss her."

Metzinger turned on the recorder and the camera. He stated the date and time and described who was in the room.

Freddie looked alarmed.

"You're doing this shit for real?"

Gert and Metzinger sat down opposite her.

"Yes, we are, Miss Winslow, as I said the other night, Sage knifed my partner. Detective Sorenson is sitting in for her."

Metzinger opened his notebook.

"Miss Winslow, I read you your Miranda rights the other day, I would like to repeat them."

"They don't last forever?"

"I'd like them on record."

"Whatever."

After Metzinger read Freddie her Miranda rights again, he studied his notebook.

"Miss Winslow, for the record, I talked to you at Sage Berenson's apartment on Sunday night."

"Yeah, more like Monday morning, me in my pajamas."

"And a robe, with a female officer present."

He looked at his notebook. "Officer Anjanette Wilcox was present as a witness."

"I guess. I don't know her name."

"I introduced her."

"Yeah, I vaguely remember. Actually, she introduced herself."

"During that interview, you changed a previous statement from before you had been read your rights. Earlier you'd said that on the evening of Daphne O'Hanlon's murder, you and Sage Berenson were at Mr. Berenson's apartment... that Mr. Berenson had gone out for a few minutes. On Sunday night/Monday morning you changed that and said that Mr. Berenson had been gone for an hour-and-a-half, drinking beer at local bars. Is that correct?"

"You know it is. You recorded it on your phone."

"Yes, I did. What we don't know about that hour-and-a-half is where you were. You said you were at the apartment but admitted that no one could verify that."

"Did I?"

"Yes, you did."

Freddie tried to change the subject.

"So, where's Sage?"

"He's in jail. Caught him on the run south of Richmond."

Metzinger hunched his face toward Gert.

"Detective Sorenson brought him back. She had some long talks with him in the transport van. We brought back his car too. '

Freddie contemplated what Metzinger had said.

"How did Sage explain the time he was gone?"

"Do you think we're comparing stories, Miss Winslow?"

"Isn't that what cops do?"

"Sometimes."

Metzinger looked at Freddie for a moment, rubbing his tongue inside his cheek as if thinking.

"Tell you what we know, Miss Winslow. We know that Sage Berenson was gone from his apartment for an hour-and-a-half around the same time Daphne O'Hanlon was murdered. We also know that the first time we came to Mr. Berenson's apartment my partner had to chase him down the street and she caught him because he stopped to look for his car. He's told us that it wasn't where he remembered parking it. Seemed like it had been moved. We also know that on the night of your mother's murder, there was a car parked opposite your house, that is, the Winslow house... the murder scene. It was a dark car, a sedan, described by a neighbor as 'a little boxy, not quite black in the dark'."

Freddie was listening. Now, her mouth was slightly open, her eyes flickering back and forth between Metzinger and Gert.

"Based on your statements we now know that suspect Sage Berenson walked to the bars, so the car was available for your use. His car is a dark green Taurus sedan. Ford probably wouldn't like it described as 'boxy', but in the dark it could look that way. Do you understand all of this, Miss Winslow?"

Freddie seemed uncertain.

Metzinger and Gert studied her for a moment.

Freddie bit her lip and looked up at the camera.

"I'm up shit creek, aren't I?"

"Tell us how far."

"Part way."

"Oh?"

"I didn't kill her."

She hesitated.

Metzinger encouraged her.

"The whole story, Freddie."

Freddie smiled dejectedly.

"You're getting personal now... friendly?"

"What do you mean?"

"You called me Freddie instead of 'Miss Winslow'. Must be a technique."

"No technique. Just want to know what happened."

"Okay, Sage had gone to get more marijuana. Said he was going to stop in a bar for a while. I felt like I was being abandoned. I felt like life was shitty. I should be in college, but I was living off poor, dumb Sage. I got in the car and drove. Ended up on Crest Street and parked just down from my house, studying it and wondering how my life there had gotten so screwed up... wondering what my future would be. I was kind of daydreaming, if you can call it that while sitting in the dark. Suddenly the front door light of my house came on. A dark figure was standing there. The door opened and there was a flash and a bang, and the figure charged forward, opening the screened door with one hand and then the lights went out. I thought, 'Shit, I don't want to be here'. I started the engine and drove off."

"What time was this, Miss Winslow?"

"I don't know. Probably after nine."

"And why didn't you want to be there?"

"I didn't want to be involved."

"Involved in what?"

"I was afraid someone might have been shot."

"Would you just leave someone to die?"

"I didn't want to get shot, too. Doesn't everyone run from gunfire?"

"Most people, yes. But this was your family."

"So, I'm a coward."

"And you didn't want to be a suspect?"

Freddie sighed, contemplating the thought.

"My feelings for my mother are no secret."

"So, you thought your mother had been shot?"

"High probability. No one liked her."

"How about the shooter? Can you describe him or her?"

"No... just a black figure wearing a hat. Just a shadow against the light, and then the light was gone."

"So, then you returned to the apartment and talked to Sage about an alibi?"

"Not till the news of my mother's death was on the TV."

"So, you didn't want Sage to know you had been gone?"

"Dummy would have said something."

Gert spoke up for the first time.

"Where'd you get the gun, Miss Winslow?"

Freddie jerked her head toward the intimidating detective.

"What? What are you talking about?"

"The pistol you shot your mother with. It was small, comfortable in your hand. Gave you power over the woman you hated."

"No! You're out of your mind."

"All you had to do was walk over to the house, pull the trigger and flick out the lights. You knew where the switch was. After all, you lived there."

"No, I never left the car."

"You'd been planning this killing for a long time. That's why you came back from college? You had unfinished business. The picture on the dormitory wall was just an excuse. Lord knows you're feisty enough to have torn it down and told the roommate off, but you were developing a plan."

"No, I came back from college because I couldn't do what my mother demanded so she cut me off."

"And that pissed you off."

Freddie turned back to Metzinger.

"I didn't kill her, detective. You have to believe me."

Gert persisted.

"What did your mother demand? Finish what you were saying."

"My mother said she wouldn't pay for college unless I wrote more books. Dad didn't have enough money to pay the whole bill. I vacillated about writing the books. I thought of doing it. My roommate's obscene picture was the last straw, like it was telling me something."

Metzinger tagged back in.

"So, you thought about writing books to have college paid for?"

"Yes."

"And you still talk about going to college."

"Yes."

Gert struck again.

"And by killing your mother you thought you could get the money to do that?"

Freddie turned to Metzinger.

"Detective, please. I can't write the books anymore. My imagination is gone. I can't do it, no matter how much I'm threatened. When I was a kid, I used to daydream about Geraldine, before I fell asleep, riding on the bus, sitting on the beach. I don't do that anymore. I guess I'm too old."

Metzinger sat back, feeling tired.

"Maybe in a different life or a different time."

Freddie sighed deeply.

"Maybe. How will I know?"

She crossed her arms on the table and laid her head on them.

"I didn't kill her."

Gert asked in a calmer voice.

"But you're not sorry she's dead."

Freddie raised her head enough to see the detectives. She sighed.

"No, I guess I'm bad that way... maybe even evil."

# CHAPTER FIFTY-NINE

A FTER THE INTERROGATION, Metzinger phoned Givens.
"I want to come talk to you."

"What? Here in my house?"

"Yes."

"No way my mother is going to allow that."

"Why the hell not? People must come visit your house."

"You're a white cop."

"Yeah, so what?"

"There's no way she's going to have a white cop come in judging her house."

"Because I'm white?"

"Way it is."

"Shit, Leslie. Then can you come out to the car? You well enough for that?"

Leslie didn't want to admit she'd been to Chick's the previous night.

"Yeah, I can do that if you don't mind Old Man Davis watching you from the stoop across the street."

"Should I mind?"

"No, he'll talk me up later, but that's on me."

\*\*\*

Street parking was full, so Metzinger had to park a couple of houses down from Givens'. As he approached her house, she burst out of the front door, pulling her coat across her shoulders. She stopped at the top of the steps and held the railing for a moment.

Metzinger shouted, "Are you all right?"

Givens breathed heavily, descended the steps, and said, "I'm fine, just moved too fast."

Metzinger tried to take her arm, but Givens shrugged him off as they walked to his car. Nonetheless, she showed acceptance as he opened the car door and held it for her.

"You didn't have to come. I'll be into work tomorrow." she said, getting into the car.

"From the looks of you, that's too soon."

"I'll be fine. What's up? I thought you were suspended."

Metzinger told her the story of his kids tracking down the doorbell recording while she nodded periodically.

"Wow," she exclaimed. "As the commercial says, 'smart kids'."

Metzinger smiled. "Indeed."

Givens laughed, holding her side, and said, "You can retire and let Ben take over."

"Maybe someday. Anyway, I've interviewed Sage Berenson and Freddie Winslow again. He's defiant, claiming innocence, self-defense and whatever he can think of. Freddie still acts annoyed with the whole thing, but she's softening. Turns out that Berenson was gone from the apartment an hour-and-a-half while Daphne O'Hanlon was being murdered, not ten or fifteen minutes like they said before. Supposedly, he had a beer and picked up marijuana at one bar and then stopped at another bar for more beers."

He gave that a second for Givens to process, then continued.

"However, Freddie didn't sit still in the apartment while he was gone. Remember how Berenson couldn't find his car when you chased him down? Well, that's because Freddie drove it while he was gone and parked it in a different spot when she returned."

Givens' interest was piqued.

"So, she drove it to murder her mother?"

"She admits driving to the house, but not the murder. Claims she witnessed it. Says she parked not far from the house and just sat there thinking about her life. She says she never left her car, but she told us the front door light came on and she saw the wood door open, but not the screened door, Says she heard the shot and a flash, and watched the assailant open the screened door, turn off the lights and leave."

"If the killer opened the screened door after the shooting, why was the victim's foot in it?"

"Don't know. Maybe it was leaning against the door after she fell, and it flopped out when the screened door was opened."

"Sounds like the killer fired quickly through the screened door. Didn't wait for O'Hanlon to let them inside."

"Makes sense. Could be the Jablonskis. We know she'd told them not to bug her... killer had to shoot before she recognized them and slammed the wooden door."

"And Freddie did nothing?"

"No. She says she knew she would be implicated. Claims she was scared."

"So, she just went back to Sage's apartment and pretended nothing happened?"

"Not entirely. She talked to Berenson and crafted the alibi they gave us. Berenson went along with it because he didn't want to be implicated either. Now both of them have independently corrected the story."

"So, what are we doing here? Are you asking me to believe her?"

"No. Just catching you up to date. I'd say Freddie is still the number one suspect. No matter what she says, she has a clear motive. She never tried to hide her animosity toward her mother. Nonetheless, she and Berenson are the only ones we know who have lied outright. Felt the need to craft an alibi."

"No one's hiding their animosity toward the dead woman. We haven't even had to play good cop/bad cop. Everyone talks. O'Hanlon may have done a good job ruling the book world, but she didn't have any friends."

"Yeah but think about it. The literary agent, who is being financially screwed, conveniently left the next day, and isn't exactly cooperative and the publisher has taken a financial hit, but that seems too impersonal for this murder... and killing O'Hanlon doesn't exactly get the money back.

Then there's Joss... annoyed...acting out with boyfriends. The whole family diminished her value as a child, and she was obviously in the right place to commit the murder, although she claims to have been oblivious to the whole thing. Hard to believe she was right there in the house and didn't see or hear anything but, her recent disagreements with her mother don't seem to go beyond typical mother/teenager stuff... arguing about whom she was dating."

"We may not know everything that happened between them."

"True, there's a lot we don't know. Always is."

Givens pondered the situation.

"How about Winslow's brother and his wife? O'Hanlon treated them like poor, inferior relatives... black sheep."

"True, clearly, they are still persons-of-interest, but it seems they had reached accommodation through Oliver and Edward's luncheons. Still, I agree we can't rule them out. We know Edward had a weapon; the one Joss took. The murder weapon wasn't a Glock, but it proves he's familiar with guns."

"And then there's pitiful Allison."

"Yes, Allison Jablonski, the illustrator. Appears very fragile, but it could be a cover. O'Hanlon evidently treated her very badly, taking out her own frustrations on the weak and defenseless was her M.O., but Allison might not be so defenseless. It's possible she didn't like being treated badly and worked up her whole condition as a cover. Premeditated over months."

"There's also her husband. His life's been changed, screwed up by his wife's dissension in to hell. If the depression is real, it must be awful to watch, to live with."

"So, where do I go next?"

Givens got her back up.

"You mean, where do we go next. I told you, I'll be into work tomorrow."

"You're hobbling."

"So, you can drive and do all the legwork. Pick me up in the morning and let's go see the Jablonskis."

"You really feel well enough? If so, do you have time to run by bars to check Sage's story?"

Givens was afraid to think too long, afraid to hesitate and give Metzinger any reason to fight her on coming back to work so soon.

"Sure, if I don't have to walk too much." *Sure hope this goes better than my night out at Chick's.*

# CHAPTER SIXTY

METZINGER PARKED BEHIND Darcy's Pub so they could enter through the back door. They walked down the hallway, past the restrooms, and then Metzinger stopped so abruptly that Givens barely avoided bumping into him.

He reached into his pocket, pulled out his wallet, and took out a picture. Its edges were badly bent where they had folded to fit in his wallet. He handed it to Givens.

"Here's a picture of Sage Berenson. Show it to the bartender and other workers. See if they remember him from last Monday."

"Hell, Drury, why don't you go? This is a white bar."

"What are you talking about? This is just a bar."

"Yeah, well I'll bet the clientele is all white. It's that part of town."

"What do you mean, that part of town? It's just a bar and I can't take the smell of whiskey."

"Whiskey doesn't smell."

"The hell it doesn't. I can smell it from here."

"Over the restroom urine?"

"Absolutely. I can smell every drink, every cherry, every drop of lemon juice, every olive... the foam on the beers. I'll take urine any day."

Then Givens looked at Metzinger's face and saw unexpected pain.

"Something I don't know about you?"

He sighed deeply.

"Lots. I just need you to take this one," he said and walked back down the hallway, out the door and into the dark.

Givens took a deep breath and steeled herself. She turned and walked to the bar, pulled out her badge, and showed it to the bartender. She felt everyone in the room staring at her. It was a feeling she had felt too often in life. She cast her eyes around in defiance.

As expected, there were no dark faces in the room. She knew in her bones that they would be watching her even if she hadn't shown her badge. Because she was black... because she was good-looking... because she was a woman.

Givens shivered and held out the picture for the bartender to see.

"We're checking on this guy. Was he here Monday evening, a week ago, sometime between eight and ten?"

The man looked wary.

Givens remembered the marijuana pickup.

"He said he had a beer here."

The man still seemed closed.

"Yeah, I think I remember him. Yeah, he had a beer."

Givens pulled the picture back and turned quickly.

She spotted Metzinger outside the front door. Apparently, he'd gone around the building. She hurried across the room and out the door onto the sidewalk as if the devil were chasing her. Once outside she stood, breathing hard, clutching her side.

Metzinger reached out to steady her.

"You all right? Can you do one more? Gilkerson's is just three doors down."

She looked at him with vacant eyes. *The poor bastard has no idea.*

As they headed down the street, Metzinger felt his cell phone vibrate. He stopped and pulled it from his pocket.

Givens was two steps ahead of him before she looked back.

He held the phone up for her to see and then answered to an angry voice.

"What the shit are you doing, Drury?"

Metzinger was startled. "Who's this?"

"Joey."

"Constantine?"

"Of course. Whitson and I have Darcy's staked out. You're screwing us up. You messing with the marijuana bust."

"No, Joey. Didn't know you were staking out Darcy's. We were checking an alibi. Nothing to do with you."

"Shit, Drury, get away from here and don't ogle around. We don't want to be spotted."

"Just need to check Gilkerson's. That a problem?"

"No, just hurry. Don't need any cops around here."

"Damn. We're parked behind Darcy's. We'll have to go back."

"Shit, Drury. They see you wandering around, they're going to panic."

"We'll hurry."

"They know you're cops?"

"Yeah, Givens had to show her badge."

"Shit."

Metzinger shoved the phone back in his pocket and they hurried on.

Givens found going into Gilkerson's a little easier... friendlier... less leering. And, yes, Sage was a regular. They were well acquainted with him. Monday night? Sure. He was there.

Walking back out the front door, she felt like she had done a twenty-four-hour shift.

They returned to the car behind Darcy's Pub, trying to look casual.

At the car, Metzinger held the car door for her. She was too exhausted to protest.

"I guess that clears Sage of one murder."

"Checking off a box for the crime report when we already knew the answers."

"So, where do we stand?"

"Tomorrow's another day."

"Jablonski?"

"For a start."

They rode in silence for a while.

Finally, Givens asked, "You got secrets you don't want to talk about?"

Metzinger didn't turn to look at her.

"We've all got secrets we don't want to talk about. Histories and pasts."

Givens studied his profile.

"Yes, we do," she acknowledged.

# CHAPTER SIXTY-ONE

As he drove home, Metzinger phoned Sarah to tell her he would be late for dinner again.

"Don't worry. We've already finished. Your plate's in the oven."

Metzinger felt her annoyance.

"I'm sorry. I was discussing the case with Givens."

"She came into work!?"

"No, I went by her house and we ran over the case."

"It couldn't wait?"

"I was frustrated. Had to talk it over with her. See where we stand."

He left out the part about swinging by the bars to check alibis.

"Okay. Come on home so I can finish in the kitchen."

Metzinger shivered. He could feel the chill.

*\*\*\**

When Metzinger got home, he stuck his head into the living room and waved to the children. Laura mouthed, "You're in trouble."

Metzinger nodded in resignation and mouthed, "I know."

In the kitchen, Sarah silently put his plate on the table along with a salad and bottle of dressing she pulled from the refrigerator. She stood and leaned against the sink. He waited a moment and then got back up and poured himself a glass of water.

Sarah offered, "There's milk in the refrigerator."

"Water's fine," he said, sitting back down.

"Okay."

"Hey, I'm sorry."

Sarah shrugged.

"We had a good dinner tonight. I wanted us all together."

"I know."

"You don't know. You weren't here."

"Sarah, you know having dinner with you all is important to me. It's always important."

"I made chicken parmigiana."

"And it's wonderful."

"Better when it was hot."

"It's still hot."

Sarah finally sat down at the table.

"So, what's her house like?"

Drury set down his knife and fork and leaned back.

"She said you'd ask that."

Now, Sarah was feeling a little guilty.

"So, what's wrong with asking what her house is like?"

"She says her mother would say we're judging her."

"Were you?"

"I wasn't allowed in the house. She came out to the car. We sat there and talked."

"And she never let you in the house?"

"No."

"Because her mother thought you'd criticize the place?"

"Not criticize... judge."

"What's the difference?"

"Criticism is all bad. Judging can go both ways."

"Would you have judged the place?"

"I don't think so. I'm in all kinds of people's houses all the time. I don't think I judge, unless it's dirty, or cluttered, or piled with trash, that kind of thing."

"Do you think their house is dirty?"

"I doubt it. Leslie's pretty neat. Her desk is cleaner than mine."

"Then, why do you think her mother was worried?"

"Jesus, Sarah, what's with all the questions? Leslie said it's because I'm white. A white cop."

"Does that matter?"

"I guess so. Would it worry you if she came into our house?"

Sarah thought for a moment.

"I don't think so. She's your partner. I'd probably try to make a good impression. Probably clean up a bit."

"The same with anyone who comes here?"

"Yeah, I think so."

Sarah became quiet, seeming to become contemplative while Metzinger finished his meal.

As he picked up his plate and took it to the dishwasher, he looked at Sarah, and asked, "Private thoughts?"

She pushed away from the table.

"Yes. Deep. Do you think I'm racist?"

"Because you'd clean the house?"

"Because I might worry about being judged by a black woman."

"More than by a white woman?"

"Yeah."

"Well, there was a time when a white woman wouldn't have cared at all... just wouldn't have wanted the visitor touching anything."

"Our grandparents?"

"Great grandparents."

"Are we making progress?"

"I wonder."

# CHAPTER SIXTY-TWO

METZINGER HAD JUST SETTLED at his desk with his cup of coffee when Lt. Ramirez called him into his office.

"It's been over a week. The press hasn't gotten too invested in these murders, but we need to get somewhere on them. What have you got?"

"Well, we've found Oliver Winslow's killer and have a confession and the murder weapon. Just can't prove it was premeditated. Daphne O'Hanlon is a different situation. We've got plenty of persons-of-interest. They all admit they didn't like the woman, but all we have is a bullet... no weapon, no witnesses, and no surveillance recordings. The neighborhood watch didn't even come through. The white-bearded trash diver alibied out."

"Your time off the case hasn't helped."

"That was a false accusation."

"Still, you put yourself in jeopardy. You shouldn't have confronted that woman."

"I didn't. She confronted me."

"Shit, Drury, you know what I mean. You shouldn't have been there."

"Hey, I'm a policeman, but I'm also a father."

"Fathers and policeman need to be circumspect. Comes with the territory."

"Okay, but it worked out. I'm back on the job."

"By yourself. Your partner's cut up. Your mind's saturated. Do we need new eyes... new minds? Do I need to keep Gert and Arley on this? They've accomplished as much as you two."

"They've been a big help, but we've got the in-depth knowledge of the case."

Lt. Ramirez shook his head.

"There's no 'we', Drury."

"Yes, there is. Leslie's coming in today. We discussed the case last night."

"She was here last night?"

"No, we talked in the car in front of her house," he said, again leaving out the part where they nearly ruined a stake-out at Darcy's Pub.

"Did you decide anything?"

"We think Freddie Winslow is the prime suspect. In questioning yesterday, she admitted she was at the crime scene. She says she was parked in a car across the street from the house that night, thinking about her life. She said she didn't leave the car but admits she witnessed the crime, although she didn't recognize the perpetrator. She says she drove off because she was frightened that she'd be implicated."

"She could have shown us her hands, allowed us to test and prove she didn't fire a gun."

"Lieutenant, in all fairness, television or no television, that's pretty sophisticated thinking."

Lt. Ramirez frowned.

"I know you're right, but it would have helped."

"No doubt. Anyway, she admits she was there. She certainly had the opportunity to commit the crime, and a motive, but we have no proof. No weapon, no gunpowder residue, no fingerprints, no DNA, nada."

"So, if you stay on the case, what's next?"

"We keep working the suspects. Hopefully, someone will break."

"So, Miss Winslow is the prime suspect. Do we need to work on breaking her?"

"I want to go back to the secondary suspects first. The illustrator and her husband."

"Why them?"

"Because O'Hanlon's issues and ego hit them the hardest."

"Okay, go at it."

***

Metzinger returned to his desk. He tasted the coffee and spit it back into his mug. *Cold as hell!*

He carried the mug to the coffee room and dumped it. After refilling his mug, he made more coffee for the next person since he caught the end of the pot.

*Bad description.* He thought, *Hell's not cold, at least I think not. There must be a better way to describe cold.*

As he returned to his desk, Arley shouted, "We're closing down the illegal marijuana sales today. You want to go along without us?"

"Where? At Darcy's?"

"Yeah. How'd you know?"

"I was there last night checking Sage Berenson's alibi. Constantine was staking it out. When he saw me, he almost had apoplexy. Phoned me in a huff and told me to get away from there."

"Lord, you were checking on where Sage got his marijuana?"

"No, just where he had a beer."

"Damn. No wonder Joey's trying to close things out. You coming?"

Metzinger shook his head.

"Waste of time. Marijuana sales are hardly worth it. It's legal in half the world. Can't you find the really bad stuff?"

Arley threw up his hands and hunched his shoulders.

"Not so bad stuff today, badder stuff tomorrow."

"Yeah, well, I'll be okay. Givens is coming in today. Oh, shit! I was supposed to pick her up."

"Tell her you had trouble getting a ride out of the motor pool."

Metzinger shook his head.

"She knows a lie when she sees it."

"Sees it?"

"It's in the face."

"You need to practice. What do you think mirrors are for?"

Metzinger rushed for the door, cell phone to his ear.

"I'm sorry. The lieutenant caught me—I'm on my way."

# CHAPTER SIXTY-THREE

METZINGER PULLED UP in front of Givens' house and double-parked. He admired the house. The front was a door-and-double-window wide. Wider than some houses in higher-priced areas of town. It was mid-century brick with a white-edged levered roof over the front door; an early version of what is today called a town house. Five steps lined with a black iron railing led up to the front stoop and it was set back by a very neat, fifteen-foot-wide, front lawn.

He sat in the car and waited, having expected Givens to be watching and rush out the moment he arrived, but she didn't. *Maybe I do expect the world to turn on my dime,* he noted.

He got out of the car, approached the house and knocked. A moment later the door was flung open, and Givens rushed out, pulling a jacket on as she hurried past him.

"Hey," Metzinger cautioned, "slow down. You don't want to fall with that wound."

Face flushed, she finished putting on the jacket, walked down the steps, slowed and walked gingerly to the car.

Metzinger watched her go as he walked down the steps behind her.

"You sure you're up to this... sure you're not supposed to be resting?"

She opened the car door.

"Now you're worried? After you worked me last night? And you're late as usual. At least I got an extra hour's sleep this morning waiting for you. Made up for last night."

She climbed into the car.

"Glad I could help out by being late."

"Yeah, always doing for others. Honestly though, I'm still tired. Might doze while we're driving. By the way, what are we doing?"

"Do you need to go by the office?"

"Aren't we pulling the Jablonskis in for interviews?"

"Hard to pull them in with the shape she's purported to be in. We're going to have to go to their apartment again."

"The interview room works better."

"I know, but I think we have to save that for later."

"You still think she might be faking it?"

"Not thinking anything. Still investigating. While we're driving, let me tell you about Lt. Ramirez. He called me in first thing this morning."

"Oh?"

"Nothing bad. Just giving me a push. Wanted to know if you and I could handle this case, what with my losing time thanks to the suspension and you being walking-wounded. I told him I was fine and that you were coming in today, raring to go."

"He buy it?"

"Reluctantly."

"Well, don't plan on me chasing anyone down Duke Street. As long as everyone behaves, I'll be fine."

Metzinger pulled into the Parkfairfax cul-de-sac where the Jablonski's lived.

"Uh, oh."

"Uh, oh, what?"

"No white Prius."

"Maybe he's running an errand, has someone staying with his wife."

"Maybe."

Metzinger pulled into a parking place and turned to Givens.

"Why don't you stay here. Take it easy while I check and see if they're home."

"Remember, the killer has a gun."

"Yeah, I won't do anything silly."

Metzinger exited the car, walked down the steps to the Jablonski's end apartment, drew his weapon, and knocked on the door, standing to the side.

Nothing happened. He knocked again and announced, "Police!"

No one came to the door.

He walked around the back and tried to peer through the terrace doors, but the curtains were drawn closed. They were sheer fabric, but not sheer enough to see anything useful. He could tell there were no lights on, not that that proved much during daylight. He gave one last try knocking on the terrace doors. Still, there was no answer.

*Darn*, he thought. *A wasted trip.*

Coming back around building and up the steps, he spotted Givens standing on the sidewalk, a few parking spaces down from their car. She was talking to a woman while holding a hand to her side.

"Mrs. Freeley says an ambulance came and picked up Mrs. Jablonski about four o'clock yesterday afternoon."

Metzinger reached out to shake the woman's hand.

"Hi, Detective Metzinger," he introduced himself, "I'm her partner."

Mrs. Freeley, hesitantly, shook his hand.

"I'm a neighbor over there." She pointed at an apartment at the end of the cul-de-sac.

"I don't like to be nosy, but it's not often an ambulance comes in here. I offered to help, but Dr. Jablonski said things were under control."

"So, the ambulance was for his wife?"

"Yes."

"Was she on a stretcher?"

"Yes, but she was awake, talking to her husband."

"Could you hear what she said?"

"A little. She seemed confused. She wanted to know where she was going, wanted to know why she couldn't stay home."

"Anything else?"

"No. Dr. Jablonski patted her arm and told her everything would be all right."

"What can you tell us about the ambulance?"

Mrs. Freeley motioned at Givens.

"I already told her."

Givens elaborated, "She didn't get the name on the ambulance, but says it was blue and white with a red stripe and a red medallion on each side. Not the usual colors. She doesn't know where it was going."

Metzinger nodded, "Hopefully, we can track it down."

He turned back to Mrs. Freeley.

"Did Dr. Jablonski stay here last night?"

Mrs. Freeley looked guilty.

"I'm sorry, I wasn't paying attention."

"That's fine, Mrs. Freeley," Givens assured her. "It's not your job. So, you haven't seen Dr. Jablonski since the ambulance left?"

"No, not since he drove off following the ambulance."

Givens shook Mrs. Freeley's hand.

"Thank you, you've been a great help," she said while handing Mrs. Freeley her card. "Please call if you see one of the Jablonskis or you hear anything about them."

Mrs. Freeley looked at Metzinger and asked meekly, "Why are the police interested in them? Are they murderers?"

Metzinger glanced at Givens and back at Mrs. Freeley.

"They're people we'd like to talk to."

Mrs. Freeley nodded.

"Persons-of-interest?"

"Right, Mrs. Freeley, persons-of-interest."

As Mrs. Freeley walked to her apartment Givens, looking culpable, turned to Metzinger and whispered, "I told her that we wanted to talk to them in relation to a murder... never said he was a killer or a person-of-interest."

Metzinger squeezed his lips together in a frown.

"You take that building and I'll take the Jablonski building. See if anyone else knows something. If you can't hold up, sit in the car and I'll finish."

When they finished their survey, they returned to the car. For a moment, they were silent, contemplating what they had learned. It was Metzinger who spoke first.

"General consensus is the Jablonskis are loners. Seldom seen. In fact, no one has seen Allison for months. They did see another woman go into the Jablonski's apartment periodically. She drove a gray Ford Fusion, but no one knows her name, and no one was concerned enough to write down a license plate number. They say Dr. Jablonski went out, but only when the woman was there. They assume he has a job but didn't know any details about it. Several people witnessed the ambulance but couldn't describe it any better than Mrs. Freeley. Sound like there was a male driver and female paramedic. They were both wearing green medical scrubs."

Listening to Metzinger, Givens noticed a woman staring out at them from the apartment above the Jablonski's.

"We're being watched."

"Probably from every apartment in the cul-de-sac. Looky-loos waiting for a shoot-out."

"Well, it's eerie."

"Okay, we can solve that by getting out of here," Metzinger said, turning the ignition key. "You learn anything I didn't mention?"

"Only that Dr. Ralph Jablonski never smiles."

"Don't guess he has reasons to."

"And no one has seen him since the ambulance left."

"Yeah, that's what my people said, too. Where do you suppose he stayed last night? And where did the ambulance take Mrs. Jablonski?"

"I guess we have work to do."

"Yep, time to play detective."

# CHAPTER SIXTY-FOUR

METZINGER AND GIVENS RETURNED to the office after lunch. Gert hurried over to greet them.

"Geez, Leslie, are you all right? Should you be back here? You staggered in here like you should still be home."

Givens protested, "I didn't stagger. Just moved gingerly. My side's a little sore."

"You look like it's a lot sore. You need to take it easy. You don't get stabbed every day."

Givens settled carefully in her chair.

In an effort to downplay her injury, she pointed out, "The report doesn't say 'stabbed'. Just 'cut'. Less impressive."

"Cut deep though... you got stitches?"

"Six big ones."

"Big ones?"

"No bikini for a while."

Arley couldn't stay out of it.

"Shit, Leslie. Get the report changed. 'Stabbed' sounds so much better, and you need to get the number of stitches included. You're damaged property. Milk the damned thing!"

Gert made a face and refocused on Metzinger.

"You're pushing her too hard," she scolded.

Metzinger scoffed.

"You think I have any control over what she does?"

Masterson shouted from his desk, "You tell her about Lt. Ramirez reading you the act?"

"I told her all about it, but he didn't read me anything. Just discussed the case. Told me to get on with it."

Gert studied Givens.

"If it's too much for you, I can take over."

It was Metzinger who responded.

"Yeah, you mean you and Arley. Hell, Leslie says she's fine. I'm fine. That's all we need."

He turned on his computer. Givens followed his lead.

"Search for blue and white ambulances with a red stripe and red medallion in Fairfax. I'll look in Alexandria and Arlington."

Givens worked at the computer keys typing in search criteria.

"Fingers crossed the database bringing up pictures."

Gert interrupted, "Hey, I can help. Fairfax is my territory."

Givens remembered that Gert lived in that area and asked, "Do you know an ambulance service with those colors?"

"How about Medplus? It's a non-emergency ambulance service in Fairfax City."

"Red stripe and red medallion?"

"Don't remember about the stripe, but there's a red circular thing on the sides."

Metzinger was excited and inquired, "Do they work outside Fairfax County?"

Gert raised her eyebrows as if to say, *the name's not enough help for you?*

"Heck if I know. Give them a call."

Metzinger brought up the ambulance service on his computer and was pleased to find an ambulance pictured with all the right colors.

He dialed the number on the screen.

"Hi, this is Detective Drury Metzinger of the Alexandria Police Department. May I ask you a couple of questions?—Yeah, okay. Do you service areas outside Fairfax, say in Alexandria?—Yeah, in the Parkfairfax area?—Yes. We're checking on a pickup there yesterday afternoon—I know, patient privacy—What about your log? Can we see that? No, I don't need a patient name. Just need to know where your ambulance went—CMHH? Okay. Got it."

Gert and Givens waited for him to hang up.

"Don't know if she should have told me that, but she did," Metzinger remarked.

Givens queried, "CMHH?"

Gert translated.

"Commonwealth Mental Health Hospital."

"You know it? Public or private?"

"Private, I think."

Metzinger scribbled in his notebook and looked back at the computer.

"In Annandale... not far. Right off Duke Street, after it becomes Little River Turnpike. Right on the road. Let's go!"

Gert held up her hands to stop them.

"Whoa, we've got a wounded detective here. Why don't I go? Arley can survive without me."

Givens pulled herself up, tying to look like steel.

"Thanks, but I'm fine."

"You don't look fine."

"It's my case and really, I can do it. I appreciate your offer. I'll let Drury do anything that requires energy."

"Or strength?"

"Or strength or running."

"Wish I could believe you. Don't you need to let Fairfax law enforcement know you're going to be in their territory?"

Metzinger looked back over his shoulder.

"Valid point. Will you give them a call?"

Gert shook her head.

"Oh, so you won't take me along, but you want my help for the shit-job."

Givens hobbled after Metzinger out to the car.

"You hear that," Givens reminded Metzinger as she gimped along. "Anything happens to me, you're going to have to deal with Gert."

# CHAPTER SIXTY-FIVE

METZINGER PARKED in the no-standing lane on the loop in front of the hospital. Remembering Gert's threat, he hurried around to help Givens out of the car. He offered her his arm, but she shook him off.

"You're overdoing the chivalry," she chastised.

"Protecting myself from Gert."

"Wise man, but you're driving me nuts."

Still, he held the front door of the hospital for her.

They entered a reception area. It wasn't spacious. The sitting area seemed exceptionally small. It was designed for ambulatory traffic, not for sitting, not for waiting.

They approached the reception counter and Metzinger said, "We'd like to see Allison Jablonski."

The receptionist studied her computer screen and hit a couple of keys as if finishing something up.

"Are you scheduled?"

Optimistically, he pulled out his badge.

"Detective Drury Metzinger, and this is Detective Leslie Givens."

"Assuming the subject of your inquiry is here, visitation is Tuesday and Thursday evenings. Family members only and only with prior doctor permission."

The receptionist pointed to a printed sign taped to the window while stating what it said verbatim.

Metzinger acknowledged the rules and said, "I understand but Mrs. Jablonski is important to a case we're investigating. May we see someone who might help us?"

The receptionist looked uncertain.

"You'd have to speak with the hospital administrator, but I hate to bother him. Is it really important?"

Metzinger was losing his patience.

"Yes, I'd say a murder investigation is really important."

The receptionist looked troubled as she dialed her phone.

Meanwhile, Givens noticed a guest register and pretended to sign it.

As the receptionist hung up her phone, she stopped Givens.

"You don't have to sign that unless you go in."

She turned back to Metzinger.

"Dr. Mallory will be out in a few minutes. You can wait over there."

She pointed to the uncomfortable arrangement of lobby chairs.

As the detectives turned toward the chairs, Givens eased over beside Metzinger.

"Ralph Jablonski was here this morning."

Metzinger turned toward her.

"Is he still here?"

"No, he signed out before lunch."

The receptionist heard them and her expression became one of concern.

"He's her husband. He's allowed to see her."

Metzinger nodded.

"Of course. It's just that's he's a person-of-interest in our murder investigation."

The receptionist put her hand to her mouth.

"Oh, my goodness, is he dangerous?"

Metzinger offered a guarded reply.

"I don't know. That's why we need to talk to him. Do you know where he's staying?"

"He's not staying at his house?"

"Doesn't seem to be."

The receptionist shook her head.

"Then, I have no idea. I don't talk to staff or visitors much other than checking people in and responding to inquiries."

Just then a man wearing a gray suit entered the lobby.

The receptionist looked relieved.

"Here's Dr. Mallory now."

Metzinger approached the man, who looked at him uncertainly.

"Police?"

"Yes."

"How may I help you?"

"We'd like to ask about a patient who was admitted here yesterday."

Dr. Mallory pointed to the receptionist and the sign.

"Yes. Gloria said you were inquiring about Mrs. Jablonski. I'm sure she told you that we are not at liberty to confirm or deny such a person is here. Patient privacy."

"Yes. We've heard. Thing is, she may know something about a murder case we're investigating, and we need to talk to her."

The doctor scowled.

"I can't discuss a patient's treatment. Visitation is extremely limited. I'm afraid I can't allow you in."

"Can't or won't?"

"Does it make a difference?"

Metzinger was discouraged.

"Don't guess so. Do I need to get a court order?"

"We'll fight it. Really, detectives, I don't think we can help you."

"She's not in good shape?"

"Sorry, I can't comment."

Metzinger twisted his mouth in thought. He gave the doctor his card.

"I'd like Gloria to phone me if Dr. Jablonski comes in to visit his wife again."

Dr. Mallory took the card and studied it.

After a moment he said, "We'll try to help, but you're putting us in a bad spot. We try to help people here. That's all we want to do."

Metzinger sighed and nodded.

"I understand. We really need your help."

The doctor squeezed his lips in thought.

"Citizen responsibility, huh?"

Metzinger met his eye.

"Exactly."

# CHAPTER SIXTY-SIX

METZINGER AND GIVENS SAT in their car deliberating.
"Do you think the APB is enough?"

Givens considered the question.

"What are you saying? You think he's on the run?"

"Could be. He's put his wife in a hospital. She's safe. Takes that responsibility off his back."

Metzinger started the car and put it in gear.

"Let's get back to the office. We need a search warrant for the Jablonski place and to check the airlines. Trains and bus lines too."

"If he makes reservations, it may flag, but if he buys a cash ticket, we might not catch it."

"Let's reemphasize the APB to the security folks, especially at the bus terminals, Union Station and the Airport Authority Police plus TSA at Reagan and Dulles."

"How about BWI?"

"Yeah, I guess them too."

"You know there are all kinds of private buses that run to New York City and other places. Not to mention rideshares and taxicabs."

"Yeah, and VRE and MARC trains, and the whole Metro system. Damn near impossible to check on all of them."

\*\*\*

Givens put in for a search warrant for the Jablonski apartment and then joined Metzinger in making phone calls. They contacted the airlines and got TSA to activate a temporary no fly order. The doctor would have to use his real name and ID to get through anywhere with security checks. Greyhound, Megabus and Amtrak were all on the lookout and the VRE conductors were checking commuter trains. They asked Arlington Police to monitor buses leaving Reston and hunted online, identifying the myriad of other bus companies and escape possibilities. The magnitude of the task was discouraging. It might even be wasted since Jablonski could drive away in his white Prius.

Metzinger wondered how many white Priuses there were in the world.

At 1:27 P.M. the call came. Jablonski had made it easy. He booked a one-way ticket on American Airlines for Detroit.

"Why the hell Detroit?" Givens blurted.

"Hell, if I know," Metzinger responded.

"Maybe he knows someone there. Could be the only seat available this afternoon. Have our communications center patch an open line with the airport authority police?"

With the airport police apprised of the situation, the detectives raced out of the police station parking lot, tires squealing.

Metzinger directed, "Check in with the comm center. Make sure we've got contact."

While Givens was doing that, Metzinger turned on his siren and headed north on U.S. 1, knowing he was fouling up a lot of traffic.

Givens questioned the siren.

"If he hears us coming, he's going to run."

"Okay. I'll kill the siren before we get there."

"Yeah, when are you going to do that?"

"Depends on the traffic, but I'll do it soon."

When they passed the Crystal Drive exit, Givens nervously pointed out, "Next exit is 233 into the airport. You better cut the siren."

"Okay."

Metzinger cut it.

"Done."

Exit 233 turned in front of old Terminal A and around to Terminal B where the airport police were waiting. Metzinger and Givens pulled up between cars unloading luggage and introduced themselves to the uniforms.

"Dave Jennings. Shelley Trollo."

Givens nodded.

"Where should I drop the car off?"

"Down and loop around to the parking lot," Trollo answered.

Givens shook her head in frustration.

"Too far. You'll never see me again."

"Okay. Pull down to Terminal C and park at the curb. I'll let the security guys know not to tow you."

Givens looked at Metzinger.

"Guess you're on your own for now."

Metzinger looked around and pointed.

"Meet you inside those doors."

"See you in a few." Givens said, as she climbed gingerly into the car and was gone.

Jennings said, "Let's get out of sight."

Metzinger passed out photos of Jablonski's driver's license picture with Metzinger's cell number written on the back.

"This is the guy we're looking for. We need to cover as many doors as possible. Do you two mind separating?"

Jennings and Trollo nodded and Metzinger continued, "You guys have radio comm, but I don't. I'll keep my cell handy for your calls."

The airport authorities moved off.

Inside the terminal, Metzinger stood back a couple of yards from the window next to the door he was covering.

As he waited, the airport shuttle bus came from his left, just as Givens came hobbling from the right. The bus stopped. Three passengers were standing in the aisle. Two got off. The third hesitated and went to the back of the bus. The bus doors closed.

"Shit!" Metzinger barked, causing heads to turn.

Metzinger burst out the door, almost colliding with his out of breath partner. He yelled with futility as the bus drove off and he got a clear view of the passenger. "It's Jablonski!"

He whirled Givens around to face the direction of the bus, forgetting she was hurt.

"He was on that bus!"

Givens hunched over, wincing.

"Shit."

Metzinger looked hopelessly at his phone and realized he had forgotten to get a phone numbers for Jennings or Trollo. *Damn. I'm getting senile.*

He looked desperately at Givens.

"Get the car."

Givens was breathing hard.

"Don't know that I can. The wound's got me."

"Okay, give me the keys. Find Trollo and Jennings and tell them to call in whatever backup they have in the parking lot, but make sure they know Jablonski may be armed. Tell them to watch out for a white Prius. I'll drive up there as fast as I can. See if they can radio the shuttle driver!"

Metzinger ran a dozen steps and realized he wasn't in shape to sprint all the way to Terminal C. Walking as fast as he could he chastised himself for being so out of shape. *If this guy gets away because I've been skipping the treadmill, Gert and Arley will never let it go.*

Once he found his car, he got in and turned on the ignition, but was blocked in by a double-parked car unloading luggage. He pounded the steering wheel in frustration. He honked. The guy unloading the luggage glared at him in anger. Metzinger turned on his flashing lights to hurry him along. The man's eyes bugged. He ran around and got into his car, and finally, with a jerk, pulled the car forward.

Metzinger peeled out into the third lane over, turned on his siren and followed signs leading to the long-term parking lot. He had to circle the whole area in front of the airport, taking forever.

Finally, he entered the Terminal B parking lot, hoping that Jablonski's car was there.

*Too many goddamn terminals, too many parking lots,* he thought, turning off the flashing lights and siren. *Shit, he knows I'm here! No hiding it!*

Arriving at the parking lot exit toll booth, he stopped the car. An attendant barreled out from the booth and started toward him, waving for him
to move the car. Metzinger held up his badge.

"We have a guy on the run. He may be armed. Get back in the booth!"

"Shit," said the attendant, running to cover.

Just then he caught sight of Givens coming across the lane for the parking lot exit.

There was a screeching of tires. A blue car wheeled down the ramp
headed toward them.

Metzinger bolted forward, noting a flash of brake lights from the corner
of his eye as he knocked Givens out of the way. Then he felt, and heard,
the Malibu accelerate and burst through the exit smashing the gate, sending it flying in pieces.

Givens clutched her side as she rolled over to get up.

"Didn't know you could move so fast, Drury."

Metzinger gaped. "Damn, you're bleeding again."

"Just a little. Call it in. Set up roadblocks."

Metzinger did so, shouting into his radio, "Yeah, our police, the state
police, the Arlington Police, and the Park Police—Yes, I said Park Police—
Cover George Washington Memorial Parkway—It's a blue Malibu! Not a
Prius!—Yeah, a blue Malibu!"

Givens choked out, "The DC police too!"

Metzinger shouted back into the car radio, "The Metropolitan Police,
too. He may cross a bridge—Yes, dammit, blue!"

He turned to Givens.

"Can you make it to the car?"

She staggered to the passenger side as he got into the driver's side."

"Where are we going?" she said between breaths, still holding her side.

As he turned the ignition, Metzinger looked at her.

"Hospital or chase?"

"Chase! Easiest exit from here is GW Parkway north."

An Airport Authority Police car, MWAA on its side, pulled up beside
them just as Metzinger took off waving at the befuddled driver.

He turned and raced through the exit, glimpsing the attendant standing with his hand over his mouth, astonished at the broken gate.

With lights flashing and siren screaming, they raced away from the airport and onto the Parkway. Almost immediately, they approached the Gravelly Point Park exit and a park police car parked in the right lane, lights flashing. A Park Policeman was standing behind it, checking cars as they passed.

The detectives pulled around past him and Metzinger hurried over to the policeman.

"You by yourself? Seen anything of the Malibu?"

"Look out! Another car's coming!" warned the Park policeman as the car whistled by.

He continued. "I haven't seen it."

"How long have you been here?"

"Since the call came in. I was already here in the park."

"Metzinger shook his head."

"Shit, even this roadblock might have been too slow. Either he didn't come this way, or he's long gone."

"The guy who's coming to back me up is watching the road as he drives. Said he'd let me know if he sees anything."

"But he hasn't?"

"No."

"Thanks for the help. I expect our guy is gone."

Metzinger got back into his car dejectedly.

"Nothing?" asked Givens.

"No," sighed Metzinger.

"Do you think he took 233 over to US 1? Our guys and the Arlington Police must have US 1 blocked."

Metzinger sighed, "But he could have gotten off at 23rd Street before they got a roadblock in place. Then he'd be lost in those numbered streets of Arlington. I'm afraid we're dependent on a random spotting. The roadblocks are too late."

He picked up the car radio and summoned dispatch. Then called Lt. Ramirez let him know they'd lost the suspect and called off the roadblocks.

Jablonski was in the wind as they headed for I-395 and the bridge exits to get turned around.

# CHAPTER SIXTY-SEVEN

INSTEAD OF TURNING AROUND at I-395, Metzinger headed west and then south, following the interstate.

Shaking off the pain in her side, Givens uncertainly asked, "Where are we going?"

"Jablonski's apartment."

"Why would he go there?"

"Where else would he go?"

"I don't know. Maybe he's running. Might be he's back to wherever he stayed last night."

"Might be lots of places, but let's start at the one place we know."

Metzinger exited the interstate at Shirlington and entered the Parkfairfax Apartment complex.

Givens inquired, "No sirens?"

Metzinger shook his head.

"Don't know if he's here and don't want to scare him if he is."

They turned into the cul-de-sac and parked next to a blue Malibu. Metzinger studied it.

"Guess he switched out the Prius for this... hoped we wouldn't recognize him."

Metzinger backed out.

Givens asked, "Aren't we going in?"

"Don't want to be an easy target. We'll park across the way."

Givens noted, "It's a basement apartment. He hasn't got a good view to the front of the building."

"Just playing it safe. People have been known to barricade themselves in and start shooting in situations like this."

"Want to call for backup?"

"Not yet."

Metzinger got out of the car, drew his weapon, and held it low by his side.

Givens followed while Metzinger directed, "Keep your weapon low. We don't want to scare anyone. If any neighbors come out, chase them back in."

They moved cautiously across the cul-de-sac, staying separated. When they reached the cars on the far side, Metzinger told Givens to get behind a vehicle with a view of the end of the building and Jablonski's door.

"Cover me from there," he directed.

Metzinger rushed past the cars to the corner of the building and stayed close to the wall as he approached the door. He started to knock and realized the wooden door was open. Only the storm door was closed. He hesitated, being sure not to expose himself through the open door. Again, he started to reach out and knock on the door frame when Givens shouted, "Get back in, lady! There may be shooting!"

It made Metzinger jump and he backed up hard against the wall. Taking a deep breath, he reached out to knock again when a voice came from within.

"Is that you, detectives? I've been waiting. You came pretty fast."

"Are you armed, Dr. Jablonski?"

"No, my pistol and the magazine are on the coffee table in front of me. It's not loaded. I don't want to shoot anyone."

"Come over and stand in front of the door, three or four feet inside with your arms raised."

"Okay but tell me you won't shoot."

"I don't want to. It's up to you."

"Okay, I'm standing with my arms up."

Metzinger took a deep breath and whirled out in front of the door, his gun aimed at it. Jablonski was standing as directed. Out of the corner of his eye, Metzinger saw Givens hurrying toward him. He reached across with his left hand and opened the screened door. He moved in, went around Jablonski, and picked up the weapon from the coffee table. As Givens came in, he handed her the gun.

"Keep him covered while I pat him down."

Jablonski stood stoically while Metzinger moved behind him.

"Arms down and behind your back." Metzinger cuffed him and moved to the front to pat him down.

"I'm arresting you for the murder of Daphne O'Hanlon."

Jablonski nodded.

"Nasty woman, wasn't she?"

"I'm not here to judge, Doctor."

"No, I know. You're just doing your job."

Metzinger faced the man and read him his rights. "Do you understand, doctor?"

Givens asked, "Out of curiosity, where were you running to?"

Jablonski shook his head in resignation.

"I don't know. Just thought I should run. The rental car was my brilliant idea of how to hide. Dumb, huh?"

"Detroit?" Givens asked incredulously.

"It was the only ticket available. I didn't do any long, careful planning. Kind of spur of the moment. I ran when I saw you from the parking lot at the hospital. Until then, I thought I'd gotten away with it."

Jablonski noticed Givens holding her blood-stained side.

"Are you hurt?"

Metzinger followed Jablonski's gaze.

"Yes. Her cut's opened. Happened when you tried to run her down at the parking lot. I'm taking her to the hospital after we deal with you."

Jablonski looked at Metzinger.

"You're just letting her bleed?"

"She says she's okay."

Jablonski glared at Metzinger.

"Maybe she is and maybe she isn't. My medical bag's in that closet over there. Get it for me."

He nodded toward the coat closet.

Metzinger was caught off guard.

"What, you want to treat her here?"

"Why not? It's what I do."

Metzinger got the bag.

Jablonski shot Metzinger a stern look.

"I can't help her while I'm cuffed."

A resigned Metzinger moved behind Jablonski and unlocked the cuffs. Givens remained quiet.

The doctor rubbed his wrists.

"Put the bag on the dining room table. You can check it for weapons."

Metzinger did. *Better safe than sorry.*

Jablonski sat in a dining room chair, his eyes fixed on Givens.

"Give your partner your gun and come over here."

Givens moved over to Jablonski while pulling up her blouse to reveal the wound.

"You've torn out two stitches. It's pretty bruised around the area."

He looked at her gravely.

"You haven't been taking care of this."

He looked at Metzinger.

"Doesn't the police department have enough people to let her take a few days off?"

"She doesn't listen well."

"And you let her get away with it. I'm supposed to do no harm, but you do lots."

Metzinger felt chagrined and annoyed.

"Yeah, and you killed a woman."

As Jablonski pulled out materials to repair Givens's stitches, he seemed to shrink.

"She was cruel."

"So, we've heard."

"She didn't need to be. She knew Allison was fragile. It was just pure meanness."

"And, as I understand it, frustration and anger."

"Doesn't excuse it."

As Jablonski worked on the stitches, he looked up at Givens's face.

"Sorry, I almost ran you over. I didn't know you'd be there. Thank God your partner saved you. I couldn't stop. When I turned off U.S. 1 and got lost in those numbered streets, 23rd, 24th, 25th, whatever, I parked the car and thought, 'I'll never get away with this and I might kill someone. They'll track me and make my life miserable. Might as well stay here—be near Allison.'. So, I found Arlington Ridge Road and drove back here."

Then, as he worked, Jablonski's mind seemed to drift back to the murder. He continued talking, but almost to himself.

"Do you know what it feels like to be a doctor and not be able to help your wife... to see her deteriorate day by day... to have to turn her over to others because you become incapable?"

Again, he looked up at Givens. "Do you know how that feels?"

Givens closed her eyes. "No, doctor, I don't."

Dr. Jablonski finished repairing the stitches and bandaged the wound. "Do no harm. That's me. Do no harm. I shouldn't have done it, but my wife was curled up in a fetal position, not eating, not talking... just kind of weeping..."

He looked at Metzinger.

"It's no excuse, is it detective? Not before the law. I try to tell myself I'm sorry, but I'm not. I set up a trust to pay Allison's bills at the hospital. The court won't take that money away, will they? She'll be all right, won't she?"

Metzinger felt uncomfortable. "It wasn't ill-gained money, was it?" Shit, he thought. Keep your mouth shut. "I don't really know anything. I'm not a member of that part of the system. What I think doesn't matter."

"It was my money. I earned it over the years, inherited some. Now it's in a trust. I don't think anyone can touch the trust. That's what the lawyer said."

He stood up and turned to Metzinger, holding out his hands.

"Can you cuff me in front? It hurts in back. I won't cause you any problems. I'll do no harm. At least, not anymore."

# CHAPTER SIXTY-EIGHT

IT WAS JANUARY, three months after the murders of Josceline and Freddie Winslow's parents.

"Would you believe she established an award for children's fiction? Put her estate into a trust to govern the award... a medal with her silhouette on one side and Geraldine Gerbil on the other side. Trying to outdo the Newberry Medal!" Freddie fumed.

She was talking to the detectives in the hallway outside the courtroom. She had just finished testifying.

The trial for Dr. Jablonski was scheduled for April, but Sage Berenson's trial for her father's murder was in full swing. It was already late in the third day. Detective Metzinger had testified, introduced his evidence and explained his involvement in the investigation.

Jimboy Drummond was brought in, against his will, by Detective Arley Masterson to testify about finding the knife and the bloody hooded jacket. It probably ended their brief friendship. Arley testified as a lead-in for Jimboy's testimony. He also introduced the recordings of defendant Berenson during the drive back from Petersburg.

Charlie Sutton testified about the hooded figure in a gray hoodie that he saw running across his yard on the day of the murder.

Audrey Hale testified to seeing a hooded figure go in and out the Winslow's back door on the day of the murder and about Jeannie Sorley going in and out the same door the next morning.

Jeannie Sorley testified to finding the body of Oliver Winslow and made an awkward presentation as to why she hadn't notified 9-1-1 immediately.

The coroner explained the condition of Oliver Winslow's body and the estimated time of death. He indicated that the victim's wounds were consistent with the knife Jimboy Drummond had found.

Manassas Laboratory sent a technician to affirm that Oliver Winslow's blood was on the knife, along with Sage Berenson's fingerprints. He further testified that the blood on the hooded jacket was that of Oliver Winslow and hairs found on the jacket matched Sage Berenson.

Repeatedly, Sage's court-appointed defense attorney emphasized that no one had witnessed the killing. No one knew what had happened. No one could prove Sage was the aggressor.

He drew from Masterson and Metzinger's testimonies that his defendant said Mr. Winslow was pushing him around and that his confession was one of self-defense. He drilled in that the knife came from the Winslow's kitchen. Mr. Berenson did not bring a weapon to the house because he did not come to Winslow's house to commit murder.

Freddie took the worst beating.

It was unclear why the prosecution made her a witness; they asked her about Sage Berenson's character and his discussions with her about the inheritance trying to show a possible motive for the killing.

The defense had jumped all over that, hammering that through her discussion about the book money and her mother's estate, she had created an emotional storm in Sage that might have exacerbated his reaction to Oliver Winslow's aggressiveness. They emphasized that Sage wouldn't have even been visiting the victim if Freddie hadn't alarmed him and made him feel like he had to do something. Freddie, they claimed, had motive to kill both her mother and father.

Released from the stand, Freddie stormed out of the courtroom and found Metzinger and Givens in the hallway.

"That damned lawyer is blaming Dad's death on me! What an abhorrent thought! How could he do that to me?!"

Givens looked at the girl and shook her head.

"Cool it. The lawyer's trying to protect his client, just doing his job. You did discuss the inheritance with Sage, worried about what it would do to you. Whether you meant any harm or not, you may have set Sage off.

He went to talk to your father on your behalf, even if you didn't tell him to. However innocent your words were, they segued into the death of your father. Sometimes, the vaguest statement can have enormous consequences, no matter that the consequences never entered your mind."

"You're saying I should feel guilty?"

"Not if you know you're innocent."

"Innocent of not being mad about the inheritance situation?"

"Innocent of premeditated thoughts of your father's death or realizations that you might have been catalyzing a murder."

"Jesus, I'm going to think about this forever! You're not helping."

Metzinger joined in.

"She's not trying to help. She's just saying you may have, and probably did, inadvertently initiate a situation that led to your father's death."

"Jesus Christ, you're no help either. Killing my father never entered my mind!"

Givens threw up her hands, "Hey, we believe you. What happened, happened."

She changed the subject.

"So, how are you and your sister making out?"

"Lord, she still has to testify about Sage busting into her boyfriend's apartment when you and your boyfriend were there."

Givens entered a rebuttal.

"My date, not my boyfriend. Be clear. I'll need to testify too. I'm the one who was stabbed."

And kidnapped at gunpoint, she seethed.

"Sage says that was an accident."

"Maybe. It still hurt and I still had to get stitches. What if he had gotten to your sister? So, I repeat, how are you and Joss making out?"

Freddie sighed.

"Fine, I guess. Gave her hell for ever thinking I'd murder her. She says she believes me but says if I hadn't flapped my big mouth about the money, Dad would still be alive. Same kind of thing you're saying now. Guess you're all right. I was paranoid and stupid. I think Joss has decided life goes on and she has no choice but to live with me. We finally got to the lawyer... found his name in mother's records. Did you hear about her will?"

"Just what you said a few minutes ago."

Freddie repeated the story about the Daphne O'Hanlon Medal.

"Wanted to be famous in perpetuity. It was all about her. The hell with her family."

"You got nothing?" Givens asked.

"Not from her. I guess that's fine. Joss and I are all right. Dad owned the house, most of the property. He left what he had to us. We're selling the house to get Joss and me through college."

"What's happening to Joss? She's only fifteen."

"I'm her guardian. Can you believe that? Eighteen and expected to be an adult. Guess I can work on it, but Joss is a hell of a lot of responsibility."

Givens sniped, "She probably thinks the same about you."

Freddie glared at her.

"Hey, let up. Joss has. You can too."

Metzinger interjected.

"So, you're living in the house now?"

"For now. Joss and me rattling around."

"Are you going back to Mary Washington?"

"No, George Mason. When the house sells, we'll find an apartment in town until Joss finishes high school. I'll commute until then. We still have Dad's Ford."

"Till then, I bet you have lots of time to kill."

"No, I'm writing a book."

"About Geraldine Gerbil?"

Freddie laughed and shook her head.

"God no. An illustrated novel about high school, a coming of age thing."

"About your life."

"Hope not. I'd rather it be original, but who knows? Mom's agent, Brigit Sanders, is giving us a leg up."

"Trying to recoup her money."

"No. That came out of Mom's estate. Didn't make it to the trust."

Givens inquired, "Illustrated, huh? Could Allison Jablonski do that for you?"

Freddie frowned and sighed.

"We talked to Dr. Jablonski about that. He was excited, but it turns out that all Allison can draw these days is Geraldine Gerbil."

"And you don't want to resurrect Geraldine?"

"No. She's part of my youth, good and bad. I don't want to relive that."

"Out of curiosity, how did you make contact with Dr. Jablonski?"

"Oh, his lawyer contacted us to be character witnesses for him at sentencing."

"That's assuming he's found guilty."

"Yeah, he says he is."

"His lawyer's going along with that?"

"He and his wife both say he's guilty, so, yes."

"Allison does too?"

"She wrote it down."

Metzinger frowned, his brows furrowing.

"How are you going to be a character witness for a man you don't know?"

"We'll talk about what our mother did to Allison... mitigation."

"I guess but I'm not sure it will do much good. The murder was premeditated... all planned and carried out. Not much emotion involved."

"Well, it can't hurt. The lawyers say that us daughters forgiving the man who killed our mother is worth a try. We'll see."

Metzinger put out his hand to shake Freddie's.

"Okay, I don't enjoy murders and I've found you a little caustic, but I like you better today. I wish you and Joss good fortune."

Freddie chuckled.

"I like me better, too."

# CHAPTER SIXTY-NINE

METZINGER WENT HOME straight from the courthouse. Sarah and Ben were in the living room.

"You're home early."

"Testified in the Oliver Winslow trial today. Came from there."

"Did it go all right?" Ben said, looking up, alert. "Did you get a satisfactory denouement of the case?"

"Not yet. Detective Givens and some others need to testify, and the Jablonski trial is still a couple of months away."

Ben looked disappointed.

"You know what 'denouement' means?"

Drury smiled.

"Context."

"Context?"

"Yeah, I guessed based on how you used the word. I can't say I'm happy about this whole thing. Sage Berenson is just a dumb, lovelorn kid, who got himself in a situation he couldn't handle. Dr. Jablonski is a frustrated man, angry about how his wife was treated by a horrible woman. He's had to watch her suffer."

Drury looked around.

"Where's Laura?"

Ben made a face.

"Up in her room, on her cell, talking to her friends about a guy who asked her to the Valentine's dance."

"What? Not the guy who asked her to the Halloween Dance after she broke up with that other dunce?"

"You mean the football player who rescued her social standing after your public altercation that ruined her life?"

"Hey, altercation is too strong a word. It was just a discussion. Besides, I saved Laura. She's bloomed since then."

"Yeah, yeah. Anyway, he's old news. The new guy lives in one of those fancy new apartments on the south side of town… wears cardigans and loafers with some kind of-grown-up pants. No jeans."

"Sounds like an oddball," Metzinger commented.

Sarah entered the discussion.

"Sounds wealthy or like he wants to stand on his own."

"Yeah, maybe. His own man or a weirdo."

Sarah responded, "Give him a chance."

Metzinger nodded.

"I won't go see his parents… yet."

Sarah frowned.

"Or ever."

Metzinger smirked.

"We'll see."

Sarah was laughing and said, "Come on into the kitchen while I make dinner."

"Yeah, I'll supervise," Metzinger replied and walked beside her.

"You can set the table, pour the drinks."

"That's the kids' job," Metzinger protested.

"Yeah, well, you're home early, so you get the honor. How's the trial going?"

"Slow. The prosecution has a million witnesses against this kid. Unfortunately, they can't find him guilty of stupidity. They'll get him for manslaughter on Winslow and assault on Leslie. He might get a few years. Still leaves those girls without parents, but I think they've been independent for years."

While Sarah stood in front of the refrigerator thinking, she asked, "Did the girls ever resolve the inheritance?"

"They're all right. Got the house, a car, and a bit of cash from the father. Not enough to make them rich."

Sarah closed the refrigerator and opened the freezer.

"How about fish?"

"What, for dinner?"

"Yes, that's why I'm cooling myself in front of the freezer."

"Yeah, fine. Have we got tartar sauce?"

Sarah pulled out frozen fish and French fries, set them on the counter, and reopened the refrigerator.

"Yeah, we have tartar sauce. So, what happened to the writer's money?"

"The woman put her money in a trust to fund the administration of an annual award, a medal, for children's literature," Drury explained while he laid the utensils out.

"Let me guess. She named it after herself."

"Yeah, her profile is on the medal."

"Will the award-winners ever know the story?"

"Doubt it."

"So, two more murders solved. Do you get tired of it, Drury? Twenty-four years of shaking out the crap people do to each other... it's been a long time... some rough times."

"And you worry about me all the time. Yeah, the really bad things get to me, and to tell the truth, there are too many of those. Fortunately, I only have the six years to go."

"Yeah, how many bodies will that be?"

"I don't want to count, Sarah. I remember too many. They keep food on our table, keep my mind engaged... I'm not sure what I'm going to do when it's over. I hate to say it, but the bodies keep me going. They pay the bills."

# CHAPTER SEVENTY

A PLEA AGREEMENT ended Sage Berenson's trial before Givens had a chance to testify. He'd serve ten years jail time, probably less with good behavior.

Metzinger didn't know how he felt about it. He always felt that intelligent killers should have the book thrown at them. With Sage, he worried about stupidity being set free.

With that trial finished, Givens and Metzinger were in the office closing out their records on the Winslow murders, knowing it wouldn't be over until after Dr. Jablonski's trial for the murder of Daphne O'Hanlon, the first murder to happen, the last one to close.

Metzinger was writing paperwork while Givens went through the material evidence again. There were a variety of items confiscated from searches of the Winslow's house and the Jablonski's apartment. Some of it was still pertinent to the cases, but some wasn't. Those items could be returned to their owners. She was separating items pertinent only to the now closed Berenson/Winslow case from evidence for the Jablonski/O'Hanlon murder trial.

She picked up the plastic bag containing the Colt 1903 used to kill the first victim. Dr. Jablonski said was issued to Allison Jablonski's grandfather when he was promoted to Army Brigadier General in 1952; a general officer's pistol. She felt its heft. It was much lighter than most, a .32 caliber. She guessed general officer pistols must be more ceremonial than police service weapons. It had never been fired until it was used in the murder. Givens was amazed it still had fired, wondered how that sixty- or seventy-year-old ammunition had still worked.

The pistol went into the evidence box along with the shell casing found at the murder scene and the bullet removed from Daphne O'Hanlon's spine.

Next, she picked up a portfolio of Allison Jablonski's drawings. They didn't seem directly relevant to the murder. Still, out of curiosity, she glanced through, admiring the artwork. Following up on so many leads, neither she nor Metzinger had really taken time to look at them. Since no more books would be written, the drawings were just historical documents in the making of Geraldine Gerbil books. Givens thought, *Now that there was a literary medal, maybe these would end up in a museum.*

Turning the pages, she admired Allison Jablonski's skill at bringing the little animal alive. Most pages were large, drawn on heavy paper, probably sixteen by twenty inches in size. In the back of the stack of drawings, she found a smaller packet of pages, standard eight by eleven typing paper, with little ink sketches. They were neatly stapled together to form a homemade comic book.

"MIGOD," she gulped. "Drury, you need to see this!"

She rushed to Metzinger's desk and plopped the comic book down. "Take a look!"

Metzinger picked up the sheath of papers and read the title, *The Continuing Adventures of Geraldine Gerbil: Mysteries of the Night.*

Gerry's in the auto seat. At last she feels alive.
Billy's at the driver's wheel,
'cause gerbils, as you know,
don't know how to drive.

In the early night-time dark, far from the house,
with stealth, we park
and through the yards I sneak,
quickly running, quiet as a mouse.

At the door I knock
and lights ignite,
doors open wide
and there she is,
a dreadful sight.

I raise my gun,
no need to aim,
and fire close,
a bang, a flame.

Her body falls and I
flip out the light,
and turn to run
quick, out of sight.

As I am leaving,
hall lights come on.
Someone is coming,
I must get gone.

Around the house I quickly scurry.
To waiting-Billy, I swift must hurry.

At last I'm safe, free once again,
as I meet Billy and drive away.
my mission's done just as I'd wished.
Revenge is mine I now can say.

Metzinger closed the pages.

"Jeezus, a damn picture book. Don't know about the poetry. Not up to Dr. Seuss standards."

"Nobody said the Jablonskis are poets."

"Obviously, but what does it mean?"

"I think it means that Allison killed O'Hanlon and Dr. Ralph drove the getaway car."

"You think so?"

Metzinger reopened to the picture of Geraldine knocking on the front door. He tapped it with his index finger.

"There's no screened door. Also, no Band-Aid on the doorbell. Was she just skipping details when drawing what happened or were these pages drawn ahead of time, planning the actual crime? Did Allison commit the murder, or did Ralph fulfill a plan she'd drawn up?"

"How the hell do I know?"

"Do you think she really did it? That he's covering for her?"

"Again..."

"I know. 'How the hell do you know'... Love does crazy things to people."

"I wouldn't know."

"Well, it does. Besides, people want to help the weak."

"If she's weak, how could she accomplish this?"

Metzinger tapped the pages of the comic book again.

"As it says, 'at last she feels alive'."

"You think that's possible?"

"Experts could probably speculate."

"Tell us what you think, at least."

Metzinger flipped through the pages again, finding the illustration where the hall light came on. He pursed his lips and tapped it.

"How could Allison know about the light ahead of time? Does it mean that Allison was there?"

"Or, Ralph told her, and she drew it later."

"Hell, you're a real killjoy. You're saying this doesn't prove a thing?"

"Not that I can tell."

"It does mean one thing."

"What's that?"

"We need to talk to Dr. Jablonski and Josceline Winslow again."

# CHAPTER SEVENTY-ONE

THE WILLIAM G. TRUESDALE Adult Detention Center wasn't far from Police Headquarters, but it was far enough to warrant taking the car.

Metzinger had phoned ahead and arranged to see Dr. Jablonski in one of the rooms where prisoners met with attorneys. This one lacked hardware for securing shackles like most police interrogation rooms. Otherwise, it wasn't much different.

An officer from the jail supplied a voice recorder and placed it in the center of the table.

As Jablonski entered the room, he nodded to Metzinger and Givens. "Detectives."

The detectives responded with similar formality. "Dr. Jablonski."

Jablonski looked at Givens.

"How's the wound coming along? They were pretty big stitches."

Givens shook the question off with her head. "Won't be wearing my bikini until June, five more months. Might get some work done on it before then. Otherwise, it's fine."

"Good to hear." His eyes swung back to Metzinger. "What can I do for you?"

Metzinger considered. "You know, I'm a little surprised to find you here. Didn't you seek bail?"

Jablonski chuckled.

"You're kidding. I'm a murderer who's already tried to run once. Bail would be exorbitant, and I have no collateral. I leased the apartment, was making payments on my car, and put everything I had into the trust for Allison. Besides, I'm happy to be here. Just wish they'd get on with things."

Givens shook her head. "Don't push too hard. This jail is better than most. Stay here as long as you can."

Jablonski laughed.

"What can I do for you? The crime is already solved."

Givens pulled herself together to get down to business and turned on the recorder.

Detective Metzinger tapped the microphone and followed standard procedures stating the date, location, and names of persons present.

Jablonski offered, "Are we starting all over again? I admitted the murder."

Metzinger replied, "Just trying to clean up details for our report."

"Okay. What do you need?"

Metzinger opened a folder and pulled out a sheet of paper on which he wrote the murder date and listed the players' names at the top. Jablonski began to get impatient.

Metzinger looked up from the paper.

"I'd like to go over what happened the night of the murder. In particular, details of what happened after the shooting."

Jablonski looked perplexed. Uncertain. A furrow was developing in his brow.

"Okay."

Metzinger continued.

"As I understand it, after you fired the shot, you turned out the hallway and outside lights. Is that correct?"

Jablonski responded slowly, as if he feared the question was loaded with implications he couldn't discern.

"Yes."

"And then you left?"

"Yes."

"Why did you turn out the lights?"

"I didn't want to be seen and I didn't want her body to be found until I was safely home."

"If you didn't want the body found, why didn't you shove the body into the house and close the door?"

Jablonski's brow furrowed further.

"That would have taken time and effort... a fair amount of effort since Daphne O'Hanlon was not a small woman. Mainly I was scared and wanted out of there."

"Were you so scared you didn't turn out the lights you thought you did?"

Jablonski shook his head.

"No, they were out. It was part of my plan. I didn't leave until every-thing was dark."

"You're sure."

"Absolutely."

"Now, tell me, as you left the front door of O'Hanlon's house, did you see the hallway light come back on?"

"What? No."

"You're sure?"

"Yes. Is there a reason you think it did?"

Metzinger glanced at Givens and back at Jablonski, deciding what to say next.

"We have a witness who says it did."

Jablonski sat in silence.

"No comment, Doctor?"

"No."

Metzinger looked at Jablonski for a minute, then looked down momen-tarily at his file. Then he pulled out the make-shift picture book and laid it on the table.

"Have you ever seen this?"

Jablonski, with a look of curiosity and uncertainty, opened the book.

In amazement, he said, "It was drawn by Allison."

"Are you sure? It's not signed."

"Yes, I'm sure."

"Turn the pages and look at it please."

Jablonski met Metzinger's eyes, then acquiesced and began turning the pages. At the end of the book, his eyes darted up expectantly.

Metzinger tapped the pages.

"Have you seen these before?"

"No."

"How did Allison know to draw these?"

Jablonski said nothing. Metzinger was sure he was weighing his response carefully, considering how it would implicate his wife. Finally, he responded.

"I told her what I had done. I guess she decided to draw it up."

"And you played Geraldine Gerbil."

"I guess so."

"And who was Billy Dilly? Who drove?"

Jablonski's answer came quickly.

"I was both."

"Why do you suppose she drew a separate driver?"

Jablonski suddenly looked tired.

"I've no idea. She was so unwell."

Metzinger leaned across the table and opened the picture book to the page where the hall light came back on. He tapped the page.

"Here's where the light in the hallway came back on. Did you tell Allison about that? A moment ago, you said you didn't know anything about the lights coming back on."

"I don't know. Maybe I did tell her that. I don't remember. I was running scared, irrational and in a panic."

"And were you irrational when you told Allison about everything?"

"Probably. I was worked up."

Givens finally merged in, offering sympathy and understanding.

"Doctor, we understand that you want to protect your wife, but the only way I can make sense of these drawings and you not knowing the lights came back on is that you are Billy Dilly and Allison is Geraldine Gerbil. Isn't Allison the only one who could know the light came back on? She must have been the one to fire the pistol."

"No... no, no. She was too weak. She couldn't have done it. She didn't have anything to do with it. She's fragile. Leave her alone!"

Metzinger put the book back in the file, closed it, and closed his notebook.

"Sorry, Doctor. I think you were an accomplice, but I'm not convinced you pulled the trigger and I will testify that I believe your wife, not you, killed Mrs. O'Hanlon."

Jablonski threw his head back and cried in frustration.

"Damn it, I've confessed! I'm guilty. Leave Allison alone! Don't be cruel!"

As they drove away from the jail, the black iron gate closing behind them, Metzinger was more distraught than satisfied.

"Dammit Givens. Am I cruel? Allison's going to be protected one way or another. Her doctors will protect her from a trial and I really don't think Dr. Jablonski pulled the trigger."

Givens spoke thoughtfully.

"Do you think contesting the confession will make a difference?"

"I don't think it's going to matter. I think the doctor is going to plead guilty, and that's it."

"Well, he is guilty... an accessory if nothing else. If Allison did the killing, someone had to drive her. Does an accessory get the same sentence as the killer?"

"Most of the time, but if the doctor pleads guilty, Allison stays safe in the hospital. That's what the man wants."

"Don't forget that the coroner's report says cause of death could be head trauma from the door, not the bullet wound. The lawyers can still argue that the wind killed O'Hanlon."

"True. That would mean Jablonski would be sentenced for attempted murder, or accessory to attempted murder. Guess he could plead out, although I don't think that would illicit much sympathy from the judge. He'd still get a hefty sentence."

# CHAPTER SEVENTY-TWO

"DAMN IT, DETECTIVES! What the hell is this? You're bringing out my ornery-self again!" Freddie screamed when Metzinger and Givens walked into the interview room.

It was no surprise that Freddie and Joss were fit to be tied.

Givens turned on the camera and the microphone. Freddie was acting ready for a fight.

"I thought all of this was over. You've got the killer. You've got the weapon. What more do you want?"

"Just trying to close things out."

"They're closed. One more trial to go, but the case is closed. How many times are you going to kill our parents? Let up and let us live our lives."

"Actually, that's what we want to talk to you two about."

"What?"

"How many times your parents were killed."

He glanced away from Freddie toward Joss. She was looking stone-faced straight ahead, although she was breathing heavily through an open mouth.

He returned his attention to Freddie.

"Most of my questions are for Joss but since you're here, as her guardian, I'd like to ask you some things first."

Detective Metzinger formally stated the time and date, for the record, and listed all persons present.

"I remind both of you that your Miranda rights have been read."

He thought for a minute and corrected himself.

"You know, Josceline, I probably haven't read you your rights. I better do it now."

He did so.

"Now, I think we're ready. Procedural t's crossed and i's dotted. For the record, I'm speaking to Winifred Winslow, who will hereafter be referred to by her nickname, Freddie. Her sister, Josceline, will be referred to as Joss."

He turned to Freddie, who slouched and looked belligerent.

"Freddie, you have stated that on the night Daphne O'Hanlon was shot, you were parked across the street from and one door down from the victim's home You have further stipulated that you were present when the shot was fired, that you heard it and saw a flash of light. I would appreciate it if you would provide as many details of what you witnessed as you can remember."

"Shit, detective. We've talked about this before."

"Before the shot, did you see the front door lights come on?"

"Yes. I said that before."

"Thank you. That's what I mean by details."

"Yeah, the lights came on."

"Did you see the figure of a person standing in the light on the stoop of the house?"

"Yes."

"Man or woman?"

"I don't know."

"Why not?"

"As I remember, he was just a shadow wearing a hat."

"I assume the 'he' you just used does not refer to a particular gender."

"Yeah, that's right."

"What kind of hat?"

"Could have been a baseball cap, I don't know."

"Not a hood?"

"No, not a hood."

"Did you see the wood door open and your mother appear?"

"Yeah. She held that door open and stood inside the screened door."

"Before the shot was fired?"

"Yes."

"Did your mother seem taller or shorter than the person at the door?"

"I don't know. The stoop is lower than the hallway floor."

"Did you see your mother fall?"

"I think so. I was starting the car... getting out of there."

"Did you see the lights go off?"

"I told you before, the figure opened the screened door and turned them out."

"Did you see the hallway lights come back on?"

"Come back on? No, I didn't notice that."

Givens noticed Joss lick her lips as if they were getting dry.

Metzinger wrote something in his notebook.

"See, Freddie, you saw more than you thought. Anything else?"

"Yeah, Dr. Jablonski was hurrying along the sidewalk in front of the house when I left."

"How do you know it was Jablonski?"

"Uh, I don't know. He confessed. There was a shadow... a figure moving along the sidewalk."

"Okay, good enough. Joss, I'll let Detective Givens ask Joss some questions."

Givens sat up straight, opened her notebook, and addressed Josceline.

"Joss, did your mother take care of you when you were a little girl?"

Joss looked hesitant.

"Yeah, of course."

"Even when you were ten- or twelve-years-old."

Joss glanced quizzically at her sister and then back at Givens.

"Yeah. I survived."

"Did she love you?"

"Yes, I think so."

"Did she love you as much as she loved your sister?"

"Uh, yeah."

"You're sure? Did she pay as much attention to you as she did to Freddie?"

"Well, yeah, but Freddie was writing the books. That made mother spend a lot of time with her."

"Even when you were young?"

"Yeah, I guess, but I didn't think about it much."

"It didn't make you feel lonely?"

"Maybe, a little."

"What did you think about Freddie writing the books?"

"Not much."

"Even when you were ten or twelve?"

"Well, yeah, I thought about it then."

"Did it make you proud of Freddie?"

"Hey, what is this? Some kind of psychology stuff?"

"Sort of. Did Freddie's success bother you... or were you proud... or jealous?"

Joss looked to Freddie who was staring blankly ahead, slightly licking her lips.

"Maybe a little jealousy at first, like when I was eight or nine."

"Jealous of her success or jealous of the time your mother spent with Freddie."

Joss thought a minute.

"Jealous of the attention."

"Whose attention?"

"My parents, who else? They were the only ones who knew about Freddie writing the books."

"So, you felt left out. Ignored?"

"That's a little strong."

"Did you feel like you were sitting on the sideline, watching a drama?"

"Uh, maybe, later. Then, I started realizing that Freddie was being taken for a ride. Told her so. I watched the arguments but didn't get into them. Just watched, kind of shook my head. She was still getting the attention. I just started bailing out... hanging out with my friends... staying away from home... meeting boys."

"You began to feel that you didn't need to be home anymore... didn't have much home life?"

"Yeah, kind of."

Freddie jumped in.

"Damn, detectives. Look at her! Does she look fifteen to you? She had every boy in miles chasing her. Of course, she left the shit at home."

Metzinger grinned at Freddie.

"Now, you sound jealous?"

Freddie looked down and pursed her lips in frustration.

"I already told you that she's the pretty one."

"Your writing success didn't match that?"

Freddie looked at Metzinger, her eyes watery with compunction.

"For me, the books are history and I never got anything for writing them. Not even the stupid medal."

Metzinger studied the girl.

"I know," he responded, and then turned to Givens, "Sorry to interrupt."

Givens scribbled in her notepad for a moment.

Joss watched the detective, apprehension clear in her face, but Givens looked up at her and smiled.

"So, to quote your sister, you 'left the shit at home'?'"

"Yes."

"But you still lived in the house... lived with it all."

"Yeah, lived in my room. Where else would I go? I'm a minor, for God's sake."

"Lived with it all, day after day?"

"Yeah. Yes. What do you want me to say?"

"Nonetheless, on the night your mother was killed, you slept peacefully well into the morning?"

"Yes."

"Just yes?"

"Yeah."

"To reaffirm what you've said before about the night of your mother's death... you came home around eight, visited with your mother in the kitchen, went up to your room, stopping in the bathroom on your way, turned on music in your room and didn't leave the room again until you went to the bathroom around midnight. And then you went to sleep."

"Yes."

"Yes, that's right?"

"Yes, that's right."

"And you didn't hear your mother being shot?"

"No."

"It would have been awfully loud since the shot wasn't muffled."

"I didn't hear it."

"Because of the music."

"I guess."

"Was your bedroom window open?"

Joss appeared momentarily uncertain, as if wondering where the questions were going next.

"No, of course not."

"Why 'of course not?'"

"It was cold outside."

"That's true. In the low forties. We had frost the next morning. Did you open the window later?"

"Yes, I did."

"And, from what I observed the next day while you were getting dressed, you slept under a lot of blankets."

"Yeah, it was cold."

"Yes, it was. Do you normally sleep with your window open when it's that cold?"

"Sometimes."

"Did you leave your bedroom door open so that you could really draw in the air?"

"Probably."

"I would say definitely. When we arrived the next morning, the wind was whistling through the house, through the front door..." Givens stopped and let Joss think.

"So?"

"Let me describe what happened to your mother."

Givens pulled papers from a folder.

"This is the autopsy report. She was shot a little after nine o'clock Monday evening. The bullet cut through the edge of her aorta, opening it to bleed, and lodged in her back between the fifth and sixth thoracic vertebrae, cutting the spinal cord. Do you know what that means, Joss?"

"Her back was broken?"

"And the lower part of her body was paralyzed. Do you know what cutting the aorta means?"

"That she bled a lot."

"Yes, and fast. It means she was dying. But do you know what else happened to your mother?"

"No."

"The side of the back of her head was caved in where the corner of the door hit her."

"Yeah, that door swings pretty hard."

"Yes, I tried it. I opened your bedroom window and it swung with quite a bang. But with the window closed, it didn't swing at all."

"Okay."

"What time did you open the window, Joss?"

Joss hesitated.

"I told you... when I went to bed."

"Around midnight?"

"Yes."

"Let me tell you some interesting things about your mother's head wound. I've practiced falling down by that door. I always end up with my head about a foot further into the hall than the edge of the door. Perhaps a paralyzed person falls differently, but the Persian rug in the entrance hallway caught my attention... it wasn't centered like most people would expect it to be. It was out of place."

"Yeah, so what?"

"With the rug moved, your mother's head was positioned for the door to hit it."

"Maybe the rug was off center before anything happened, or she flailed her arms and moved it. Who knows?"

"Right, who knows. But there's another interesting thing."

Joss said nothing and waited.

Givens wanted her attention.

"You listening?"

Joss flinched.

"Yeah."

"There were three wounds to her head. First, she was hit by the door. Then her head moved, and she was struck again, lower on her head, and then yet again causing a third wound."

"So?"

"Thereafter, the door kept hitting that third spot. The strikes were not as hard as the first three hits, but there were several, and all in that same exact spot."

"Yeah, so she fell, and the door hit her, didn't swing as hard every time. Wind gusts?"

"Maybe. But you know what is interesting. All three wounds bled."

"Why's that interesting?"

"Because they wouldn't have bled after she was dead... after her blood settled."

"What?"

"The medical examiner says she would have died fairly quickly from the severed aorta."

"Uh, huh."

"But you just told us that you didn't open your bedroom window and start the door swinging until three hours later."

"We don't know that it didn't swing before. Like if there were gusts."

"The thing is, without your upstairs window open there weren't any gusts. You say you didn't open it till around midnight. The initial head wounds were made much earlier than you opened the window, so, something else made the door slam, for example, a person slamming the door hard into Daphne O'Hanlon's head three times."

"Because her head was bleeding?"

"Right. You've got it."

"The medical examiner might have been off. Maybe she didn't bleed to death as fast as he thought."

Givens decided to fudge.

"Another interesting fact is that we have a witness who says the hallway light came on after the shooter left. Right after he left... requiring someone from within the house to turn it on... while you were supposedly upstairs listening to music."

"Yeah, I was. What else did the witness see?"

Givens drew in a breath in frustration.

"Let me suggest, Joss, that you heard the gunshot. You came downstairs, flipped on the light and discovered your mother's body... you repositioned the body so that the door would hit your mother's head... you banged the door against her head to ensure she died."

Freddie threw up her hands.

"Geez, detective. You're inventing all this. Why would Joss do that... you said our mother was bleeding to death. The medical examiner said so."

"It's called a coup de grâce, Freddie... surety."

"Baloney, detective. Did your magic witness see all this? Have any other fairy tales to tell?"

"No."

Givens stared at Joss who returned a defiant glare.

"You know what you did, Joss. You need to 'fess up."

Joss's confidence had grown since her sister had spoken.

"I didn't do anything, detective. If you can prove I did, arrest me."

Freddie rose and Joss followed.

"Is that all? If you think Joss is going to confess to something she didn't do, then you're spitting in the wind. This isn't Perry Mason with confessions out of the blue. There's no magic confession to be found, so we'll be leaving now."

At the door, Freddie turned back.

"You have a confessed killer, detectives. You have one body. Why do you need two disparate murderers? Why isn't one murderer sufficient?"

Metzinger responded, "We want the truth. Dr. Jablonski may have confessed to protect his wife."

Freddie countered with exasperation, "I would think that was his right... a husband's right. What do you want, detective? What do you need?"

"I need to close the case. I need justice."

"And who defines the justice you seek, detective? You?"

"No. That's the jury's job. I just provide the facts."

"Yes, the facts as you see them. Are Detective Givens' conjectures facts?"

"We'll provide them as possibilities."

"So, you decide the facts and the possibilities?"

"Yes. It's our job."

# CHAPTER SEVENTY-THREE

AFTER THE ACCUSATIONS, Joss and Freddie returned to their car in front of police headquarters and settled in their seats.

"Do you think we'll ever have to go in there again?" Joss asked.

Freddie scowled.

"Almost a goddamned second home. Our mother's going to be a ghost in our lives, following us forever."

"Nah, we'll shake her loose."

"Not if Metzinger and Givens can help it."

"How? They can't prove anything."

Freddie turned quizzically to Joss.

"Did Givens have it right? Is that really what you did?

Joss finished snapping her seat belt.

"Let's get out of here. I'm not saying anything."

"You think they can hear?"

"They could have a parabolic antenna or something."

"Good Lord! Do you really think so?"

"Or you could be wearing a wire."

Freddie was appalled.

"Christ, you really are paranoid. You thought I was going to kill you and stupidly hid at Earl's. Even Sage found you. Hell, the thought of killing you never occurred to me. Now you think I'm working with the cops. Didn't you hear me covering for you in there?"

"Yeah."

"Okay, cut out the shit. Did Detective Givens have it right?"

"Not sliding the rug. It must have slid when she fell."

"Damn!" Freddie exclaimed. "You hit her three times?"

"Hard as I could. Each with added value."

"Because our mother said you had no value?"

"Damn right."

# CHAPTER SEVENTY-FOUR

METZINGER SAT SLUMPED at his desk again. It had become routine. Givens brought him a cup of coffee from the break room.

"Sorry it took a while. I had to make a new pot."

Metzinger scowled. *I'm tired of this case. God, I hope the next six years doesn't drag on like this... Sarah's right. I should take a cushy corporate security job.*

Givens sat at her desk, sipping her own coffee.

"So, what do we do? Close the case? To keep it open, we need to answer unanswered questions."

"Hell, you know there are lots of questions."

"I know, and I agree. But what's the loose end that keeps this open when we already have a confessed killer?"

Metzinger groaned.

"Okay, lets run through this again."

He sat up straighter and encapsulated the investigation.

"1. O'Hanlon's murder has no fingerprints, no DNA.

"2. Nothing, except a seven-page picture book drawn by a woman with psychological problems and an ancient general's pistol.

"3. We know the victim was shot with the pistol and that it belonged to the Jablonskis but we also have an autopsy report saying the head wounds may have killed her before the gunshot did."

He sighed.

"The hanging thread is the damned picture book... Does it reflect things Allison observed? Was she there when O'Hanlon was shot? Dr. Jablonski says he committed the murder while his ailing wife was home and that he told her about it later... why would he tell her about it? Did she make the book after the murder, based it on what her husband told her? We don't know. The picture book could have been written before the crime as a plan... either way, either Jablonski could have been the gunman. They both had access to the weapon."

"True," Givens agreed.

"And there's the question of the hall light coming back on again. One page in the story book corroborated Freddie Winslow's claim that she was sitting in her car across the street and saw the light turn off. Another says the light came back on. Freddie didn't see that because she had presumably driven away. We have no witness that saw it. Only a picture in a comic book."

"Also, true."

"Your scenario fits what facts we have, with an extension to the comic book... Joss heard the gunshot, went downstairs, found her mother bleeding out and bashed a lifetime of turmoil out against her mother's head. One of the Jablonskis fired the gun and Joss attacked separately. Problem is, the evidence against Joss is a single drawing made by an unstable woman who is a suspect in the murder her husband confessed to. Fanfuckingtastic."

Givens took a sip of her cup of coffee.

"My theory about Joss is all my conjecture. Not even circumstantial. I think the defense will have a field day, especially with a mentally ill witness who's in the hospital and was suffering severe depression at the time of the murder. Any case against Joss is dead in the water, even if she is guilty. We can't prove that the head wounds killed the victim before the bullet. Jablonski's lawyer will blame the headwounds and Joss's lawyer can blame the bullet. Even if the medical examiner gets on board that the blows to the head killed her, the lawyers can still blame the wind."

Metzinger scribbled on the calendar mat on his desk.

"Well, we know the gunshot would have done the job, eventually. That's enough to say one of the Jablonskis at least attempted murder, even if they're not the killer. Based on Dr. Jablonski's confession, he went to the house with a gun intent on killing O'Hanlon for hurting his wife and he left believing he'd murdered her. That's enough to close our case file."

"Is that three potential murderers, a murderer and a killer, or a killer, an accomplice and an accessory? Accessory after the fact? I'm getting confused about the definitions of murderer and killer... The important question is, do we say something or just hope mitigating circumstances get Dr. Jablonski a light sentence?"

Metzinger shook his head.

"As Freddie said, who am I to judge. I say we write it all up and leave it to the judge and jury."

"So, who writes it up?"

"We both do... equal blame."

# CHAPTER SEVENTY-FIVE

IT WAS A MONDAY morning in late March, three weeks before the murder trial of Ralph Jablonski. Metzinger and Givens were still waiting to finalize their report on the Daphne O'Hanlon murder. They had turned in everything they had for the trial. Unfortunately, the Commonwealth Attorney wasn't happy with what they had. They hoped it would blow over. It didn't.

The call came into Lt. Ramirez.

He was still fuming when he entered the bullpen and headed for Metzinger's desk.

Speaking loudly, he broadcast halfway across the room, "Metzinger, we're due at the courthouse, Shannon Jennings's office, in half-an-hour. Get your shit together and be ready to talk. Be ready to explain yourselves but be circumspect."

Givens tried to hide by hunching her shoulders.

"Only Drury needs to go?"

Lt. Ramirez turned to her.

"Good luck with that. If I have to go, I'm taking every culprit I can find with me. Get up and find your armor. Be waiting for me outside the Commonwealth Attorney's office when I get there."

He wheeled around back into his office, slamming the door behind him.

Givens looked at Metzinger.

"We did all we could do."

"Yeah," replied Metzinger, leaning back in his chair looking defeated. "But we knew we were dumping the prosecutors with nothing but what ifs and maybes. We knew Jennings wouldn't be happy. She wants solid guilt, no wishy-washy stuff. Get yourself together and let's go. We have to be there before the lieutenant."

***

Metzinger was pacing in the hallway outside the Commonwealth Attorney's offices. Givens stood by the wall, leaning her head back against the coolness.

Metzinger spoke, "You ever wondered what it felt like to the French nobles loaded in carts headed for the guillotine?"

"Hell, Drury, we just tried to be honest. We're not miracle workers."

"Supposed to be. Supposed to solve cases. Discover the clues and connect them together. Locate suspects. Find motives. We did those things. It didn't work."

Lt. Ramirez arrived.

"You ready? No excuses. No bullshit. Okay?"

Metzinger and Givens nodded, but Metzinger thought, it's not bullshit. It's the way it is. If Shannon Jennings can solve it, let her do it.

Lt. Ramirez approached the receptionist, said he was there to see Mrs. Jennings, and he was told to wait. A few minutes passed before Jennings emerged from her office carrying a file. She was fully dressed for court in a power suit. Pearls hung around her neck. She looked ready for a trial.

"The conference room ready, Betty?"

"Yes, ma'am."

Attorney Jennings marched across the reception area to a glass door. She spoke to the space in front of her.

"My office only has two chairs. We'll meet in here."

She opened the door, entered the conference room, pulled out the chair at the head of the table, sat down, opened her file, and spread out some of its papers.

The two detectives and the lieutenant stood nervously inside the door. They had all been in this room before and didn't like it.

Jennings looked up and, without speaking, waved at the detectives to sit.

She tapped the papers with the fingers of her right hand.

"What is this shit?"

Finally, Ramirez spoke.

"Looks like the report on the Daphne O'Hanlon case."

"Not just a case. A goddamn murder. A murder that's not solved. A murder with a confession that means crap. He pleaded 'not guilty' at the indictment so it had to go to trial! You have a murder confession, and you question it? You have a murder weapon, a motive, and a confession! You and the medical examiner have turned the whole case into a circus and I'm the prosecutor who has to take it to trial. We can't ignore a confession, even though you've draped it in gobbly-goop."

She stared down one detective after another.

Metzinger finally spoke.

"We couldn't ignore what the medical examiner said. I talked to him. He wouldn't back off."

"So, now, the fucking defense can argue that the wind killed beloved children's author Daffy O'Hanlon. Do you think we should prosecute the wind? Sage Berenson stabbed Mr. Winslow to death in an altercation because O'Hanlon was killed by a breeze? Does it all make sense!?"

She tapped the report again.

"This damned report has more monkey wrenches than a plumber's truck."

Again, she waited, listening to the silence.

"Detective Metzinger, Detective Givens, you were in this room with me just a few months ago when we were dealing with that dumpster baby murder case, another screw up. You let the murderer run and get himself killed in a police chase, and the doctor involved in getting a baby made for himself blew himself up while you watched. Left me with a participant so dumb he didn't know what was going on. Just like THIS a solid case vanished."

Metzinger sat forward to speak but Lt. Ramirez clamped his hand on the detective's leg. In frustration, Metzinger sat back fuming. Hell, I wasn't even assigned to the case when the baby doctor ran. We sat right here and decided there was no case. With you, we decided. We all agreed. What the hell?

Jennings picked up her papers, stared at them, put them together, tapped their edges on the table to align them, and looked morosely at the detectives.

"You have anything to offer... anything useful? Anything more than conjecture? Anything better than a Hollywood script about a woman and the wind?"

Givens had had enough, and she was sitting where Lt. Ramirez couldn't reach her.

"Mrs. Jennings, we interviewed a myriad of people, all of whom had motive. Yeah, Mrs. Jablonski has depression problems, mental problems, but that doesn't exclude her from committing murder. There just isn't much evidence. There's the generals' pistol that either one of the Jablonskis had access to, and the picture book detailing the crime. We couldn't ignore it. Perhaps it's conjecture, but it couldn't be ignored."

Jennings glared at Givens, sighed and grimaced.

"Yeah, it's what you've given me. Crap, or no crap, it's what I have to work with."

She stood up and walked out of the room.

Lt. Ramirez breathed deeply.

"I think we're excused."

As they rose from their chairs, Metzinger looked at Givens.

"I think you've replaced me on her list."

"Yeah, big mouth."

# CHAPTER SEVENTY- SIX

THE COURTHOUSE HALLWAY looked like a police conference. The patrolman who originally responded to the 9-1-1 call was there. Migliano and Prothro were there. Metzinger and Givens were there. So was everyone else materially involved with the O'Hanlon case at 410 Crest Street.

The postman, Bennie Hastings, was at the end of the hallway looking out the window.

Freddie and Joss sat on a bench away from the police, across from the medical examiner.

The postman and the Winslow sisters were the only ones not studying papers to refresh their minds.

It was nine-thirty. The trial had started at nine. No witnesses had been called.

Suddenly the door to the courtroom opened and the court bailiff came out holding a paper from which he read.

"Detective Drury Metzinger, Miss Winifred Winslow and Miss Josceline Winslow are asked to remain here as possible witnesses. The rest of you are excused."

Bennie Hastings ran up to the man.

"Is Bennie Hastings excused?"

The man sighed.

"Only the three I named are required to stay. Don't know about a Mr. Hastings. He's not on the list."

Metzinger spoke up.

"What's going on? What's with the trial?"

The bailiff hunched his shoulders and wrinkled his brow.

"The man pleaded guilty."

"Guilty of what?"

"Murder... err... attempted murder."

Just then Shannon Jennings came out. She called the Winslow girls and Detective Metzinger together.

"Jablonski pleaded guilty to attempted murder," she explained. "The judge called me and the defense attorney for a sidebar and asked for the medical examiner's report, then she took us to her chambers. I told her the cause of death was indeterminate and would clearly serve as a defense. Doctor Jablonski's attorney agreed. Finally, the judge agreed to accept the plea. I recommended seven years, but the judge wouldn't agree. She demands that the jury set the sentence. She has a jury and wants to use them. We all want to get on with it, so the jury is being sworn in as we wait. You three are my witnesses. Both the defense attorney and I will question you about the circumstances and Jablonski's motive."

Metzinger questioned the approach.

"Aren't you going to ask about the hallway lights coming back on?"

"Conjecture, detective, and irrelevant now. Don't you dare muddy things. Let's get it over."

The girls rolled their eyes.

Metzinger saw them.

"I saw that. I'll remember," he rebuked.

Metzinger entered the courtroom as the first witness.

Freddie whispered behind him, "Justice, detective. We're looking for justice."

Both attorneys asked questions related to Allison Jablonski's work as an artist for the Geraldine Gerbil books... about her being fired... about how Mrs. O'Hanlon's treated her and about the state of her health....

Freddie and Joss testified in mitigation.

Little was asked about Freddie having written the books. Only that as she grew older, she couldn't do it anymore, that maturity limited her childhood. Nothing was asked about Freddie's resentment or Joss being treated as if she had no value. Nothing was said about the light coming back on.

Dr. Jablonski was called to testify on his wife's deteriorating health and hospitalization. His testimony was the most gut-wrenching moment.

The jury returned a sentence of five years.

With time off, it could be two-and-a-half.

That was it.

As Freddie and Joss followed Metzinger out of the courtroom, Freddie taunted.

"You part of the system, detective? Good system. Don't you like the way it works? The doctor did all right. I bet he thinks five years is worth it. Justice, detective... it's called justice."

Metzinger tried to hold his tongue, but he couldn't help himself.

"It's about conscience girls, not just justice," he rebuked. "I had hopes for you, Freddie. Thought you had potential, but you've regressed. Conscience, girls. That's what you need to think about."

The girls looked at him with mild disdain.

Metzinger continued.

"I have a conscience with no dead people on it. I'll lie awake for a few days thinking about your sense of justice, wishing you had a conscience, but I'll get over it. It will be absorbed into the detritus of my years on the police force."

Freddie sneered.

"Justice. That's all we know about, detective. It's all that matters. You're talking to the wind."

Metzinger sighed hopelessly. "Yeah the wind."

He turned to Joss. "Do you hear it, Joss... the wind blowing. Do you hear the sound as the door hits your mother's head?"

He strung out the sound.

"Ka-thunk!....... Ka-thunk!........ Ka-thunk!....... and maybe a crack when her skull fractured."

Freddie made a face.

"Wrong sound, detective. How about Ding dong?"

She turned and walked away. "Ding dong ... ding dong."

*What the hell?* thought Metzinger.

*Ding dong... damn... ding dong... the witch is dead.*

*The wicked witch is dead.*

# BOOKS BY J. STEWART WILLIS

GESTATION SEVEN

DEADLY HIGHWAY

THREE DEGREES AND GONE

ONE VOTE

If you enjoyed this book give it a star rating
or leave a review with your bookseller or on Good Reads.

Reader reviews and word of mouth are
essential to authors and small presses.

Reviews don't have to be fancy. Every word helps.

THANK YOU!

#jstewartwillis   #bairinkbooks   #GeraldineGerbil

READ... REVIEW... REPEAT

# ABOUT THE AUTHOR

J. STEWART WILLIS began imagining characters and story plots in between the work of life.

The stories percolated in his mind and finally, after years of imagination, he determined to get them down on paper and into the world. His first novel, *Gestation Seven,* was published in 2017.

"Requiem of Geraldine Gerbil" is set in Northern Virginia where Mr. Willis grew up.

He graduated from the United States Military Academy, served in Taiwan and Vietnam with the 173rd Airborne Brigade, earned his Ph.D. in physics, and returned to West Point to serve as Professor of Physics for 16 years.

After military retirement, Mr. Willis went onto a second career with a tech firm working with the Department of Energy before he was elected Mayor of Washington, Virginia for 9 years.

He now lives in Charlottesville, Virginia.

*Learn more about J. Stewart Willis at*
*www.jstewartwillisbooks.com*

Made in the USA
Las Vegas, NV
15 May 2021